I willed myself to sit [illegible] faintly hear footsteps approaching. Footsteps coming down the marble-floored hall. They must be coming toward me because the clicking grew louder. Feeling very disoriented, I couldn't be sure about anything. Be still! I told myself again. Get hold of yourself. Don't act hysterical. It will only make things worse. Worse? How could things get any worse?

Suddenly I heard a key fit into the locked door. My heart began to pound. I was totally helpless. . . .

DEADLY PARADISE

Vicki Mason White

FAWCETT GOLD MEDAL • NEW YORK

A Fawcett Gold Medal Book
Published by Ballantine Books
 Published in the United States by Ballantine Books, a division of Random House, Inc., New York, and simultaneously in Canada by Random House of Canada Limited, Toronto.

http://www.randomhouse.com

Library of Congress Catalog Card Number: 96-96331

ISBN 0-449-14978-1

Manufactured in the United States of America

First Edition: October 1996

10 9 8 7 6 5 4 3 2 1

CHAPTER 1

I awoke to blackness, and the taste of fear and blood in my mouth. My arms were tied securely behind me, and my ankles were bound so tightly that I had very little feeling in my feet. Apparently when I was chloroformed and tossed into the closet, I had landed on my face with enough force to cause my lip to split and my nose to bleed. My head was throbbing, and every molecule in me wanted to panic and begin thrashing about in claustrophobic hysteria. Of course, it would do me no good at all. . . . Thrashing about rarely does.

I was lying facedown, and it took a great deal of maneuvering and acrobatics to work myself into some kind of an upright position. I was enormously uncomfortable. I tried to concentrate on breathing slowly and deliberately through my nose, but about all I could manage was snuffling. In my seventeen years of teaching second and third graders, I had surely learned self-control. Only I had never been gagged and tied up before. The air in the closet was stifling, making me even more nauseous.

I willed myself to sit still and listen. I could hear very faintly footsteps approaching. Footsteps coming down the marble-floored hall. They must be coming toward me because the clicking grew louder. Feeling very disoriented, I couldn't be sure about anything. *Be still!* I told myself again. *Get hold of yourself. Don't act hysterical. It will only make things worse.* Worse? How could things get any worse?

Suddenly I heard a key fit into the locked door. The

doorknob turned. The closet was instantly flooded with light and cool, fresh air. The brightness blinded me, and I blinked and squinted, trying frantically to make out what was happening. I couldn't focus very well, but I could see two tall shapes standing over me. My heart began to pound. I was totally helpless.

"Luca, Luca! Why did you allow this? *Tsk, tsk.* This is a terrible mistake, and certainly Mrs. Hanson did not merit this kind of rough treatment."

I knew the voice. My head felt like it was stuffed full of fuzzy insulation, and I still could not focus my eyes. But the voice . . . It belonged to Nikki's husband, Carlo. Egotistical. Powerful. Violent.

Quickly he untied my arms and legs and removed the awful rag from my mouth. I responded by snuffling loudly through my nose. I must have been an attractive sight. I could just imagine what several hours in an airless closet could do for one's appearance. Had I lost all sanity? Why was I thinking about my appearance at a time like this? My sluggish brain registered no response. My thought processes were slow and muddled.

"Luca, carry her to the bed," commanded the voice in control. "Careful, careful, she's not a side of beef. She's our houseguest."

Luca, all two hundred and fifty pounds of rippling muscles, bent over me and did as he was told.

"Are you all right, Mrs. Hanson?" the powerful voice spoke again. Commanding. Treacherous.

I tried to focus my eyes, but there seemed to be a half dozen Lucas and at least as many Carlos floating around me. It was very disconcerting. I tried to speak, but all I could manage was more snuffling.

Carlo offered me water, and I slurped and coughed and finally swallowed some. It tasted slightly of the blood from my split lip, but it was soothing.

"Take it easy, Mrs. Hanson, uh, Catherine," said Carlo.

"Try to relax and calm down. This was all a terrible mistake. I'm very sorry. Truly sorry. Soon the drug will wear off, and you'll be okay. Try to sleep."

Of course. I have always found it easy to relax in the company of people who have tied me up and drugged me.

Unfortunately, I found myself in danger of slipping back into the deep hole of blackness. I tried to stay awake, but the drowsiness was overwhelming. Maybe I would just go to sleep and wake up at home in Kansas, and all of this would just be a bad dream. . . .

I awoke, and it was dark. According to the numbers on the little gold clock next to the bed, it was four o'clock in the morning. My body was covered with beads of cold sweat. I remembered. No, I am not Dorothy, and I am not in Kansas, and for that matter, I'm not in the Land of Oz either. I was caught snooping in Nikki's room, and somebody didn't like it. They didn't want me to have Nikki's diary, which they snatched away when they grabbed me. There was something important in that diary, and that's why I was drugged and tied up.

Fear, like a giant wave, engulfed me once again, making it difficult for me to breathe. For some stupid reason, I remembered myself as a kid scared of the dark, and how my older sister had taken pity on her pathetic, fraidy-cat sister, teaching me how to help control my fear by taking slow, deep breaths.

I tried it. It didn't work very well. Unfortunately this fear was founded not on imagined bogeymen, but on events that had really happened. This was life-and-death stuff. Nevertheless, I forced myself to slow my breathing. Finally my eyes adjusted to the dark, and I sat up in the bed. Trembling slightly, I switched on the bedside light. Hallelujah! My clear vision was back. I could see that I was in familiar surroundings.

This was the same room that I had come to stay in only a few days ago, as an invited guest. It was very large, like all the other rooms I had seen in this house. All the furniture was quite massive, designed on a grand scale. It would have been vulgar—the huge, king-size canopy bed, the enormous dresser, the bulky armoire, and the overstuffed lounge chairs—if not for the beautiful, delicately flowered wallpaper that softened everything and somehow gave the room the appearance of a flower garden in bloom. Ruffled pillows and curtains of matching fabric in pastel pinks and blues gave the entire bedroom and adjoining dressing area and bath an air of springtime. If a couple of butterflies had come flitting out of the wallpaper, it would not have seemed the least bit unnatural. For a brief time, the airy lightness of my surroundings made me forget the mess I was in.

My breathing seemed normal now, but I still felt woozy. I did a quick inventory and determined that there were no broken bones. Still, every inch of my body ached. I felt my nose gingerly to make sure that it wasn't broken. It seemed stupidly vain to be worried about my nose in light of more imminent dangers, but I was relieved to discover that it was only sensitive and sore, not broken.

I was thirsty, and looking at the bedside table, I discovered a large lead-crystal pitcher filled with water and a matching old-fashioned tumbler beside it. Pouring myself a full glass, I tried to sip it slowly. I considered the possibility that my captors were brutes, but not totally heartless. Or at least, they didn't want me to die of thirst.

I decided it was time to check out the situation. Sliding carefully out of the bed, I stood on rubbery legs. They seemed a little wobbly but adequate to support the rest of me all right, and so I walked slowly and carefully to the door. Placing my hand on the knob, I turned it, and instead of finding it locked, discovered that it rotated quietly and easily.

Cautiously I opened the door and peered outside. The room I occupied was located at one end of a hallway that led to the main stairs. The hall was dimly lit by a large hexagonal skylight that allowed the light of the moon to spread its soft luminescence from the center of the house outward.

My first inclination was to run like the wind. Run, run

quickly out of this house, away from the danger, away from all the troubling bits of information that were now swimming aimlessly around in my head like millions of microscopic organisms in a vat of pond scum. Run and keep on running until I was safely back home in my own little brick house in Hamilton, Kansas. Unfortunately, that was not possible, since my present location was a small, secluded, privately owned island somewhere in the Caribbean, thousands of miles away from my home.

I needed time to think and sort things out. I needed a plan. I needed advice. I needed a SWAT team to get me out of here. Two out of four would have to do.

Noiselessly I closed the door, hobbled back into the room, went into the bathroom to relieve my bladder, and then climbed back into the giant bed. Taking another large swig of water, I propped up some pillows behind my neck and back and began to think. I needed to review everything that had happened to me in this house and in the weeks before I had arrived here.

CHAPTER 2

Mark, my twenty-one-year-old son, had just graduated from our local university. Valedictorian, summa cum laude. A plethora of scholastic honors. He had received a full scholarship to Harvard Law School and would begin classes in the fall. I was so proud of him I could hardly contain myself.

My graduation gift to him was a summer vacation in Europe with three of his best friends. On an elementary school teacher's salary, it had taken me eons to save up for it. I knew how very hard Mark had worked, and so it was worth every bit of the scrimping and extra tutoring I had had to do.

At the moment, his six-foot-four frame was sprawled on the den floor and dressed in a torn football jersey, a pair of wrinkled madras shorts, and holey tennis shoes. He looked more like a skid-row reject than a college graduate.

"Come on, Mom. What are you going to do with your summer? And don't tell me you're going to spend it painting the exterior of the house."

Silence.

"Well, Mom, I'm waiting."

I grinned sheepishly.

"Mark, I'm going to paint the house."

"Mom, that doesn't count. I realize we can't both go to Europe, but you do have a life, too. Look, the Parkers have been after you for a long time to spend a couple of weeks with them at their lake cabin. And then, of course, there's Chuck MacDonald. He's always wanting you to go camping. Take a week, take two weeks, and live a little. Get away from this place for a while. Take a *vacation*!"

"Okay, okay. What a nag. I'll think about it, all right?"

"Mom!"

"Mark, I said I'll think about it!"

Mark was probably right, although I hated to admit it. He usually was right. When Alex, my husband and Mark's father, had died of a sudden stroke at the young age of thirty-three, Mark had changed almost overnight from a typical "me-oriented" ten-year-old into a wise and responsible head of the household. I hadn't intended for that to happen. In fact, I had tried to discourage it, but like many things in life, it just happened anyway. Of course, Mark played football and baseball and went to proms and parties, but underneath the baseball cap and the oily teenage skin, he had really been a man masquerading as a kid.

When the kitchen sink sprang a leak, and we couldn't afford a plumber, who conned Billy Webb's dad (a plumber) into fixing the sink in exchange for a month of free lawn mowing? Mark did. Who fixed flat tires and put up storm windows? Who talked me into getting more exercise and replaced my sugary breakfast cereal with a healthier high-fiber brand? Who could, at the ripe old age of thirteen, balance the checkbook in a matter of minutes after his college-graduate mother had unsuccessfully tried for hours and was still two hundred dollars short of being correct? Mark did, and somehow managed to have great fun doing it.

I was still looking at Mark when the phone rang. Mark answered it. His face was animated.

"Hey, Mom, it's a transatlantic call for you."

Puzzled, I took the receiver.

"Hello?" I answered.

Nothing but lots of static rumbled back at me.

"Hello? Hello?" I said.

"Hello," a voice replied. "This is a transatlantic call for Mrs. Alex Hanson. Is this Mrs. Hanson?"

"Yes."

"Go ahead with your call, please," she said to the other party.

"Catherine, it's Nikki."

"Why, Nikki, hello!"

Nikki had been my best friend throughout our four years of college. We had met at freshman orientation and had become fast friends. Our own personal lives had geographically separated us for most of the last twenty or so years, but we had always managed to keep in touch by mail and occasionally by phone. I hadn't actually seen her in several years.

Nikki's voice was muffled by static.

"Catherine, I'm so glad I caught you at home."

"I'm glad, too, Nikki. I've been meaning to write you a long letter now that school is out for the summer."

"Catherine, that's why I'm calling. I want you to come out and spend the summer with us. You must come, Catherine, we have so much to catch up on. Please say you'll come. We could have such a wonderful time. Say yes, because I won't accept no for an answer. We're long overdue for a reunion. The 'twins' have been separated much too long!"

"Nikki, it sounds wonderful, and you know I'd love to see you. I do need to think it over. . . ."

Mark's animated expression had suddenly turned cloudy and disapproving.

"Catherine, I promise you it will be a summer you won't forget. And besides, I need your advice on some things. Please say you'll come. The island is beautiful now, and the weather is gorgeous."

Her tone had changed somewhere in there from exuberance to urgency.

"But, Nikki, it would be so expensive. We simply can't afford it. Remember, I'm sending Mark to Europe as a college-graduation gift. As much as I'd love to come, I don't have the money."

"Catherine, stop worrying about the money. We can certainly afford it. Carlo and I have already arranged for your air-fare to Miami. From there, you'll be picked up in our private jet and flown directly here to our island. I've got everything arranged. All you have to do is say you'll come. A letter is on the way explaining everything."

"Now, wait, Nikki. That's extremely generous of both of you, but I still need time to think about all of this."

"Great, Catherine! Sorry . . . Can't hear you . . . well . . . sorry . . . Damn this bad connection . . . want you to come . . . important to see you . . . letter on the way . . . need your advice . . . We'll enjoy . . . tomorrow . . . love to Mark . . ."

Her voice faded out in a roar of static. The conversation was over.

Mark let out a whoop of joy and spun me around.

"Mom, this is going to be a summer you'll never forget!"

Funny, Nikki had used those exact same words.

CHAPTER 3

The next few weeks flew by in a whirlwind of activity. Now there were two of us preparing for lengthy trips.

Immediately after Nikki's phone call, I questioned the whole idea of going to visit her, and Mark continued to challenge me about my feelings. He asked me to give him a list of reasons why I should not go. I replied as follows:

"One. You know I don't make rash decisions. This is totally out of character for me. I'm a planner and an organizer. For heaven's sake, Mark, I'm a Taurus!

"Two. I haven't actually been with Nikki for years. What if we don't get along anymore?

"Three. This is a big one. I've never met Nikki's husband before. What if our personalities clash? Three months is a long time to spend with anybody."

Mark listened closely to my protests. Then he smiled.

"Mom, I love you, but you're undoubtedly the biggest procrastinator I've ever known in my life. You need a change. You need a vacation. You need a chance to put your life here in proper perspective. For the last nine years, you've done nothing but put me first before everyone and everything else in your life. This is an extraordinary opportunity to get away from your routine and return refreshed and revitalized. It's an excellent chance to think about yourself and how you want to live your life."

"Yes, Mark, but I . . ."

"Please listen, Mom, I'm not finished. To address your second point. You and Nikki have managed to keep in touch over the years. I've heard you mention many times that you wish you could spend time together again. This is that chance, and I think you would always regret it if you passed it up. Finally, you mention your concern about Nikki's husband. According to Nikki's letters, he works most of the time and travels a great deal, so I don't think that'll be a problem. Besides, I don't believe Nikki would ask you to come if she thought it wouldn't work out. We know her husband is a millionaire, and Nikki has written in her letters to you that she's very happy in her marriage. So forget that argument. This is perfect for you. Go and enjoy yourself, so that while I'm in Europe having a great time, I can feel good about the wonderful summer you're having, too."

We stared silently at one another. Finally I grinned.

"Okay, I give up. You and Nikki win. I'll go!"

Mark gave me a triumphant grin and hugged me.

"We all win on this one, Mom."

Nikki's letter had arrived by special delivery within a day after our brief phone conversation. She had sent it before I had even agreed to come. She was true to her word. The letter included all the travel details I needed.

The night before Mark left for Europe, our next-door neighbors, the Parkers, invited us over for dinner along with a few other mutual friends.

Millie and Bob Parker were my oldest and closest friends. At the risk of sounding corny, they seemed like family to Mark and me, especially since we had no other living relatives. Some things about Millie reminded me of what little I remembered about my older sister, who died in a car accident over thirty-five years ago. Bob was like a big brother. They agreed heartily with Mark that I should definitely go to visit Nikki, and that really helped me to stop worrying about the trip and begin looking forward to it instead.

Bob and Millie were in their late fifties but looked much younger. They were both fitness buffs who liked to ride bikes, play tennis, and jog. Bob was the superintendent of schools in our town, and Millie was the principal of the elementary school where I taught. Their two daughters were adults, married with babies of their own. For as long as I had known them, Bob and Millie were my ideal couple.

It was a lovely evening. The intense heat of the day had mellowed into a pleasant warmth, and the air was heavy with the scent from the many rosebushes that bordered the Parkers' well-tended backyard. There were about fifteen of us enjoying the evening. We gorged ourselves on succulent, spicy barbecued ribs and fresh corn on the cob from Bob's outdoor grill and plump, homemade rolls and luscious blueberry pie from Millie's kitchen.

Good conversation accompanied dinner and dessert. Everyone wished Mark and me bon voyage, and the party began to break up. As I started inside to give Millie a hand with the dishes, Chuck MacDonald gently took hold of my elbow and drew me aside.

"Catherine," he said in his quiet, serious voice, "I'm going to miss you a lot."

"I won't be gone that long, and I am coming back."

Oh no, Chuck, not here, not now. We had already had a lengthy conversation, or rather conversations, about this same subject. Chuck and I had been friends for years. And that was all it was, or so I thought. A month earlier, he had told me between innings of a college baseball game that he was in love with me and wanted to marry me. A romantic moment it was not, since at the time of his declaration, I was seriously contemplating a large wad of gum stuck to the bottom of my shoe that threatened to keep me cemented to the stands for the rest of my life. I had not had a clue about his feelings toward me. Stunned, I told him in a kind way that I thought of him as a good friend, and that was all. His pronouncement had put a real strain on things, though, and I knew it would be difficult for us to simply be "friends" from then on.

Chuck's blue eyes looked down into my brown ones.

"Even so, I will miss you, Catherine. I wish you'd miss me, too."

Time for me to exit.

"Chuck, I . . . I hope you have a good summer. I'd better go help Millie in the kitchen. I think she's being overwhelmed by rib bones and corn-on-the-cob carcasses."

He smiled wistfully and walked away.

Chuck MacDonald. Forty. Never married. Still lived with his mother. Kind to animals and people. Very quiet. Polite. Mild-mannered. Hard-working. Tall, lanky, and pleasant looking. He owned and operated a large, well-stocked hardware store in town. Made a good living, too. Almost everyone I knew, including Chuck, thought we were perfect for each other. Everyone except me. Chuck was a nice guy, but he was not for me. There was no spark between us, just a comfortable, friendly feeling. I knew there had to be fire and passion, too. That's what I'd had with my husband, Alex, and I didn't expect it would ever come along again. Once in a lifetime was rare. Enough said.

My flight for Miami was scheduled to leave the day after Mark's. This left me with little time to do what I always did best: worry. Bob Parker had once told me that if black belts were awarded for brooding, I would have earned the mother of all black belts. I had finally convinced myself to look forward to the trip and actually enjoy it. I felt excited and tingly, like a kid on Christmas Eve, as I neatly packed my wonderful new summer clothes: shorts and tops, swimsuits and cover-ups, summery dresses and barely-there cocktail dresses—purchases made at a nearby factory outlet for women's clothing, well known for attractive, discounted clothes at low prices. The clothes were not designer quality, but they were respectable copies, very stylish, and looked much more expensive than they actually were. Only a few days before, Millie had persuaded me to raid my secret stash—money I had saved for buying house paint—and use the money on some much-needed new clothes. The painting would have to wait until next summer anyway. I didn't want to arrive at Nikki's gorgeous home looking like somebody's poor relative. At any rate, looking at the newness of my purchases made me feel alive and young and adventuresome. I was ready for my luxurious vacation in an exotic place. Enjoying the company of my best friend. Sun. Fun. Relaxation. Good food. Servants everywhere. Uh-huh. I could handle that fine, thank you.

CHAPTER 4

The next morning at six o'clock, Mark and I loaded up my trusty, old Honda Civic and began our drive to the Kansas City airport. It was a bright, sunny day, an auspicious beginning for Mark's travels in Europe. At first, Mark and I talked freely about the fascinating summer that lay ahead of us. We laughed and joked and gave each other advice, keeping the conversation on a light note. But as we drew closer to the airport, we grew silent, and an air of seriousness settled upon us.

"Mark," I said, turning my head to look briefly into his eyes, "I want you to know how truly proud I am of you. Not just of your impressive scholastic accomplishments, but of you as a person. You're a sensitive, compassionate man of integrity, very much your own person, but like your father in many ways." I glanced at him again. His profile was strikingly similar to his dad's, and the close resemblance made my heart ache. The well-chiseled, classic features and the thick, sandy blond hair were all legacies of his late father.

He smiled wistfully.

"Ever since you were a boy, you've been filled with a zest for life. You've known instinctively when to work and when to play, and how to keep the two in proper balance. Your *joie de vivre* is one of your most endearing qualities." I swallowed hard, struggling to hold back the tears that would keep me from saying what I needed to say. "After your father died, I wondered how I could survive, how I could possibly go on without him, the center of my life. But then I looked into your eyes, and I knew that somehow you and I would have to continue on. And we did, Mark. You and I built a good life together. We managed to pick up the broken pieces and put them back together in a new way. Being your mother has brought me more happiness than I could have ever dreamed possible. And now, here you are. A young man with your whole life ahead of you. My heart is just . . . overflowing. You're a wonderful son, and I love you very much."

I smiled at him, as the tears I had fought so hard to hold back began streaming down my cheeks.

His voice was soft as he spoke.

"Mom, pull over there, into the parking lot."

I eased the car into the first available spot and turned the ignition off. Grabbing a tissue, I blotted the tears.

Gently he took my hand.

"Mom, I'll never be able to thank you for everything you've done for me. I owe you so much. Without your support, I could never have come this far. After Dad died, you had to shoulder all the responsibility for raising me. You were always there as parent, friend, or confidant, whatever the situation required. We've laughed and cried together, shared the bad and the good and all the in-between. We've forged a bond, you and I, that neither time nor distance can ever break. I love you, Mom."

We hugged each other fiercely, silently acknowledging the commitment we had to each other.

It was time to go. I started the car.

"Ready?" I asked, forcing myself to smile. Once again, I was assuming the role of Mom. Back in control of my emotions. Putting on the brave face for both of us.

"Ready," he answered, smiling back at me.

I pulled out of the parking lot and drove to the passenger drop-off zone. Earlier Mark and I had agreed that he would go on alone to meet his friends at the flight gate.

We got out of the car, and Mark took his bags out of the trunk and set them on the curb. We hugged again, he kissed my cheek, collected his bags, and disappeared into the terminal.

Exhausted from the rush of emotions, I got behind the wheel and wearily maneuvered the car into the correct lane to get back on the freeway. I sighed. We'd said some pretty heavy things to each other. Today we both faced the reality that our lives would never be as closely interwoven again. Soon after his return from Europe, Mark would be leaving for law school. And I would have to look closely at my own life, and how I wanted to live it. I was losing a major piece of my identity.

Change was here. Now. The future had arrived like a cunning burglar who sneaks undetected into a house and steals the family heirlooms, while the family sleeps soundly.

Mark was gone. He was on his way. Suddenly, I felt very alone.

The drive home was long, and I restlessly switched the radio dial from one station to another trying to occupy my mind with something other than my own thoughts. Talk shows seemed to dominate the airwaves, and I listened to everything from "Interviews with Teenage Werewolves" to "Problems of Midget Hookers." Finally, after a long three-hour drive, I pulled into my driveway. The minute my car turned into the drive, Bob and Millie shot out of their front door as though on cue.

"We know you've got last-minute packing to do, but you have to eat, Catherine. I've thrown a few things together for a light supper, so come join us," urged Millie.

"Okay, I'd like that."

"Catherine, you must be exhausted from getting Mark ready for his big trip and getting yourself ready to leave, too," remarked Bob.

"You're right about that, Bob. Hopefully, I can get a decent night's sleep tonight. Most likely, I'll be too excited to sleep, in which case I'll settle for napping on the plane."

We went inside the Parkers' house and down a central hall

to the kitchen. Millie's kitchen was a large, roomy one built circa 1940. It had been remodeled recently, though, so that everything was modern and up-to-date. Fortunately, the redecorating had tastefully left much of the kitchen's original charm intact.

Millie's kitchen was decorated in crisp blue and white. As usual, everything was in perfect order, clean enough to pass any stiff military inspection. The round oak table was set with a cheerful blue-and-white checked tablecloth and coordinating blue china. A full plate of generously filled tuna salad sandwiches occupied the center of the table, surrounded by heaping bowls of fresh fruit salad, baked beans, potato salad, chips, sweet pickles, and homegrown tomatoes.

I laughed.

"Millie, I love these little 'thrown together' suppers of yours. A sumo wrestler would find this meal satisfying."

"Thanks, Catherine. I suppose it has to do with growing up in a family with six brothers. You can't imagine how much food my mother had to prepare three times a day to feed that crew."

The three of us chewed companionably in silence, enjoying the delicious flavors of the meal Millie had prepared. It appeared that we were all ravenous from the way we were eating. Bob broke the silence.

"Catherine, tell us more about your friend Nikki. What's she like?"

"Let me show you a photo of her first," I said, digging into my handbag for my wallet. I took her picture out and laid it on the table in front of Bob.

"What do you think?" I asked.

Bob shook his head. "I don't understand."

"What do you mean?"

"Well, I . . . this is a photo of you, Catherine. I thought you were going to show us a picture of Nikki."

Millie snatched the picture from Bob and studied it herself. Puzzled, she shook her head, too.

"I don't get it, Catherine. Is this some kind of joke?"

"It isn't a joke. It really is a picture of Nikki. We met, years ago, waiting to enter the college auditorium for our first freshman orientation session. There were several hundred freshmen just standing there, milling around in a big group. All of a sudden, I was standing eye to eye with this girl who looked almost exactly like me. Well, she did look exactly like me. She was dumbfounded, and so was I. It was the strangest feeling I've ever experienced, as if someone had stolen my face and my body. It was almost Orwellian."

"Well, well," Bob chuckled. "The resemblance is uncanny. You're almost doubles. It would take a real expert to tell you two apart."

Millie and Bob inspected the photo carefully again.

Millie looked up from the picture. "I can't believe it, Catherine. She looks just like you. Is this a recent photo?"

"Yes, it's only a few months old. Actually, I liked her short hairstyle in the picture. I showed the photo to my hair stylist, and she copied it on me. It was a sure thing. I knew it looked nice on Nikki."

"I love it on you, Catherine," remarked Millie, returning to her study of the picture.

Meeting Nikki that day at Bascombe College was startling to both of us. I remembered that Nikki had come to my dorm room after the orientation, and we had stood side by side in front of the full-length mirror on my closet door comparing our likenesses.

"Oval face," said Nikki.

"Large brown eyes," I said.

"Upturned nose . . . I always wanted it to be perfectly straight," she said.

"Our mouths are identical."

"Uh-huh."

"Height. I'm maybe a half inch or so taller than you, Nikki. I'm five-foot-five. What about you?"

"You're right, Catherine. I'm about five-foot-four-and-a-half inches."

"This is weird! Even our hair is the same. Dark brown, and we're wearing it in a bob with bangs."

Nikki and I stared at the twin reflections in the mirror. She touched her face. "My skin tone is a bit darker than yours, Catherine."

"I think you just have a deeper tan than I do, Nikki. You're from the South, right?"

"Yeah. I probably just get more sun than you do."

We both had small frames and wore a size six dress. Our shoe size was a bit different. I wore a seven, and she wore a six.

"Amazing!" she said.

"Amazing!" I agreed.

Millie brought me out of my memories and back to the present by offering me a refill of iced tea.

"Catherine," Bob said, "I've seen people who resemble one another before, but this is definitely the closest I've ever seen. Are you two related?"

"No, we checked into that ourselves because we were so curious, but we found nothing. It's also extraordinary that we would actually meet each other. I wonder what the odds of that happening are."

"If you were standing next to each other right now, would we be able to tell the difference?" asked Bob.

"Well, there are a few very subtle differences, like moles, but, no, I'm certain you couldn't tell us apart. Of course, our personalities are totally different. Nikki was always more flamboyant and outgoing than I was. I'm the cautious one, and she is more adventurous."

"But you've kept in touch all these years?" Millie asked.

"Oh, yes. We were very close in college. After graduation, we went our separate ways, but somehow we've always managed to keep in touch through letters and sometimes phone calls."

"You married Alex right after graduation, didn't you?" asked Millie.

"Yes, and Nikki went off to New York to try to break into the theater. She loved acting and was really quite good in the college productions. It was tough, though, and after a year of waiting tables, living in a scuzzy apartment, and getting chorus-line jobs in shows that rarely opened, she decided to give it up. I think her life would have been a lot different if she had actually gone home to Tampa."

"What did she do?" asked Millie.

"She thought she was in love with a young actor who was having about as much luck as she was. They eloped and struggled to survive on their tiny combined salaries. Unfortunately, he drank, he beat her up, she forgave him, he drank, he beat her up, and she forgave him. Finally he broke her arm, her jaw, several ribs, and of course, her heart. She ended up in the hospital, and she divorced him. It tore her up."

"What happened then?" asked Bob.

"After she recovered, she went into modeling and did well. Mostly catalog stuff, but they liked her look, and she had steady work. She made a decent living and shared a nice apartment in New York City with another model. About a year later, she met another very handsome, charming guy who was an attorney. It looked as though she had found the right person to share her life with, but then she found out he was married and had two children. Nikki was hurt and angry and had no intention of being a homewrecker. She broke up with him, but he couldn't leave it alone. He got a divorce and finally convinced her to marry him. She did, and her euphoria lasted about a month before she discovered that he was sleeping around. Nikki divorced husband number two after only two months of marriage."

"What did Nikki do then, Catherine?" Millie asked.

"She got back on her feet, and, using the skills she had learned from her business minor, opened a fancy dress shop with a modeling friend of hers who had lots of money. The shop did very well, and it looked like Nikki was on her way. Once again, she fell in love. This one was a rich plastic surgeon who had come into her shop to buy a gift for his mother. Two months later, they were married. He was wonderful to her, and they were anxious to have a family. They tried for a year with no luck and Nikki went to a specialist who told her she was sterile. She went through all kinds of painful and expensive procedures trying to restore her fertility, but nothing worked. I believe they really loved each other, but Nikki couldn't handle the fact that she could never give her husband children. Eventually it poisoned their relationship, and she divorced him."

"Poor Nikki. Life really threw her some bad curves," said Millie. "What happened next?"

"She returned to work; she had remained a partner. Lonely and deeply depressed, she started drinking. She clobbered herself with alcohol for a couple of years. Her business partner didn't give up on her, and finally she talked Nikki into going to AA. She went, and it was miraculous. Nikki's been sober for two years now."

"Her life sounds like a soap opera," remarked Millie.

"Yes, it does. But that's not the end of the story."

"You told us that she has remarried. How does this husband compare with the others?" asked Bob.

"I honestly don't know much about him. I know he is an enormously wealthy businessman of Italian descent. He's handsome, of course, and seems to have made Nikki very happy. They've only been married for a little over a year, but I think things are going well. I received a letter from her a month ago, and she seemed quite contented."

"It's about time," said Bob, and Millie and I nodded solemnly in agreement.

CHAPTER 5

That night I fell into a deep sleep almost instantly. Morning did come early, but I had finished my packing the night before, so I didn't feel rushed at all. I was excited but definitely in control. I showered, dressed, and applied my makeup carefully. I made the bed and did a rapid check of my suitcases and closet, making doubly sure that I wasn't leaving anything essential behind. Satisfied, I went to the kitchen and breakfasted on the last of the orange juice and a toasted bagel.

I glanced at my watch. It was seven-thirty. Time for Millie and Bob to pick me up. I walked through the house to make sure all the windows and doors were locked. Bob and Millie would be checking the house, but I wanted to make their job as easy as possible. I carried my bags to the small front entry hall and set them down. The doorbell rang, and I opened it to Millie and Bob who whooshed into the house and commandeered my bags. They completely ignored my protests that I could carry something and zoomed out to load my things into the trunk of Bob's new Buick. That left me standing in the open door with only my purse. All of a sudden, I felt oddly sentimental over leaving my home for such a long time. My eyes passed lovingly over the fireplace mantel filled with photographs: Alex and me toasting each other as a young bride and groom deeply in love; Alex and me in tennis whites wearing broad smiles and holding rackets; Alex and me clasping each other tightly and waving a SOLD real estate sign; and a plethora of pictures of Mark at different ages, such as Mark blowing out the candle on his first birthday cake, Mark in swim trunks holding a diving trophy in the sixth grade, and Mark and me smiling victoriously after his college graduation.

A horn beeped. Bob stuck his friendly balding head out the driver's-side window and called, "Catherine, we promise to keep the shrine in perfect condition while you're gone. Come on, or you'll miss your flight."

"Coming!" I yelled back. *'Bye, house. See you in August.*

Bob was in rare form and kept Millie and me laughing all the way to the airport. I always felt he had missed his calling and should have been a stand-up comedian. The drive didn't seem long at all. At the gate, I hugged my friends.

"Catherine, don't worry about your house. We'll take care of the yard and keep a close eye on everything. And don't worry about Mark. He's having the time of his life. For goodness' sake, enjoy yourself and come back to us refreshed, revitalized, and renewed!" Millie advised.

"I will, I promise. I'll try to dash off a card every once in a while to let you know I'm okay. I'll miss you two. Thanks for everything." We hugged again.

The flight to Miami began pleasantly. The skies from Kansas to Miami were reported to be clear and calm. I had a window seat. It had always been my favorite. Although Alex and I had made our home together in the small town of Hamilton, Kansas, population twenty thousand, we were by no means hicks, or strangers to flying for that matter. We had always enjoyed traveling, and whenever we had the money and the opportunity, Alex, Mark, and I had flown to a new city to explore and enjoy what it had to offer.

The center seat was soon occupied by an old Gypsy-like woman. She wore bright orange slacks and an electric blue blouse. Heavy gold hoops hung from her ears, and at least ten thick gold chains adorned her neck. As soon as the flight took off, I knew she was sound asleep because of her loud snoring.

To her left, on the aisle, sat a skinny teenage boy of about sixteen. He was dressed in baggy shorts, torn T-shirt, and thongs. His blond hair was very short, and he looked like a typical teen, except for the small gold ring protruding from his right nostril. He appeared to be totally engrossed in a paperback book but was constantly fiddling with the ring in his nose. Rather disgusting.

I settled happily into my seat planning to enjoy the flight as marking the beginning of my vacation. From a small carry-on bag, I pulled out Lawrence Sanders's latest suspense novel. I sighed contentedly and began reading. I was just beginning page three, when I had the uncomfortable feeling that someone was staring at me. Slowly I turned my eyes to the left. The old woman was now wide awake and blatantly staring at me. I thought perhaps she would get her fill and look away, but she continued to stare. I was beginning to feel very uneasy. Finally I felt I had to say something.

"Excuse me, ma'am. Is something wrong?"

As I turned to face her, I realized that she was even older than I had previously thought. Her dark, weathered complexion resembled ancient leather. Her once black hair was almost all white and stuck out in all directions like that of the Troll dolls that have remained so popular. Her mouth spread wide into a mostly toothless grin as she spoke. "Why, no, dearie. I was just admiring your hands. They're so lovely, and your fingers are long and graceful-like."

"Thank you." Oh, God, I felt like I was in the middle of a Grimms' fairy tale. She was really a horrible-looking little creature.

"Now, dearie, give us your palm, and I'll tell you what your future holds."

"Oh, no," I replied pleasantly but firmly, consciously leaning away from her toward the window. "Thank you, but no . . ."

"Now, dearie, don't be afraid. Nothing bad could happen to someone as lovely as you. I read palms all the time." Before I knew what was happening, she grabbed my left hand with lightning quickness and gripped it tightly between her rough, clawlike hands.

There was nothing to be gained from making a scene even though I was annoyed and repulsed by her aggressive behavior. In fact, she had better get this over with quickly because I had just decided to move back several rows to an unoccupied seat I had spotted at takeoff. I was not going to be bullied by this strange little woman.

"Okay, what do you see?" I asked impatiently.

She was still staring intently at my palm, scrutinizing every detail carefully. She clutched my hand firmly, and with a gnarled index finger, lightly traced the lines of my palm. Evidently she took this stuff seriously.

"Wait, dearie. I must be certain about what I see," she practically growled.

I shuddered. All right. Enough was enough. I had had it with her. Scene or no scene, I was going to get up and move now.

I gave her one last angry glance, but she was still totally engrossed in my palm. As I started to pull my hand away, she held onto it screeching, "No, no, no! God in heaven have mercy on you!" A look of absolute horror covered her face, as though she had seen something too terrible to acknowledge.

CHAPTER 6

She let out a bloodcurdling scream, her eyes rolled up into her head, and she collapsed forward, with her head in her lap, still clutching my hand.

Totally unnerved by her screams, I tried to pull my hand away from her viselike grip, but I couldn't. The cabin was in complete pandemonium. Confused and afraid, some passengers crowded into the aisles. Two flight attendants reacted quickly to restore order by herding people firmly back into their seats. The senior flight attendant, a heavily made-up woman in her early thirties, rushed to our row of seats.

"What happened?" she shrieked at me very unprofessionally.

"I . . . I don't know. This woman sitting next to me wanted to read my palm, and she started screaming. I don't know anything about her. . . . She's still gripping my hand. Maybe she's fainted or had a heart attack. . . . I don't know."

The teenager on the aisle was white-faced. He sat as still as a piece of stone. In the background, I could hear the two other flight attendants speaking in low, calm voices trying to reassure the other passengers that the plane was not going to crash and that we weren't being hijacked.

I finally worked my wrist free and sank back into my seat.

The frustrated flight attendant felt for the old woman's pulse and determined that she was still breathing. The flight attendant was clearly irritated. Frowning, she consulted the flight list, found there was a doctor on board, and with the help of two big, burly farm types, carried the old woman to the first-class section.

In a few minutes she returned, still looking exasperated that something like this incident would dare occur on a flight she was attending.

"Are you sure you don't know anything about the old lady, or what caused her to pass out?" she barked impatiently. I was really getting tired of her questioning. She was treating me like some kind of criminal who was withholding evidence.

"No, I'm sorry. I can't help you. I don't know anything about her. How is she now?"

Glancing around quickly, she leaned closer and lowered her voice. "Lucky for me, there was a general practitioner on this flight. Damn! I'd hate to give her mouth to mouth! She gives me the creeps. Anyway, he brought her around with some smelling salts. He says her heartbeat is erratic, and he's certain she's suffered a heart attack. He's used some medication to keep her fairly comfortable for the time being."

"Oh, that's terrible. What can he do for her on the plane?"

"Not much. We'll have to turn around and take her back to Kansas City for immediate treatment."

"I see. It's fortunate that we're still fairly close to the Kansas City airport."

"Fortunate for her but not for me. Losing all this flying time will mess up everybody's schedule, particularly mine. Shit! I have a late lunch date in Miami with a sexy linebacker from the Miami Dolphins. This little episode really screwed that up for me!"

So much for compassion. I guess they can't teach you everything in flight attendants' school.

My mouth was dry, and I felt shaky, but I didn't want to ask Miss Congeniality for a glass of water. In her present state of mind, she might throw it in my face. I tried to compose myself. I was still trembling slightly, and my hand hurt from the old lady's viselike grip. Within minutes, the pilot announced that we were close to landing.

As soon as the plane rolled to a stop on the runway, two paramedics raced onto the plane, loaded the old woman onto a stretcher, and with the plane doctor in tow, hurried into an ambulance waiting on the landing strip.

Soon the pilot's voice came over the intercom again and reminded everyone to stay in their seats and prepare for takeoff. In preparation for the departure, the harried flight attendant charged up the aisle checking to see that seat belts were fastened. After all, it was her duty. She paused at our row of seats just long enough to speak to me. She leaned across the teenager, ignoring him as if he were an inanimate object. Her voice was slightly hushed as she spoke.

"What a crazy! She's a nut case. She kept moaning and muttering, 'Oh, God. Oh, God, no! That poor woman. There's danger in her future, and it's coming soon!' "

For a moment, it looked as if a genuine thought had passed through the flight attendant's brain, because she looked me straight in the eye as she said, "Good Lord! She was talking about you." Then she turned and thundered up the aisle.

A cold chill ran down my spine. *Happy vacation, Catherine!*

I spent the next hour of the flight trying to get my mind off the whole unfortunate episode. I'm a very practical sort of person who is not superstitious. Frankly, I've never given any real credibility to fortune-telling. I don't see it as a science, but as a type of diversion that's entertaining at school carnivals and county fairs, as long as you don't take the predictions seriously. Therefore, I told myself, it was important to forget the entire incident. I picked up my novel once again and determined to immerse myself in it.

Evidently I had done a good job of losing myself in my reading, because the next thing I knew, Miss Congeniality was passing a lunch tray to me.

Sizing it up as typical airline fare, I sighed and decided to make the best of it because I was starving and had no choice. The meal consisted of some indeterminate kind of chicken concoction over rice, a green salad, a roll and butter, and a creamy-looking chocolate dessert thing. The food didn't taste like much of anything, but on the other hand, it was edible. The chicken was rather chewy, but that was understandable, considering that it could have been cooked and frozen for two years before appearing in its present form on my plate. I was up to the one hundredth chew on the same chunk of chicken, when the teenager on the aisle scooted over into the seat next to me and smiled at me shyly.

"Dude, that was some weird grandma sitting here!" he remarked.

"Uh, yes, I guess you could say that."

"I was, like, really bummed out over the whole thing. I mean, like, was she heinous or what?"

"She was pretty strange all right."

"Did she, like, put a hex on you or something?"

"No, she just wanted to read my palm and tell my fortune. I told her no, but she did it anyway. Did she frighten you?"

"Like, affirmative, dude. She was too weird to be weird. It made me think, though, like, how many weirdos are really out there in the world? It boggles the mind, dude."

"True. By the way, I'm Catherine Hanson. And you are?"

"Beau Matson."

"Well, Beau, I'm glad to meet you. Would you mind if I ask you a question?"

"No problem."

"Does the ring in your nose bother you at all? Is it uncomfortable?"

Beau evidently liked this topic because his whole face lit up.

"Like, you noticed my nose ring! Cool! You know I've had it for about two months, and it's not sore anymore, but, like, it does itch sometimes. I've also got this weird bogus fear that something will happen, and I'll accidentally sniff the backing up into my brain, and I'll be history! But it's cool, that's why I like it. It's cool!"

With that, he winked at me and slid back over into his own seat, where he resumed the reading of his paperback book entitled *Surfing the World Over*.

After lunch, I was sufficiently tired from chewing to fall asleep. I napped dreamlessly until the pilot's voice woke me with his announcement that we would be landing in a few minutes. I did a quick touch-up of makeup and hair, and then obediently brought my seat into the proper upright position. According to the pilot, we were only thirty minutes behind schedule because en route the air currents had helped us make up time.

According to Nikki's instructions, I was to deplane, and one of Carlo's employees would be waiting to help me pick up my bags and shuttle over to the smaller airstrip devoted to private planes. Carlo's jet, complete with his personal pilot, would be waiting to whisk me off to the private island.

Carlo's "man" was not difficult to spot since he was holding a printed sign with large block letters reading CATHERINE HANSON. He was about my height, thirtyish, dark mustachioed, slender, pleasant looking, and impeccably dressed in a lightweight beige tropical suit.

I walked over to him and said, "Hello, I'm Catherine Hanson."

He smiled, bowed slightly, and pointed to a plastic name tag pinned to his lapel that read EDUARDO.

It soon became obvious that our entire communication was to consist of subtle facial expressions and appropriate head movements and gestures, such as nods, raised eyebrows, etc.

As we were walking to the baggage pickup, I asked him if he spoke English, but he merely raised his eyebrows and politely placed a gentle, but firm hand on my arm to guide me successfully through the baggage claim section. We picked up my bags, then boarded the tram, and finally arrived at the area where the Lear jet was parked.

I had never flown in a Lear jet before, and I can say that it was quite impressive inside and out. Eduardo gestured for me to follow him onto the plane as he dutifully carried my luggage and led the way. The interior looked expensive and luxurious with lots of taupe-colored leather. He nodded his head toward a vinyl-curtained area at the back of the cabin, and then raised his eyebrows. I translated this to mean that that was the restroom. Gratefully I made use of the facilities.

Surveying the cabin, it appeared that it would seat about seven adults quite comfortably. I selected a spot that I thought looked comfortable next to a window and seated myself. My host had disappeared momentarily, but he returned with a silver tray filled with scrumptious-looking tuna salad and ham sandwiches and a chilled glass of white wine. I selected a delicate tuna sandwich, nodded approvingly at the wine, and thanked him.

Eduardo nodded his head in acknowledgment and then lightly tapped the seat-belt strap.

"Oh, yes, I'll put it on now. Thanks, Eduardo."

With a little smile, Eduardo clicked his heels together and disappeared into the cockpit. Clicked his heels?

I couldn't help wondering if he could not speak English, could not speak at all, or if he was practicing to be a mime. At any rate, I was full of questions, but Marcel Marceau was not the one to answer them.

I enjoyed the delicious sandwich and the wine. It was light and satisfying. I was surprised that I was hungry, but I knew that the time change was playing havoc with my internal clock. I felt myself beginning to relax, far removed from the unpleasant incident on the plane. I eased back into the sumptuous leather seat. The wine was relaxing my tense neck muscles, and it felt good. I wanted to watch the scene below me, but I slipped into a brief nap. Only a few minutes later, Eduardo was lightly tapping my shoulder. I opened my eyes quickly, noted where I was, and stretched. I felt remarkably refreshed and clearheaded. I had never been a napper before, but look at me now. Two naps in one day. So this is how Reagan managed to complete a successful presidency. All of those snide jokes about his daytime sleeping habits were definitely unwarranted.

Eduardo smiled at me, leaned across me, and tapped on the window. I looked out and saw Puerto Rico spread out below. I could see the green bullet-shaped island, and El Morro fort, which was (according to my reading) symbolic of Spain's four-century rule over Puerto Rico. Nikki had mentioned in her letter to me that their island lay about thirty minutes northeast of Puerto Rico. We flew over more of the beautiful Caribbean, and then Eduardo sat down in the seat beside me and buckled his seat belt. He was an enigma. I made a mental note to find out more about him from Nikki.

Aware that we would be landing soon, I used my compact to powder my nose and put on fresh lipstick. In only a matter of minutes, Eduardo leaned across me once again and pointed toward the window.

We were approaching the island. The ocean was deep blue and vast below us, but coming up quickly was the island, which resembled a big green glob lined with a pale sandy color.

The pilot was a well-seasoned one because our landing was practically perfect. The plane touched down on the runway very gently and came to a controlled stop. Eduardo popped up, dashed to the cockpit, and then back to the cabin. He checked out the window to be certain that the steps were lined up to the plane properly and held out his hand to assist me. He opened the door, secured it, and then gestured for me to step out.

As I stood at the doorway of the plane, I took everything in at once. The sky was bright blue and cloudless, and the air was pleasantly warm, stirred by a slight breeze that barely ruffled my hair. Nikki stood at the bottom of the steps. Slender and bronzed by the sun, she wore a crisp, red sundress and red sandals. Dark sunglasses hid her eyes, but not her wide grin.

"Catherine! You made it!" she yelled.

"Nikki! It's great to be here," I called back. I walked down the steps, and we hugged each other.

"You look sensational, Catherine. You've kept your figure. Honestly, you could pass for thirty."

"What about you? You look sensational yourself. Your new life must agree with you, Nikki." I really thought she was too thin, but like a good friend, I didn't mention it.

We chirped on and walked arm in arm to the gleaming black limo. The chauffeur, attired in dark suit and tie, held open the back door for us, and we slid in. I heard the luggage being loaded into the trunk, and then the driver got behind the wheel. He steered the car briskly onto a blacktop road that looked practically new.

"Our house is only a ten-minute drive. Of course, nothing is very far away from anything here. The whole island is only seventy-five square miles in area."

"Nikki, from what I've seen it's beautiful." I peered out the tinted window and took in the azure-colored ocean to our left and the green-covered mountains on our right. Brilliant accents of red splashed the hillsides with color. The smooth, macadam road was practically deserted.

"What are those trees with the large red flowers called?" I asked.

"Oh, those are royal poinciana. Elegant looking, aren't they?"

"And the really tall trees with the large tulip-shaped blooms?"

"African tulip trees. They're abundant on this island and on Puerto Rico."

"They're lovely. Very exotic."

A lot of tropical-type vegetation hugged the roadside, and there were several different varieties of palm trees bordering the road.

"It's a far cry from Kansas," I muttered.

Together we gazed out at the beauty flowing past us. I was transfixed by the untamed lushness of the island. It truly was a paradise. My vacation was beginning to look promising once again.

"We're almost there," said Nikki.

The road continued to wind gently, following the contours of the island. Soon the driver slowed the car down and turned onto a narrower road that had only one lane. The driver used a remote-control device to unlock huge white wrought-iron gates. They swung slowly open, and a small guardhouse stood empty on the left. We drove on and soon the house was in sight. I don't know what I had expected, but nothing as large and elegant as what I was seeing.

"Nikki, it's gorgeous. It looks like Tara from *Gone with the Wind*."

"Yes, it does. Carlo has always been enamored with the South and its exquisite homes. It was always a dream of his to live in a southern-style mansion, and he made it come true."

The magnificent house and its landscaping were breathtaking. The whole picture was straight out of the South all right, but instead of magnolia trees and Spanish moss, there was a wide variety of palms and a profusion of flowering tropical plants.

Our driver expertly brought the car to a gentle stop on the circular drive in front of the house.

"Thank you, Milo. Please take Mrs. Hanson's things in to the 'spring room' so that Inez can unpack them."

"Yes, ma'am," he answered. I hadn't taken notice before, but Milo was a rather large, bulky-looking Italian man in his fifties with a big hooked nose and a menacing stare. Frankly, his appearance was downright frightening.

He opened the door of the limo for us, and fortunately, Nikki was closest to the door and took his hand as she got out of the car. I followed her, politely declining any assistance. Milo went to work unloading the trunk, and Nikki and I walked up the huge steps of the large pillared porch, complete with white wicker furniture, and into a spacious entry hall.

I looked around at the gleaming white marble floor, the

dramatic, curved staircase, and the massive crystal chandelier suspended above us from the sixty-foot-high ceiling. I realized my mouth was hanging open, and I closed it quickly, glad that none of my second graders were here to see how their teacher could gawk just like they did.

While I was still gazing up at the massive dome-shaped skylight that formed the high ceiling over the large entry hall, I heard a slight noise. Glancing to my right, I saw a petite Hispanic woman, sixtyish, dressed in a starched black-and-white long-sleeved uniform, standing next to Nikki. She seemed to have materialized out of nowhere.

"Good afternoon, señora," she said in a voice delicately laced with an accent. She bowed very slightly.

"Hello, Inez. Inez, this is Mrs. Hanson, my good friend."

"It's a pleasure to meet you, Mrs. Hanson. Please forgive me for staring, but you do look so much like Señora Cappelli."

"I'm glad to meet you, Inez. I understand about the staring. Everyone does when they see us together."

"I'll go upstairs now and unpack your things, Mrs. Hanson. Will that be agreeable to you?"

"Well, no, thank you. I mean, that isn't really necessary, Inez. I'm used to doing that kind of thing for myself."

Inez's face remained expressionless.

"Catherine, let Inez do it for you. You're on vacation, remember? You could use a little pampering," said Nikki.

"Oh, well, of course. I just didn't want to cause you any bother, Inez. Thank you."

Inez nodded and moved soundlessly up the stairs. I was beginning to think that everyone who worked here floated a couple of inches above the ground.

"Come on, Catherine. While she's unpacking your things, we can relax out on the terrace. You've had a long day of traveling. There's the powder room to your left. When you're ready, come straight along the dining room, and out through the terrace doors."

I headed for the bathroom. The fixtures were pure gold and everything else was marble. It was the most glamorous bathroom I had ever seen.

The terrace was huge. It was filled with a dizzying array of comfortable chairs that could easily seat fifty people. There were lounge chairs and club chairs of every size and description, all white wicker and cushioned in turquoise-and-white coordinating patterns. I felt like I was a guest at a four-star resort hotel.

Nikki and I stood at the railing of the terrace and looked at the amazing view. We could see out over a sloping hill and sandy beach to the beautiful Caribbean, which sparkled like a rare and precious jewel.

"You realize you may never get rid of me," I said to Nikki, who had just poured me a glass of iced tea.

She laughed.

"It does have that effect, doesn't it? Unfortunately, amid all this beauty, there is one drawback."

"And what is that?"

"Aside from the house staff, there are virtually no other people on this island. Carlo does quite a bit of traveling to Miami and New York. Sometimes he has to be gone for weeks at a time. When he's away, it's very lonely for me here."

"Do you ever go with him, Nikki?"

"I did in the beginning, but when he has business meetings, they can go on night and day. He just doesn't have time for me then, and I hate being in a hotel with nothing to do. Shopping and eating by yourself become very tiresome. I've found that it works out better for me to just stay here."

"How do you fill your time, Nikki? This place is a virtual paradise, but I imagine too much of a good thing can be tedious."

"I do love it here. It's so beautiful. You can see how perfect it all is, but it's isolated. Soon that will all change, though. Carlo and I are building a small luxury hotel on the other side of the island. It's about two-thirds of the way finished. Carlo has had me in on the designing of it from day one, so I've had that to occupy my time. I've been working very closely with the architect and the interior decorator, and it's kept me from going bananas. Once it's completed, I'll be helping to manage the hotel, of course."

"Nikki, that sounds very exciting. When will the hotel be finished?"

Nikki frowned. "Well, things have slowed down for a while. But that's only temporary. We need some additional financing. The hotel is costing more than Carlo thought it would originally, so he'll be returning to New York soon to take care of it."

"I know it's none of my business, but are there any problems about getting the financing you need?"

"No, not really. It's just that Carlo will need to get more backing from some of his friends. We had hoped it wouldn't be necessary, but these types of ventures often incur additional expenses."

"Would it be possible for you to show me the hotel while I'm here?"

"Of course, I'd love to show it to you. It's going to be unique and very posh."

"I'm sure things will go well, the building will be completed soon, and before you know it, you'll be playing Leona Helmsley, queen of your own hotel."

She made a face. "She ended up in prison, you nut."

"Sorry, bad reference. Nothing negative intended, Nikki. Just be sure and order your tiara well in advance of the grand opening."

"Thanks, pal!" she said, throwing a paper napkin at me which I managed to dodge.

Then Nikki launched into a barrage of questions about me, my life, and Mark. I filled her in on the high points of my basically humdrum, quiet life. As always, she was an attentive listener, an attribute I had always appreciated. Nikki had a way of making you feel that everything you said was very important. She seemed completely engrossed in all my stories. Somehow, all the years seemed to melt away, and I felt as close to her as I had been when we were college roommates.

"Nikki, it really is great to see you again. I'm so glad you made it possible for me to come. It feels like only yesterday that you and I were sitting up late after a date and having a heart-to-heart talk."

"I feel the same way, Catherine."

A rustling sound caused me to look around. It was Inez, in her black-and-white starched uniform, standing obediently directly behind me.

"Excuse me, Señora Cappelli. You asked me to remind you of the time. It's five P.M. now."

"Oh, thank you, Inez. Catherine and I have had such a good time catching up that I did lose track of the time. Catherine, cocktails are at six-thirty. I though you'd like a chance to rest a little and freshen up before dinner."

"Sounds like a good idea." Nikki led me back into the house, through the large dining room and living room, and up the stairs. At the end of a long, wide hall, Nikki swung open a door.

"We call it the 'spring room' because of its light, spring colors. I think you'll find everything you need. Don't hesitate to press 'one' on your phone, and Inez will be able to help you with anything."

She swept briskly out the door. The spring room was spacious, decorated in pretty, feminine pinks and greens. Elegant but comfortable. Large French doors opened out onto a small balcony. Balmy ocean air swirled in gently, bringing with it the fragrances of heavenly, exotic flowers. I took a deep breath and sighed. Yes, this was wonderful.

Across the room was the door to a large walk-in closet. True to her word, Inez had obviously unpacked everything, because all my clothes were hanging neatly, and my shoes were lined up in precise military fashion. A large mahogany dresser contained my other things folded in the same organized, exacting manner. My toiletries were displayed neatly on a silver tray in the gold-and-marble adjoining bath.

I took a long leisurely soak in the tub, washed my hair, and fluffed it dry outside on the balcony. I admired the lavish side garden that was overflowing with gorgeous, tropical flowers.

Sitting at the dressing table, I carefully applied my makeup. Never one to lay it on with a trowel, I nevertheless believe in the transforming magic of foundation, powder, blush, mascara, eyeliner, and lipstick applied with a light and practiced hand. I chose a hot pink dress with simple lines, not too short and not too revealing, and a pair of high-heeled gold sandals. A fine gold chain and matching earrings completed the look. One last glance in the mirror told me that I was ready to meet Nikki's husband and whoever else was present for dinner.

I descended the stairs slowly, wanting to soak in the atmosphere of the house. Although its exterior was definitely southern colonial, the inside reflected a tastefully elegant eclectic look. Below me in the entry hall, I saw Inez arranging a huge bouquet of exotic flowers in a large crystal vase, the centerpiece of a massive, round mahogany table. Another Hispanic woman, twentyish, stood next to Inez, and appeared to be the direct recipient of the older woman's anger.

Although Inez appeared to be furious, she kept her tone low so that I couldn't distinguish exactly what she was saying. The younger woman was getting a real tongue-lashing and was wringing her hands in distress. Inez delivered a powerful slap across the younger woman's face, and the poor thing burst into tears retreating immediately down another hallway. I stopped where I was. My presence hadn't been noticed yet, so I decided to appear ignorant of the awkward situation by waiting a few minutes before continuing down the stairs.

As soon as my heels touched the marble floor, Inez turned away from her flower arranging and attempted a pleasant look.

"Good evening, Mrs. Hanson. They're waiting for you on the terrace."

"Thank you, Inez." She was a sharp-faced woman whose

attempt at a smile didn't soften her features one iota, but instead made her look like someone who could use a strong dose of milk of magnesia. I clicked off down the hall.

Nikki was standing, gently leaning against the far terrace wall. She was elegant in a pale yellow sheath dress that clung to her curves and set off her deep tan. In her hand was an old-fashioned glass filled with what looked like ginger ale, and next to her stood a tall, dark, attractive Italian man whom I assumed was Carlo. Carlo had his arm around her waist and was speaking in a low, intimate voice. She laughed, and he pulled her to him kissing her passionately on the mouth. Once again, I felt it was appropriate to slow down my arrival and not interrupt this private moment. I waited a few minutes as they slowly separated and turned toward me.

As soon as she saw me, Nikki's face lit up.

"Catherine, this is my husband, Carlo."

Carlo smiled. "Catherine, it's wonderful to meet you in person at last. My Nikki has told me so much about you. But now, meeting you in person, I see why she refers to you as her twin. You're lovely! I'm overwhelmed by your resemblance to Nikki. It's startling and rather disarming, too, I must admit."

"Yes, it is, Carlo. Nikki and I are used to it, but it always seems to have this same effect on people."

"I want to welcome you, Catherine, to our little island paradise."

"Paradise seems to be a perfect word for it. It's simply breathtaking, all of it, from your gracious home to the island itself. Thank you so much for making it possible for me to come. I'm very happy to be here."

Carlo took my hand and kissed it. His dark eyes sparkled as he spoke. "It's our pleasure to have you here. My Nikki has been wanting to have you visit for a long time. I'm glad to make her wish come true. Thank you for coming."

Suddenly Eduardo appeared and handed me a crystal glass of champagne. The sounds of soft, samba music wafted across the terrace. Four Puerto Rican musicians expertly sailed their hypnotic music out onto the pleasantly balmy night air. Hearing the voices of several people in conversation, I noticed three new people for me to meet.

Carlo did the honors in his gracious manner.

He introduced me to Laura Masters, his secretary, and Luca Romano, his chief of security and personal assistant, and Alberto Albergetti, his business partner.

We talked for a few minutes, and then Eduardo appeared to announce that dinner was ready to be served.

A large round dining table complete with white linen cloth and candles was set for us. Carlo seated me to his left, Nikki to his right, and next to me sat Alberto, and then Laura, and then Luca. Champagne was poured all around, except to Nikki, who had Evian. Carlo raised his glass in a toast.

"In honor of Catherine, Nikki's good friend and our new friend. *Salud!*"

Everyone raised his glass to the toast, and the evening began.

The dinner was as exceptional as our surroundings. Crab and lobster, delightful green salad, spicy vegetables, and a freshly baked herb-flavored bread all elegantly served by Eduardo and the young woman who had been slapped by Inez. The champagne flowed, and I made a point to sip it slowly.

The conversation was relaxed and amiable. Alberto, Carlo's business partner, seemed to be a polite, reserved man. Although he was rather quiet, he did manage to hold up his end of the conversation. His homely appearance was in direct contrast to that of the handsome Carlo. Alberto looked about fifty-something, almost completely bald, with dark olive skin, piercing black eyes, large nose, and protruding ears. His five-o'clock shadow was exceptionally heavy, and I determined that by the end of dinner, he would be fully bearded once again.

"Catherine, Nikki tells me that you have a son," said Carlo.

"Yes, his name is Mark. He's just recently graduated from

college. Right now, he's enjoying the summer in Europe. In the fall, he'll be attending Harvard Law School."

"He must be an intelligent young man. He's been awarded a full scholarship, too, I understand."

"Yes, that's right. I think his brilliance comes from his father, who was an exceptional history professor."

"He's a lot like his father, then?"

"Yes, very much. I regret deeply that his father is not alive to see how well Mark has done and how much he's accomplished. He would have been proud."

Carlo's face clouded over. "Such a shame. The pride a father feels for a good son is the crowning glory of a man's life. The greatest accomplishment he can have is a worthy and honorable son, strong in mind and body."

With Carlo's pronouncement, an uncomfortable silence fell across the table. He stared into the candlelight with the expression of a man who had lost everything. Or was I misreading this altogether?

Carefully I glanced at Nikki to see how she was reacting to all of this. She looked painfully grim. I realized that before this evening, her eyes had been masked by her sunglasses, and only now could I see the dark circles under her eyes.

Finally, after long minutes of uncomfortable silence, Laura Masters attempted to change the subject.

"Catherine, you're going to love the weather here. Most days are so perfect that I find it hard to concentrate on my work. By the end of the summer, you'll return home totally rested and beautifully tanned."

"And terribly spoiled, too, I'm afraid."

Everyone laughed, even Carlo and Nikki.

"Every day I try my best to get Carlo and Alberto to finish early, so I can sneak in at least an hour of sun," said Laura. "Catherine, these guys are real slave drivers. We work five days a week, sometimes six, and our days start early at seven."

Carlo smiled and nodded in agreement. "I'm afraid she's right, Catherine. Alberto and I are workaholics. There's a lot to do and not enough hours in the day. Sometimes it takes Nikki and Laura together to get us to call it a day."

Nikki smiled weakly, but she had not regained her original exuberance since Carlo's statement about fatherhood. I wished I could say something to make her feel better, but I knew it would be wrong to discuss it in front of the others.

Laura seemed to be a congenial type and good at keeping the conversation going. She apparently had been raised in New York City, as had Carlo and Alberto. We all took part in a lively conversation about professional baseball. Everyone except Luca, that is. Nikki brightened up again and told us a funny story about her and Carlo's last visit to New York, and how she had actually caught a foul ball at Yankee Stadium. I couldn't help noticing that Luca Romano, Carlo's personal assistant, smiled and nodded occasionally but never initiated any conversation. Luca was a massive man, very muscular. Probably a weight lifter who spent hours developing his body, but not his brain.

Dessert arrived and was served graciously by Eduardo and the young woman. I learned that her name was Elisa. She had a natural beauty and grace about her. As she placed before me a handsome portion of the delicious-looking key lime pie, I sneaked a peek at her face and saw that she was attempting to hide a rather nastily bruised and swollen cheek with makeup.

Everyone lingered over coffee, good-naturedly complaining that they had eaten too much. Finally Carlo stood, and the rest of us followed suit. Eduardo reappeared to offer the men Carlo's prized Cuban cigars. After lighting up they walked over to talk to the four-piece band that had artistically played their sambas, rumbas, tangos, and cha-chas softly throughout our meal.

Laura stretched her arms and yawned, politely covering her mouth.

"Please excuse me. It's been an awfully long day, and I'm exhausted. As I explained earlier, Catherine, we do put in a lot of hours. I hope you and Nikki will excuse me. I'm going to call it a night." I had thought earlier, when we were introduced, that she was a rather slender woman. In reality, she was slim, all except for her tummy, which looked to be a slightly pregnant one, if I were still capable of seeing straight after the long hours of traveling I had put in that day.

"I'm tired, too, Laura. Catherine, you must be worn out yourself." Nikki sighed deeply. She did not look well.

I agreed. "It sounds like we've all had a full day. Nikki, the dinner was lovely. Thank you for a great evening. Now I think we all need sleep."

We said our good nights to the men, who teasingly proclaimed to be superior in stamina because they could stay up later than we ladies who were conking out at ten o'clock. Carlo expressed concern over Nikki, who was usually a night owl. They embraced and kissed lightly on the lips, and she urged him not to stay up too late. To me, they seemed every bit the loving couple.

We parted ways at the stairs, as Nikki's suite was in the other wing and so was Laura's. I gave the secretary one last look as she turned to go in the opposite direction. Thirtyish, olive-skinned, tall, shapely, sensuous, and sexy even with a pregnant tummy. Her mane of dark, shoulder-length hair was thick and shiny.

I waved to Nikki, and she waved back. I hoped I could remember my way back to my room. It was such a large house, and I wasn't exactly sure which room was mine. I just kept walking and recognized my room because Inez happened to be standing in front of the door, apparently waiting for me.

"Mrs. Hanson, is there anything else I can do for you tonight?"

"No, thank you, Inez. I'm going to bed now. It's been a long day. Oh, is breakfast served at a particular time?"

"No, Mrs. Hanson. Señor Cappelli, Miss Masters, and Mr. Albergetti eat early, around six-thirty. Often they eat together in the building that houses their offices. Señora Cappelli breakfasts around ten. I take a tray to her room. But there is nothing formal about breakfast. We will serve you at whatever time you wish. Perhaps I could bring you a tray. Señora Cappelli wants you to relax and have a leisurely breakfast."

"Thank you for the information, Inez. Uh . . . doesn't Mr. Romano eat breakfast?"

She gave me that milk-of-magnesia look again.

"Mr. Romano eats his breakfast in the kitchen around six o'clock." She sniffed as though she smelled something unpleasant. "Good night, Mrs. Hanson."

"Good night." I regretted that I hadn't had a chance to talk to Nikki again. But I knew we were both tired, and whatever we needed to talk about could easily wait until morning.

CHAPTER 7

I awoke at about midnight with a terrible thirst. Of course, it was the champagne. Wine always made me thirsty. I switched on the table lamp by the bed and went into the bathroom. A large marble vanity occupied one side of the spacious bath, and there I found a silver pitcher of icy cold water and, naturally, a lead-crystal goblet. I poured a full glass and gulped down the whole thing. I refilled it and sipping slowly, carried it back to the bedroom. Sitting on the edge of the bed, I turned out the light. The full moon spread a soft glow through the open French doors. A gentle warm breeze stirred the sheer curtains covering the doors. With glass in hand, I stepped out onto the balcony. The night was clear, and the stars appeared very bright against the dark, midnight blue sky. Everything was still, except for the friendly chirping of the crickets. I thought about Mark and hoped his night sky in France was as beautiful as mine was here.

Suddenly I heard the low murmur of voices and determined that the sound was coming from the garden below me.

"This whole situation is impossible, and you know it," said a man's voice.

"It is not impossible. I don't expect you to understand anyway. I just need for you to go along with me," a woman answered.

"I don't know what good that'll do. How do you expect people to believe that you and I . . . that you and I . . ."

"That you and I made love, and that you got me pregnant? Why don't you think they'll believe that?"

"Because," the man said, "because you're so beautiful and I'm so . . . I'm so ugly."

The woman's tone softened.

"That's not true. You're not ugly. And besides, they will believe it if we say it's true and act like we mean it. Please, I need your help. . . ."

"The whole story seems so implausible. You know I want to help you, but it seems like something from *Beauty and the Beast*. A nice fairy tale, but not very realistic . . . but, all right, I'll do it, if that's what you really want."

"We have to convince them that it happened the evening of the big party in San Juan. Everyone was drunk, including you and me. We'll just say that we had been drinking too much, and that we got caught up in the moment. It was a one-night thing, a fluke, a mistake."

"You just don't seem like the type not to take precautions."

"We were drunk, plastered, smashed, remember? People lose their heads in the heat of passion and act irresponsibly. Even normally reliable and level-headed types like me and you."

No one said anything for several minutes.

"Okay, okay. I'll do my best to make the story believable. You know I'd do anything for you, Laura."

"Thank you, Alberto. All I ask is that you follow my lead and make this a convincing performance."

It seemed that I had just overheard a very private conversation. Thankfully, they hadn't seen me on the balcony so I stood very still, waiting until they moved away. I heard muted footsteps walking across a side patio and then into the house. I went back into the bedroom and climbed into bed.

It was going to be difficult to fall asleep after hearing the secretive conversation. I told myself to forget it and go to sleep. I wished that I hadn't heard anything. After all, it was none of my business. I was here on vacation, and I didn't want to get involved in somebody else's problems.

I had no idea what time I fell asleep. But the next time I looked at the bedside clock, it read ten A.M. I hadn't intended to sleep that late. I jumped up, took a quick shower, made up my face, and put on a matching pink knit shirt and walking shorts. I hurried downstairs to find Nikki.

I found my way to the dining room and saw that an elegant sideboard was laid out with a help-yourself type of breakfast or lavish coffee break, whichever the case might be. Steaming coffee, freshly squeezed orange juice, fresh fruit, and a scrumptious-looking assortment of sweet rolls. Seeing no one else in sight, I decided to serve myself a quick breakfast and then find Nikki. It was well after ten-thirty now, and most likely, she was wondering if her lazy guest was going to sleep all day.

"Good morning, Mrs. Hanson. Can I get you anything else?" came a voice from out of nowhere. I jumped.

"Oh! Good morning, Inez. You frightened me. I didn't notice anyone else in the room."

"I'm sorry, Mrs. Hanson," she cooed as though I were some idiot child. "You must still be a little edgy from your long trip." She always seemed to be lurking somewhere. Lurking. Intrusive. Intrusive Inez. It had a certain ring to it.

"Maybe so. Have you seen Señora Cappelli this morning? I didn't intend to oversleep. I wanted to have breakfast with her."

"I took a tray in to her just a few minutes ago. She doesn't appear to be feeling too well."

I finished the last bite of my raspberry Danish and dabbed my mouth lightly.

"In that case, I'll go see how she is."

"Mrs. Hanson, perhaps you shouldn't disturb her. She's trying to rest."

"Oh, I won't stay long."

This did not seem to please Inez at all. However, she collected my dishes and marched off to the kitchen with a disapproving look on her face.

I wasn't really sure which room was Nikki's, since I had not been given a grand tour of the house yet. I knew it was in the other wing, upstairs, so I just kept walking. As it turned out, all the doors were open until I got to the end room. The door was closed. I tapped lightly.

"Nikki? Nikki, it's me, Catherine."

Silence.

"Nikki, it's me. Can I come in?"

Finally I heard her say softly, "Come in."

I opened the door. The room was twice the size of mine and was decorated in soft blues and peach. The heavy damask curtains were closed. Across the room in a huge king-size bed lay Nikki. She was propped up on a stack of pillows, looking very small beneath the big canopy that was swathed in yards of elegant blue satin moire. She wore no makeup. Her hair was disheveled, and her skin was very pale. The dark circles under her swollen eyes were quite prominent, and she looked as if she had been crying. A lot.

"Nikki, are you sick?" I asked, perching lightly on the side of the bed.

"No, I'm not . . . well . . . yes, in a way I am. I'm sick and tired of being this way."

"What's wrong?"

Nikki lay there in silence struggling with some internal turmoil.

"I might as well tell you, Catherine. You'll figure it out anyway. . . . I . . . Well, I've started drinking again. . . . Last night, when I excused myself early, I wasn't really tired. I came back here to drink, in secret, so no one would see me."

My spirits sank.

"But I thought you were doing so well, Nikki. I thought you were off the stuff for good. You'd been sober for two years, and I thought . . . well . . . I hoped you were really on your way to a new life with Carlo."

"I was fine for a while. But then Carlo had to start traveling, and I got so lonely. I tried hard, Catherine. I really did, and I thought I was finally over it for good. But any alcoholic will tell you that it's never really over. It's just a lifelong battle that doesn't end."

She burst into tears.

I embraced her, hugging her as tight as I could.

"Oh, Nikki, I'm so sorry. I had no idea. What can I do to help you?"

She didn't say anything but continued to sob her heart out. Finally she sighed and dabbed at her eyes with a tissue. She gave me a weak smile. "Thanks, Catherine, I'd forgotten how comforting it is to have a good friend to unload on. It's really therapeutic to be able to talk to you about this."

"What can I do to help you? Obviously there's no local chapter of AA here. What does Carlo say?"

"Carlo is very unhappy with me. I think we were really building a strong marriage, but then this thing came up. I'm seeing a psychiatrist now in San Juan. Carlo insisted on it. It's just that I'm afraid I'm never going to beat this thing."

"Do you think the doctor is helping?"

"Yes . . . a little . . . I suppose. The doctor wants me to come to San Juan and stay in the sanatorium there for a few months. He thinks that's the only way I'm ever going to resolve this thing. He wants me to come now, but I wanted to have one more chance to do this on my own here. I'm afraid I'll lose Carlo either way, but I've just got to try one more time. That's . . . uh . . . that's one of reasons why I invited you. I knew I would feel strong having you here. I believed this was the one thing that could save me. I'm sorry. I don't mean to put so much pressure on you, Catherine. I need your support now and your friendship."

"Nikki, I don't know what I can do. Of course, I want to help you, but in the end you know you have to do it yourself. I can't be your watchdog. You'd hate me."

"Oh, I'm not asking you to do that, Catherine. I know it's up to me. But if you're here for a while this summer while Carlo is gone, I know I can get strong. With you here, we can play tennis, swim, take long walks, talk . . . have fun. If you don't want to stay, I'll understand. I should have told you before now. But I was afraid you wouldn't come at all. Please say you'll give me a chance. Just stay for a little while."

I was overwhelmed by what she had said. This was a big order. I had a lot of doubts, but I agreed to stay. At least for a while. I was touched by her faith in me, but doubted seriously that my mere presence alone could actually prevent her from drinking. Still, she was my friend, and if I could help her at all, I wanted to give it my best shot.

She seemed greatly relieved. She hugged me again.

"Thank you, Catherine. Thank you so much! I can do it, you wait and see. Now, let me take a quick shower, and we'll get on with the day." Her tear-stained face broke into a wide grin, and I could see the old Nikki shining through. The one with gutsy determination and grit.

We spent the rest of the morning outside in the glorious sunshine. After playing a couple of sets of tennis—we each won one set—we found a shady spot under a tall palm and sat down to enjoy the delicious picnic lunch that Inez had packed for us.

Nikki and I scrubbed our hands with moist towelettes.

"I feel much better, Catherine. I love to play, but there's seldom anyone around to play with."

"Does Carlo play?" I asked, munching on a stalk of celery.

"Sometimes, but he rarely has the time. When he's not in meetings with Laura and Alberto, he's conducting business over the phone."

"It's a shame he has to work so hard. However, I'm sure it takes a lot of money to support this lifestyle, and that means long hours."

"There's really more to it than that. Carlo grew up very poor in New York. His father was a school janitor, and his mother died of tuberculosis when Carlo was only five. He was the youngest of eight children. When Carlo's mother died, his father left home. Just vanished one day, leaving all the children alone. They had no other family, and all the children were sent to the state orphanage. Soon, Carlo was adopted by a wealthy couple who became abusive. He was beaten, kicked, and whipped on a regular basis. The father was a well-respected judge, and no one ever suspected him of any abuse. He claimed that Carlo was clumsy and fell a lot. No one dared to question him. When Carlo was ten, he ran away because he knew he couldn't live that way any longer. He managed to survive on the streets and ended up living with and eventually working for the head of a mafioso family, the Cappellis. Mr. Cappelli, Luigi, deployed his personal attorneys to investigate Carlo's adoptive parents. The attorney discovered that the judge and his wife had been killed in a car crash soon after Carlo ran away. Having become quite fond of the boy, the Cappellis used their 'influence' to formally adopt Carlo. The Cappellis treated Carlo well, provided a home and family for him, and after he graduated from high school, sent him to Columbia University. After graduation, Mr. Cappelli set Carlo up in a legitimate business, owning and managing several Italian restaurants. That was how he began, but the rest of his success is largely due to Carlo's own drive. He can never forget how he started out in life."

"I guess that explains his long hours with little time off. He probably doesn't know how to play, because he never had a real childhood."

"Yes, it's hard for him to relax."

"Do the Cappellis still live in New York?"

"No. They were all murdered a couple of years after Carlo graduated from the university."

"My God! What happened?"

"There was a terrible fire one weekend. Carlo was living in his own apartment in New York City. That weekend he was out of town on business. The rest of the family was at home together. . . . It's hard for me to tell this. . . . I'm sorry . . . Well, Mr. and Mrs. Cappelli and their four daughters were all home for the weekend. It happened during the night. A raging fire started while they were asleep and killed them all. The authorities thought it was arson, but their investigation turned up nothing. Carlo was devastated. His whole family was wiped out. There was a lot of speculation that it might have been a rival Mafia family who murdered the Cappellis. Catherine, Carlo has lived with the terrible memory of that weekend for many years."

Nikki's eyes were filled with tears.

I handed her an extra napkin to wipe her eyes.

"Carlo still has horrible nightmares of the fire. He says he feels guilty that he wasn't killed, too. Sometimes I see him, even now, staring off into space. He says he can't stop going over it in his mind."

"How tragic! It must have been horrible for him."

"Yes, it was. Carlo said that for a long time he hardly had the will to continue living himself. Of course, that was years before I met him. He also lived through a succession of bad marriages before we found each other."

"It sounds like you've both been through a lot."

"Yes, that's true, Catherine. That's why I have to get myself straightened out. Because we do love each other very much, I've got to stay sober to make this marriage work." Her face looked sad again.

"Nikki, I don't mean to pry, but since you've involved me in your private lives, there's something I need to ask you."

"Go ahead, Catherine. You can ask me anything."

"Well, last night at dinner, I had the impression that Carlo either had a son and lost him or is disappointed because he never had one."

"He did have a son, Carmine, with his first wife, Annette. He divorced her because of her severe drinking problem. He tried to get custody of Carmine, who was two at the time, but Annette's attorney was just more devious than Carlo's was. Soon after the divorce, Annette went on a drinking binge that lasted for days. Carmine, who was unattended throughout that time, fell to his death from their apartment window on the twentieth floor. Carlo has never gotten over it."

"Did he know that you were an alcoholic when he married you, Nikki?"

"Yes, but we were so much in love. He said it didn't matter. Besides, I had been sober for months, and he never saw me drinking. That's why I can't let him or myself down, Catherine. We've got some problems, but I think they're caused by my drinking."

"I understand, Nikki. And he never fathered any other children?"

"No, his second wife, Zara, had a daughter, Nina, from a previous marriage. After Nina's birth, Zara had her tubes tied. I want to make this marriage work, Catherine. I *have* to make it work. There are problems, but I know we can straighten them out. This is a last chance for both of us. If we fail . . . I mustn't . . . I have to . . . So much is riding on this. . . ."

Two shrieking sea gulls overhead interrupted Nikki.

For a few minutes, we both sat very quietly thinking about the tragic stories she had told me.

Finally, she stood and began putting things back into the picnic basket. She attempted a brave smile.

"Now it's time for a swim. I'll race you to the pool!" she yelled. We were eighteen again.

We changed quickly into swimsuits in a poolside dressing room and had a nice, relaxing swim in the Olympic-size pool. Afterward, Nikki and I sat in the sun and enjoyed its soothing warmth. It wasn't long, though, before we started feeling a bit sunburned, so we decided to head inside, she for a short nap, me to dash off a few letters. I needed to write a note to Bob and Millie. I could tell them about how picture-perfect this place was and also about my weird experience with the Gypsy lady.

I returned to my room and reached out to turn the crystal knob on the door, when a noise from inside caused me to stop. It sounded like someone was opening and closing drawers.

And rapidly, too. Pulling them open and slamming them shut. I decided to open the door.

It was Luca. He closed a drawer quickly and turned around, grinning sheepishly at me.

"What are you doing in my room?" I asked, trying to keep my anger under control.

"Mrs. Hanson, I'm sorry. I know what this must look like, but I wasn't snooping. This was my room for several months before you arrived, and I'm missing some cuff links. I felt sure I must have left them in here, and I came to find them."

"I see, and you didn't think to wait until I was here to ask me if you could look for them."

"Well, I knocked, but you're weren't here. I didn't think you'd mind if I just came in and looked."

"You assumed quite a lot, didn't you? You should have waited until I was here. That would've been the right thing to do. Please respect my privacy in the future."

He gave me a lopsided grin.

"If I'd known you were going to make such a big fuss, I would've waited. I really think you're blowing this thing out of proportion, Mrs. Hanson. Sorry to bother you."

He wanted to exit, but I was standing in the way. I realized how large he actually was. He moved toward the door, forcing me to step aside. His size was naturally intimidating.

"Did you find what you were looking for?" I asked as he moved past me into the hall, intentionally brushing up against me. "You know, Luca, the missing cuff links?"

He gave me a supercilious look.

"Yeah, I did. See?" He held up two flashy gold cuff links.

"Must have a hot date to require those," I said sarcastically.

"The only kind of date I ever have, Mrs. Hanson," he replied with a smirk.

I watched him walk off down the hall with his swaggering gait, the kind that egotistical athletes always affect.

I went back into my room, shut the door, and locked it.

I opened the drawers to see if any of my things had been

disturbed. He was a neat searcher, I'll say that for him. If I hadn't caught him in the act, I would never have known he'd been in my room. I felt angry and violated. And I didn't believe his story about the cuff links either. Being a second-grade teacher had taught me to be a bit on the suspicious side.

I spent the rest of the afternoon writing to Millie and Bob, taking a shower, and getting dressed for the evening ahead. The letter to the Parkers was light and cheerful. After all, why should I burden them with all the odd bits of disturbing information that I was privy to? I wished that I could write to Mark, but since he and his buddies would be on the move most of the time, there would be no address for me to write him. He had promised to drop me a card now and then to let me know he was all right.

I assumed that cocktails would be about the same time as yesterday, so I worked on making myself look presentable. As I considered my choice of dinner attire, I wished that I had been somewhat more conservative in my selection of dresses. When Millie was helping me shop, I had had this carefree attitude of "letting go and letting loose" on this vacation. Now that I was here, and knowing some of my housemates' little secrets, I felt uncomfortable exposing too much of myself, physically and emotionally. Unfortunately, I had a choice of slightly sexy, revealing, or seductive. Finally I chose a black, low-cut little number that seemed to be as acceptable as any of the other dresses.

I was just adding pearl earrings and a pearl choker, hoping that the necklace might distract the eye upward, when the telephone rang. I jumped, a habit that was becoming uncomfortably customary for me.

"Catherine?" It was Nikki.

"Hi. Did your nap help?"

"Oh, yes, I'm feeling fine now. Catherine, I'm sorry I forgot to tell you that cocktails are at six-thirty. It's almost that time now. Will you be able to make it?"

"Of course. I just assumed we would meet somewhere around that time. I'm all ready."

"Good. We have guests this evening. The architect and the interior decorator for our hotel. They just flew in an hour ago. I think you'll like both of them. It should be a fun evening."

"Sounds good. Should I come down now?"

"Yes, of course. See you in a couple of minutes."

" 'Bye."

On the way out, I squirted a touch of Estée Lauder's Private Collection behind each ear. As I closed the door I wished I could lock the room from the outside. Since Luca's unannounced visit, I felt especially vulnerable.

I set off toward the terrace, and on the way almost crashed into a gentleman I had not yet met. He was coming out of the room next to mine. I was busy looking down at my left leg checking to make sure I didn't have a run when we bumped into one another.

"Oh, Nikki, I'm ever so sorry," he said. "I'm just too clumsy. Please forgive me, my dear."

"I'm sorry, too. I should have been watching where I was going." I realized I was looking down into the face of a very short man. He was at best only five feet tall, and with my super-high heels on, I definitely towered over him.

"But I'm not Nikki. I'm Catherine Hanson, Nikki's good friend from Kansas."

"What? You're not Nik . . . Oh . . . oh . . . yes, now I remember that Nikki said you were almost identical. Still, I had no idea . . . It's incredible . . . You do look like twins! It's amazing! Oh, I'm sorry to be so rude, it's just that I can't believe . . ."

"Everyone has the same reaction. Nikki and I are used to it."

"Catherine, I'm Jeremiah Stephens, interior decorator. I'm very happy to meet you."

"I'm glad to meet you, too, Jeremiah."

"Well, my dear lady, let us proceed to dinner. I promise not to step on your toes as we go." He was a pleasant little man, immaculately dressed in a light-colored tropical-weight suit and a pale yellow shirt, accented with a matching yellow scarf around his neck and a fresh yellow hibiscus in his buttonhole. He was slender, with a full head of wavy brown hair and a very neatly trimmed mustache. His skin was lightly tanned, and he looked like he was in his mid- to late thirties. His face was cute and round, with the kind of cheeks that maiden aunts can't resist pinching. In fact, he looked more like an adorable little doll than a man.

We walked briskly out to the patio and were greeted warmly by Nikki, Carlo, and Alberto. Luca and Laura had not shown up yet. Next to Nikki and Carlo stood a tall man who held himself very erect. He was distinguished looking, around sixty. His hair was all white. Something about him reminded me of a somber rendition of the debonair actor Cesar Romero.

When Carlo introduced me to Richard Hilliard, the architect, we shook hands, and I was struck by his coldness. He seemed polite, but very aloof, in direct contrast to the effervescent Jeremiah Stephens.

Nikki looked beautiful in a slinky, white, backless knit. Evidently she was accustomed to Richard Hilliard's rather cool personality, because she seemed truly glad to see him and kept linking her arm through his. In fact, Nikki, definitely in a party mood, led him onto the dance floor. (The little combo from the previous night was back.) They made a striking couple, and out on the dance floor their rumba would have made Ginger Rogers and Fred Astaire jealous. As I was enjoying watching the magic couple dance, the cherubic Jeremiah took my hand and soon I found myself dancing, too. Although I towered over him, Jeremiah proved to be a talented dancer himself and led me successfully through a samba, a dance I hadn't tried since the high school cotillion.

The sensuous, upbeat music was infectious, and soon Luca, partnered with Laura, joined us on the dance floor. Carlo followed suit with a young woman I had not met yet and who had just come out onto the terrace. She was dark-skinned, vastly overweight, and not the least bit attractive. Her face seemed to be fixed in a permanent scowl, making her features appear even more unattractive than they were. The musicians, encouraged by the number of dancers their music had attracted, kept extending the length of the song, and it lasted a full ten minutes. With the conclusion of the selection, everyone clapped enthusiastically. I noticed that everyone was smiling except the young woman.

Eduardo appeared and offered liquid refreshment to everyone, in the form of a large yummy, tropical, mixed drink that quenched the thirst but proved to be lethal if you drank more than one.

Carlo wiped his brow with his handkerchief and hung his coat carefully over the back of a chair.

"Catherine, I want you to meet my stepdaughter, Nina Migliazzo."

I gave Nina a brilliant smile and shook her sweaty hand. She returned my gesture with a snarly expression. I wasn't sure how to interpret that.

Carlo seemed unperturbed. He was probably used to her sour disposition. Interestingly enough, no one else seemed to care either.

"Catherine, Nina is the daughter of my second wife, Zara. She lives with her mother in New York not far from Richard and took the opportunity to come out for a short visit."

"How lovely. This place is really a paradise, isn't it?"

Evidently politeness was not one of Nina's strong points. She gave me a vacant stare and yelled to Eduardo, "Hey, Eddie, bring me another one of these pink drinks, okay?"

Carlo looked away, seemed to regain his composure, and turned to me once again.

"Catherine, you look ravishing this evening." His eyes dropped from my face to my cleavage in one smooth sweep.

"You and Nikki are so much alike in every way. It would be a man's ultimate dream come true to have two very beautiful women who were identical in personality and . . . uh . . . form."

Slightly embarrassed, I blushed deeply. A result of my Kansas upbringing. A response over which I had no control.

"Nikki and I are very different in personality, Carlo. I'm surprised you haven't noticed that yet."

He licked his lips and flashed me another gleaming smile.

"My answer to that, Catherine, is *vive la différence*!"

Eduardo appeared and motioned that dinner was ready, and Carlo set about seating us. Luckily I ended up between the pleasant Alberto and the friendly Jeremiah.

Dinner was another culinary success, thanks to the chef I had yet to see. The chicken was succulent and seasoned perfectly, and the vegetables were crisp and garden fresh. I hadn't eaten a meal here that wasn't visually appetizing as well as top-notch in taste. After dinner, a beautiful dessert was presented. Nikki had seemed particularly bubbly and full of life all evening, so I was surprised when she quietly apologized and asked to be excused when the coconut-cream pie arrived. I hoped she wasn't leaving to do some private drinking.

"Please don't let my absence dampen your evening. I would be very unhappy if I thought you wouldn't all remain and enjoy yourselves. I just have a touch of indigestion and need to lie down. And let me add that the indigestion has nothing to do with the excellent dinner. It's just me. I've been having a little problem with it lately."

All of the men stood, Carlo kissing her cheek, and the rest of the group behaving in a respectfully subdued manner acknowledging the exit of their charming hostess. Carlo offered his assistance, but she declined. Each one of us expressed concern and wished her good night.

"Has Nikki been having digestive problems lately, Carlo?" I asked.

"Sometimes. It goes in cycles really. She has a very delicate digestive system that seems to get out of kilter rather easily if she doesn't watch what she eats."

"Has she seen a doctor?"

"Yes, the last time our doctor was visiting the island. A month ago, in fact. He warned her about spicy foods."

"Do you have a regular doctor?"

"Well, yes, in a manner of speaking. Dr. Laurenza lives in San Juan and has limited his practice now. He comes out whenever we need him. It's a short trip by air."

"Does she have some medication?"

"Oh, yes. Don't worry, Catherine. This happens from time to time. It's nothing serious. She'll be fine after a good night's sleep."

"I hope so." It seemed to me that only Jeremiah and I showed any real concern. His cherubic little mouth turned downward in a frown.

Nina, who sat next to her stepfather, was glassy-eyed as she reached the bottom of her third drink, and the straw made a loud gurgly sound as it sucked in nothing but air.

"Papa, I need more," she whined like a spoiled child.

"No, Nina, you've had quite enough," he said firmly. He snapped his fingers in the air, and Eduardo appeared instantly.

"Eduardo, please assist Nina to her room," said Carlo in a hushed tone.

Eduardo nodded and tried to hoist the ponderous Nina up out of her chair. It obviously wasn't going to work since Nina outweighed Eduardo by at least a hundred and fifty pounds. He propped her back up carefully in her chair and went off in search of reinforcements. Carlo asked the men to join him for cigars, and excusing themselves, they walked off to look out at the ocean. Eduardo returned soon with Milo, the chauffeur.

Together they hauled the whalelike Nina away. It was not a pretty sight.

Only Laura and I remained at the table.

"Well, I think I'll excuse myself, Catherine. It's close to eleven, and it's been another full day."

As we started back into the house, Laura began to talk.

"That horrid girl Nina. I don't know why Carlo lets her come here. She isn't his real daughter, you know."

"He introduced her as his stepdaughter. Has she been here many times?"

"Oh, she comes every few months or so. I don't like her at all. She always has such an ugly disposition, and when she comes she never spends time with Carlo. She just eats and drinks herself into oblivion. Altogether an unpleasant person."

"She certainly didn't seem very friendly. Is she on good terms with Nikki?"

"Oh, I think Nikki tolerates her like the rest of us do, but they don't have any kind of relationship, if that's what you mean. Nikki tried to be especially nice in the beginning, but when she discovered that Nina wanted nothing to do with her, Nikki backed off."

"Nina looks young. Does she go to college or work?"

Laura laughed. "Are you kidding? That fat cow? She just sits around and gives fucking orders to people. Her mother, Zara, got a huge settlement from Carlo and lives in a posh uptown apartment. They have lots of servants, and Nina doesn't give any of them a moment's peace. She just sits on her fat ass and barks out orders. Oh, yes, and when she's with Carlo, she always calls him 'Papa,' which seems to temporarily summon his paternal feelings for her, making him forget momentarily what a pain she really is."

"If she's so obnoxious, why does Carlo let her come here?"

Laura yawned. "I have absolutely no idea. Listen, I'm sorry I used such crude language to describe her. I wouldn't want you to think that I talk that way all the time. It's just that I find her intolerable."

"Of course, I understand."

CHAPTER 8

I awoke early the next morning. I had been restless all night, unable to find a comfortable position for sleeping and unable to relax. All kinds of things kept buzzing around in my head, none of which made any sense. I decided to go down to the beach and take a walk by the ocean. I hurriedly brushed my hair, brushed my teeth, washed my face, and applied a minimum of makeup. Next, I put on a T-shirt, walking shorts, and walking shoes. Hopefully, I wouldn't run into a single soul. I felt like being alone.

Once I reached the main floor, I saw no one as I walked across the terrace to the steps that led to the beach. The sun was already warm, even though it was only seven o'clock, and it felt good on my face. In front of me, I saw lots of palm trees and a well-trodden trail that wound along the beach. The ocean looked picture-postcard perfect. The sand was white, sparkling beneath the bright sun. Taking off my tennis shoes and socks, I carried my footwear as I enjoyed the simple pleasure of walking barefoot in the gently warmed sand. I smiled to myself as I meandered along the shore, reveling in the solitude of the morning. After I had walked about a mile on the empty beach, I came to some rocks that jutted out into the water. I climbed up on a rather flat-looking one and sat down to enjoy the view of the beautiful blue Caribbean. Only a few minutes had passed when I heard the sound of running footsteps coming my way.

It was Jeremiah, the interior decorator, jogging. Dressed all in white, he was decked out in appropriate athletic attire right down to the latest in running shoes. When he saw me, he waved his hand vigorously, and ran over to me.

"Good morning, Catherine! Mind if I join you for a few minutes?"

"Please do." The rock was a large one, probably big enough for ten people to sit on comfortably. He climbed up and sat down next to me.

"I can tell you're a regular jogger," I said.

"Yes, it's something I've been doing for about fifteen years now. I love it. It makes me feel great and keeps me in shape."

"I admire your dedication. I like to walk, but I'm not nearly as disciplined as you are about keeping to a regular schedule."

He pulled a water bottle off a hook attached to his waistband. "Would you like some? I haven't drunk from it yet."

"No thanks, you go ahead. You're the one that needs it."

He took several long swigs from the bottle.

"Catherine, I must tell you I still do a double take because you look so much like Nikki."

"Maybe I should just wear a big name tag and that'll eliminate the guesswork."

He laughed and took another long drink of water.

"I don't think that's necessary. As long as you don't mind being erroneously called Nikki every once in a while."

"I don't mind at all."

Together we gazed appreciatively out at the ocean. He was an easy person to be around.

"Beautiful place, isn't it?" Jeremiah remarked.

"Yes, it is."

"When Richard first contacted me about the hotel, I had no idea what this island would be like. We flew out and looked at it, and it was totally wild, like a jungle. I knew the island had great potential, but I was absolutely stunned by all the work that Carlo had had done by the time I returned a few months later. He had crews working seven days a week to turn this place into the paradise it is now. I have to hand it to him. He's transformed it into a virtual Shangri-la."

"It must have been terribly expensive."

"You can say that again. This place is worth millions. Of course, the key thing was getting possession of the island in the first place."

"Did Carlo pay outright for it?"

"According to the story, he won it in a poker game. The former governor of Puerto Rico, Juan Dominguez, loved a good poker game; it was really an obsession with him. Anyway, a few years ago, Carlo was in town, and the governor, who was always ready for a challenge, invited him to a game with very high stakes. Carlo upped the bet, the governor folded, and Carlo won this island. Being the ultimate bluffer, Carlo was never asked to reveal his hand, so no one ever really knew what cards Carlo actually held. It's rumored that his hand that night contained not one matching card."

"That's quite a story."

"Yeah, it's indicative of the way Carlo is. A shrewd businessman all the way. He's tough on the people who work for him, but he also expects a lot from himself."

"Have you known Carlo for a long time?"

"Not really. I met him through Richard. Richard and I do a lot of work together. I was grateful he brought me in on this," he said, stroking his mustache thoughtfully.

"Is your clientele large?"

"Not really large, just extremely rich and willing to pay for the very finest. I'm rather selective myself. I depend mostly on recommendations. It's what my business is built on. Fortunately, I've been rather popular with the wealthy. My jobs usually take a long time because I'm a perfectionist, and I insist on everything being done precisely the way I plan it. I will tolerate nothing less than the best from the people who work for me." He paused to take another drink of water.

"Besides, with me in charge, rich men don't have to worry

about their wives getting involved in expensive and embarrassing affairs with the interior decorator." He winked at me.

"I suspected it, but I wasn't certain."

"Now, my dear, you needn't be embarrassed. It's your Kansas upbringing, darling. Don't be ashamed of the fact that you were taught to be polite and always respect the feelings of other people."

"I suppose you're right, Jeremiah. I don't like being judgmental."

"Keep in mind that I pride myself on presenting myself to new people as a professional first and foremost. However, since I rely heavily on referrals, new clients have already been told by their friends that I'm gay. And, as I've said, you'd be amazed at how many wealthy guys feel perfectly comfortable knowing that I'm spending many hours alone with their wives. Many of them also believe that my homosexuality is proof that I possess some great innate artistic ability and a natural aptitude for decorating. Can you believe that?" He laughed.

I laughed, too.

"Catherine, I've met all kinds of people in my business. I can say that it has been my pleasure to work for some incredibly beautiful, intelligent women with a great deal of character. Some of them are goddesses, works of art themselves. And it's a shame to see all that loveliness go to waste on husbands who are totally immersed in making money, or who would rather play golf every weekend with the guys, or who prefer to jump in the sack with some cheap whore rather than give their own beautiful wives the attention they definitely deserve. Personally, I believe in monogamy. That's the kind of relationship I have with Charles."

"Charles?"

His eyes shone.

"Charles is my significant other, my everything really. We've been together for ten years now, and we're both totally faithful and committed to one another. Do you have someone, darling? You are a lovely treasure yourself. You need someone in your life."

"No, not now. He died many years ago," I said softly, and sighed.

His eyes filled with sympathy. He patted my hand in an affectionate gesture.

"Have you eaten breakfast yet, dear?"

"No, but I'm starving. Don't ask me why, I certainly haven't missed a meal since I've been here. And the chef is very talented, don't you think?"

"Absolutely. Carlo spirited him away from a big fancy Miami restaurant, you know. He pays him big bucks."

"I can understand why." I glanced at my watch and realized it was nine o'clock.

"Jeremiah, I think I'll head back to the house now. I want to check on Nikki. I hope she's feeling better."

"I need to get back, too. Perhaps we can grab a quick bite together. I'm supposed to meet with Richard and the others at ten-thirty."

We began walking briskly back.

"Jeremiah, did Nikki have stomach problems the last time you were here?"

"Let's see, we were here in March. No, I don't remember her having any problems then. At least she said nothing about it. I hope she's okay. Perhaps she's gotten hold of one of those tough viral things—the kind that plays havoc with your whole system. She certainly looked green last night, though, didn't she?"

"Maybe I'll skip breakfast and see how she's doing."

"I think that would be a very thoughtful thing for you to do. Catherine Hanson, you are an extremely nice person."

"So are you, Jeremiah. I'll see you later."

He left for the dining room, and I set off for Nikki's room. As I approached, I saw Inez coming out and closing the door behind her.

"Inez, how is she doing this morning?"

She held a finger up to her lips.

"*Sshh.* She's sleeping now. Please don't disturb her, Mrs. Hanson."

"I just want to see how she is, Inez."

Inez shook her head.

"She's not feeling well, but she's sleeping now. I must ask you to let her rest. Please excuse me. I have some things that need attending." She turned to walk away and then stopped.

"If you can't find anything to do, you might go to the library. It's quite extensive, and I'm sure you could find something to read. It's downstairs, right off the living room."

"Thank you, Inez."

I turned to follow her directions but walked slowly, waiting for her to turn the corner. After a few minutes, I returned to Nikki's room. Twisting the knob slowly, I slipped inside. The room was completely dark and hot and stuffy. I could hardly breathe. I walked over to the bed. Nikki looked awful. She was very pale but two red blotches accented her cheeks. Beads of perspiration clung to her upper lip.

Gently I laid my hand on her forehead. She was burning up. I went to the window nearest the bed and opened it. Fresh sea air came flowing in.

Nikki stirred slightly, and I went back over to the bed.

"Nikki, are you all right?" I asked, taking one of her hands in mine.

Her eyelashes fluttered, and she struggled to focus her eyes.

"Catherine, is that you? Sorry . . . I'm . . . party pooper. I'm really sick . . . vomiting . . . diarrhea . . . Carlo called Dr. Laurenza . . . said to give me more medicine . . . says it's a nasty virus . . . I'll be okay . . . feel so sick and weak . . ."

"Nikki, I'm sorry. I can sit with you for as long as you like. I'll go get a cold washcloth for your forehead."

"It's okay, you don't need to stay . . . don't want you to catch this . . . I feel so sick, so sick." She struggled to sit up but was too weak and fell back against the pillows.

"Cathy . . . must get up . . . help me to the bathroom . . .

can't get up by myself . . . so weak . . . room is spinning . . . Is it spinning? . . . Cathy . . ."

I tried to help her. I managed to support her a little, but her knees started buckling, and she fell back against the bed. She fainted, and I worked hard to get her back onto the bed.

I dashed to the bathroom, prepared a cold washcloth, and hurried back to put it against her wrists and forehead.

"Nikki, Nikki."

She stirred and then opened her eyes.

"Catherine . . . sorry . . . please . . . hand me basin . . ."

I spotted the basin and brought it over to her. I held her head as she vomited. She was really sick, and after a while she wasn't bringing anything up, not even bile. It was just dry heaves.

I took the basin away and wiped her hands and face with the washcloth. She looked ashen.

"Now lie back and rest, Nikki. I'm going to have a talk with Inez. I think Carlo needs to call the doctor and have him come and take a look at you."

"No, Cathy . . . I'm okay . . . only a virus . . . gave me medicine to make me sleep . . ."

"Well, I think I'd better sit with you for a while. I don't want to leave you alone now."

I glanced at Nikki again. For the moment, she gave the illusion of being peaceful. She lay very still, but I didn't think that was a good sign.

Her eyes fluttered open again. She seemed startled and confused, clutching at the sheet beneath her as though she felt she were falling. Her eyes reflected terror.

"Cathy? Cathy, are you there?" Her eyes searched wildly for me in an obvious state of panic.

I reached out and took both of her hands in mine.

"It's okay, Nikki. I'm here. I won't leave you. It's okay." I tried to sound as calm as possible.

She clung to my hands fiercely like a frightened animal.

"Cath . . . I have these weird nightmares. . . . They seem real. . . . I feel so strange . . . so sick . . . so sick . . ."

I patted her hands.

"Just try to relax, Nikki. I'm here."

She nodded her head weakly, and as she lay back against the pillow, I could see some of the tension slipping away.

"Cathy, please stay with me a while. Don't leave me. I've been vomiting since last night. . . . I feel so odd . . . I'm afraid."

"I will, Nikki. I'll stay."

"Okay," she said, sighing deeply and finally closing her eyes.

I placed my fingers lightly on her pulse. It seemed oddly irregular. One minute racing, the next it was very slow.

I perched on the side of the bed and held her hand. For fifteen minutes, I sat as still as a stone, watching her sleep. She lay totally motionless. I gently laid her hand down on the sheet. I watched her face, and she didn't move. Then I slowly placed both feet on the floor and stood up. Nikki slept on her back snoring softly.

I tiptoed across the vast blue-carpeted bedroom, turned the squeakless knob, and went out into the hall.

Inez was headed straight toward me. Anger was written all over her pinched little face.

"Mrs. Hanson! I distinctly asked you not to disturb Señora Cappelli. You have deliberately disobeyed me!"

We were standing face to face now, and she placed her hands angrily on her skinny hips as if to emphasize her wrath.

"Now look, Inez, I think we'd better understand each other. Number one, I don't take orders from you, and two, Mrs. Cappelli is an adult and does not need protection from me, her friend."

She was still spewing steam like a raging bull. It took every bit of composure she had to keep from blowing up. I could almost see the wheels spinning in her head, as she determined that she would be out of line if she rebuked me. After all, she was the servant, and I was the guest.

"Do you understand that she is quite ill?" I asked.

Finally she took in a deep breath and exhaled slowly, still trying to control herself. At last she spoke.

"Of course I do, Mrs. Hanson. I'm only following doctor's orders, which are that she must have complete quiet and bed rest. And excuse me if I say so, Mrs. Hanson, but that includes you, too."

"I believe that Mrs. Cappelli's condition is getting worse. She doesn't act like a person with a common twenty-four-hour stomach virus. She's very ill. This is serious. I believe it is imperative that Carlo speak with the doctor again. In fact, I believe that Dr. Laurenza needs to come and examine her immediately."

"I will tend to her needs!" She started to enter the room, but I put out my hand and touched her on the arm.

"Inez, wait. Mrs. Cappelli is seriously ill. You must talk to Mr. Cappelli immediately. She could die of dehydration if we don't do something soon. Are you going to talk to Mr. Cappelli, or shall I?"

I gave her my firm eye-to-eye "I mean business" stare that always got immediate results from my second graders.

She stopped.

"Very well, I will talk to Señor Cappelli. But you stay out of the room." Her black eyes snapped at me.

I was totally exasperated. Even second graders listen to reason once you explain the facts to them.

"Inez, listen to me. Mrs. Cappelli is very ill and should not be left alone. I'll stay with her until you return. Remember to tell Mr. Cappelli that his wife has a high fever, extreme weakness, delirium, vomiting, and diarrhea. It is absolutely necessary that something be done immediately. Is that clear?"

She did not answer but whirled away, hopefully to talk to Carlo.

Quietly I opened the door and went back inside. Nikki was still sleeping. I carried the vile-smelling basin to the bathroom, emptied the contents into the toilet, and rinsed it out with hot water in the lavatory. I scrubbed my hands with soap and hot water and returned the basin to her bedside. I sat down in a small blue velvet chair next to the bed so I could watch Nikki.

I stayed there for what seemed like a long time. I was very worried about my friend. As I waited, I kept checking my watch impatiently wondering what was taking so long.

It was already afternoon. I had missed breakfast, and my stomach growled, but I couldn't have eaten anything anyway. I was much too worried.

My impatience was building. What in the hell could be keeping Inez? I watched Nikki stir restlessly and then turn over onto her side facing away from me.

Finally the door opened. It was Inez. She looked so smug that I felt like smacking her. She motioned for me to come outside into the hall. I did, closing the door carefully behind me.

"Well, what did Mr. Cappelli say?"

She gave me a wickedly triumphant smile.

"He said," she replied as if talking to an idiot child, "that there is no reason for you to be overly concerned, because he will take care of everything."

"What exactly does that mean?"

"It means, Mrs. Hanson, that he will take care of everything. In his own way, in his own time."

Having delivered her little speech, she brushed past me and added, "Have a nice lunch, Mrs. Hanson. I'll stay with Señora Cappelli." I felt like a time bomb ready to explode.

She was almost through the door, when she stopped and, feigning forgetfulness, added, "Oh, by the way, you have a long-distance call which you can take on the phone at the end of the hall." And smiling sweetly, she disappeared into Nikki's room.

Aggravated, I glanced down the hall, spotted the phone, and hurried to answer it.

"Hello?" I said.

"Hello, Mom. It's Mark."

"Mark, it's wonderful to hear your voice! How are you, and how is your trip going?"

"Great, Mom. We're having a really good time. How about you? Is everything okay?"

I forced myself to lie enthusiastically.

"Oh, yes, everything is fine here. The island is incredibly beautiful."

"Good. I told you so, Mom."

"Uh, yes, Mark, you did. Where are you now?"

"We're in Paris. What a city! You've got to see it, Mom. There aren't words to describe what it's really like. You just have to see it and experience it."

"Everything's okay, then? You and the guys are enjoying yourselves. No problems?"

"Oh, no. We're fine. Just wanted to say hello and make sure you're all right. Guess I'd better go. We're taking a tour bus outside the city and into the countryside. Our bus is about to leave, so I have to go. I'm glad you're having a good time, too, Mom. Give my best to Nikki and her husband. Love you!"

"Okay, Mark. Glad you called. I love you, too. 'Bye."

Frustrated, I walked toward the dining room. I couldn't have told him anything. He would only worry. Somehow everything would resolve itself here. I sighed. It was always lonely being a single parent.

CHAPTER 9

I had to eat something. I needed energy in order to think straight and put things into perspective.

It was one-thirty, and the dining room was empty. My stomach growled. I longed for a simple peanut-butter-and-jelly sandwich on white bread. Something basic that would stick to my ribs. I pushed through the swinging door into the kitchen. Several young men were taking clean dishes out of a commercial-size dishwasher and putting them away as they chatted companionably in Spanish. When I appeared, they stopped talking and looked very surprised. Evidently no one except kitchen help ever walked through that door.

"Hello, I'm sorry to bother you. I'm just going to make myself a sandwich. Don't mind me."

They looked puzzled. My Spanish was really limited. I hadn't used any of it since college, at least a hundred years ago.

"*Perdóname,*" I said. Oh, brother! That's all I could recall.

They exchanged quick looks of amusement, and then cast their eyes downward to avoid breaking out into full-blown laughter. I decided to go on about the business of making myself a sandwich.

The kitchen was large and efficient. There were ample cabinets, counter space, ovens, and commercial-style ranges all in gleaming stainless steel. Everything looked spotless under the bright fluorescent lights.

I spotted two large Sub-Zero refrigerators across the room. Opening the door to one, I discovered the makings of another elegant evening meal. I opened the second and found enough milk, butter, eggs, cheese, juice, and other perishables to feed a small army. While I was standing there trying to figure out where the pantry was, the swinging kitchen door flew open revealing an enormous black man. He wasn't fat, just tall and massive. He was wearing a white T-shirt and gigantic white Levi's covered by a pristine white apron that tied behind his neck and around his waist. Black letters spelled out THE BOSS across his chest.

As soon as he saw me, his face registered surprise. Okay, it was unanimous. The kitchen was off-limits to civilians. I decided to explain my presence in hostile territory, noticing that the three kitchen helpers looked nervous and had immediately put their unloading task into high gear.

"Hi. I'm Catherine Hanson, a guest. I'm sorry to intrude on your kitchen, but I've missed breakfast and lunch due to extenuating circumstances, and I just wanted to make myself a quick sandwich. I hope you don't mind; I'll be out of here before you know it," I confessed, babbling like some naughty child who's just been caught sneaking cookies before dinner.

The man wore an angry frown on his broad face. He looked mad enough to fillet me with one of his special knives that appeared to be readily available. The massive man with the shaved, gleaming head stared at me with his piercing black eyes for an uncomfortably long time. I began to perspire.

All at once, he threw back his head and roared with laughter.

I didn't have a clue as to what was going on.

When he finally stopped laughing, he took out a big white handkerchief and wiped the tears that were running down his face.

"I'm sorry, Mrs. Hanson! Did you honestly think I was going to swallow you alive?" He shook his head and chuckled again.

"Uh . . . well, no . . . of course not . . . maybe!" I could see the humor in the situation now, and I managed to relax and laugh at myself.

"I'm sorry, ma'am. I shouldn't have been teasing you like that. I'm a dramatic fellow, to tell you the truth. Sang gospel and also musical theater on stages across the country for close to twenty years. Guess I never got it out of my system. Ma'am, I am Genesis Revelations Jefferson." His shiny face beamed, as he gave me a grandiose bow and then reached out his huge ham of a hand to shake mine. His handshake felt warm and firm.

"I'm glad to meet you, Genesis. You really had me going there."

"I know, I know."

"I'm a little upset today. I'm not usually so gullible."

He smiled kindly and added in a gentle tone, "I understand, ma'am. We all have days like that. But what's this I hear about your not having had breakfast or lunch?" He raised his bushy eyebrows.

"That's true."

"Well, ma'am, I have a reputation to uphold. I'm not gonna let anybody starve to death while I'm around. Let's see now. . . . Uh-huh, you look like a lady who could use a nice gooey peanut-butter-and-jelly sandwich."

"How did you know?" I asked.

"Ma'am, I've been feeding people since I was just a kid. Learned how in my mama's kitchen back in Alabama. There were twelve of us kids at home. All boys, and my daddy, too, of course. My mama used to turn out heaps of good food every day. I used to stand around and watch her cook. She was a genius in the kitchen, she was. Anyway, one day when I was ten, I was watching her cooking away, and she turned from the stove and said, 'Genesis, quit standin' there gawkin', boy! Give me a hand fryin' this catfish your daddy and older brothers caught today.' Ever since then, I've been a specialist in cooking, eating, and figuring out what folks want to eat."

He laughed again and proceeded to move quickly about the kitchen gathering the ingredients for my sandwich. As he moved, I could see how agile he was for a man his size. I was impressed with the deftness of his hands, as he created the neatest and most delicious peanut-butter-and-jelly sandwich I've ever eaten in my life. For good measure, he added some fresh pineapple on the side and a tall glass of ice-cold milk.

Carrying the plate of food and milk, he gestured for me to follow him across the room to a long stainless-steel table. He set my food on the table, and in mock dramatic fashion, pulled out a chair for me as though I were the queen of England.

"Thank you, Genesis. This looks wonderful."

Humbly he nodded his thanks.

"This is delicious," I managed to say between bites of the sandwich.

"Enjoy your lunch, ma'am." He turned to go.

"Wait, Genesis. Could you sit down for a minute, please?"

"Sure, ma'am." He pulled out a chair next to me.

"Genesis, did you think I was Nikki when you walked in?"

"I sure would have, ma'am, but I had just been over to see how Mrs. Cappelli was, so I knew she was sick and flat on her back in bed. And, before you came to the island, Mrs. Cappelli told me all about you and her and showed me some pictures, so I knew that you two look almost like twins."

"Did Inez let you in to see Nikki?"

"Oh, no, ma'am. She wouldn't let me say hello or nothing. I just went by to see if Mrs. Cappelli was able to eat anything at all, because I would have fixed her something special. Mrs. Cappelli is a very fine person."

"Yes, she is."

"But that Inez! She's a mean one if I ever saw one. She was as mad as a wet hornet and told me that Mrs. Cappelli was too sick to eat and too sick to see anybody and for me to go back to the kitchen where I belonged."

"I understand. I'm not on Inez's list of favorite people either."

"Mrs. Hanson, how is Mrs. Cappelli really feeling?"

"She's very ill, and I've got to find Carlo and talk to him

myself." I wiped my mouth with the napkin. Not a crumb remained on my plate.

I pushed back from the table and stood up.

"Do you know where Carlo's offices are?" I asked.

"Yes. Go out this side kitchen door that leads through the pantry and then outside. You'll see a one-story building with big pillars, in the same general style as this big house we're in now. Go through the French doors and you'll find yourself in a good-size sitting room. Walk straight through the room and you'll come to a wide hall. His personal office is the first door on the right." He paused and looked back at the three young men. They had finished their work and were standing quietly in a row looking at their feet.

"Okay, boys, good job. Be back here at five o'clock sharp tonight. Understand?"

They nodded in unison, took off their aprons, hung them neatly in a service closet, and left the room.

"Sorry, but around here you never know who might be listening."

I wanted very much to pursue the meaning of that remark, but I needed to find Carlo as soon as possible.

"Was there something else you wanted to say, Genesis?"

"Yes, ma'am. Uh . . . are you sure you need to speak to Mr. Cappelli in person? You could call over there first, you know."

"No, I don't want to waste any more time. Besides, Laura Masters would probably just tell me he was too busy to see me or find some other excuse. I must see him now."

"Well, okay, but when you do see him . . . uh . . . be careful how you talk to him, Mrs. Hanson."

"What do you mean, Genesis?"

"I mean, ma'am, without saying too much, that Mr. Cappelli has the personality of a chameleon. Do you understand?"

"I think I do, Genesis. I'll proceed diplomatically. Anything else?"

"Be careful, ma'am. You're a good person, like Mrs. Cappelli. If I can help you, let me know. I live down the beach in the small, white frame house. It's about a five-minute walk, along the main terrace steps, to the beach, and to the right."

"Thank you so much for the great sandwich and the advice, Genesis."

"You're welcome, ma'am. Good luck."

I followed Genesis's directions right up to the French doors of the building, which looked more like a small but elegant residence than of a place of business. I paused outside the door, then opened it. Genesis's description was right on track. The sitting room was beautifully decorated with antique furniture of dark mahogany upholstered in pale blue-and-white chintz. A grandfather clock stood majestically to my right, dutifully ticking away the minutes. I heard no other sound.

I walked straight back and saw the wide corridor ahead of me. I was almost to the first door on my right, Carlo's office, when I heard voices. The door was halfway open. I walked slowly up to the door and peered into the room. No, the voices were not coming from his office. Slowly I walked down the hall, noting that the other doors were closed. The hall opened up into a large room. Inside was a beautiful indoor spa. Large, probably accommodating fifteen to twenty people. I saw no one here either. I walked into the room and heard voices again. I saw a door marked LADIES and one marked GENTLEMEN, and the third door stood open. I walked over and was about to knock to announce my presence when what I saw caused me to put my arm down, and stand there in total shock.

The room inside was partially darkened. The area was softly lit by an ornate fixture that hung over a bed. As my eyes adjusted to the dim lighting, I could see clearly into the room. I was shocked by the sight. A big four-poster and lying on it stark naked was Elisa, the pretty housemaid whom Inez had slapped. Her slender wrists were tied with heavy ropes to the headboard. Her ankles were shackled together with a man's leather belt.

"Carlo! Carlo, hurry up!" Elisa yelled. She twisted her wrists impatiently against the restraining ropes.

An interior bathroom door opened, and Carlo came out, totally naked.

"What's the hurry, honey? We've got the rest of the afternoon. The others have all gone back to the house. Nobody's gonna bother us."

Still dumbfounded, I could not move. I felt rooted to the spot. It was hard to breathe.

Elisa giggled.

"Ooh, baby, you are so sexy," she cooed.

Carlo laughed and lay down next to her. He stroked her long dark hair, her cheek, her throat, her breasts.

"Come on. I don't like it when you tease me!"

"Yeah, but I do, baby."

"Untie me so I can touch you."

Carlo got up and strutted around the room again.

"Untie me!" she insisted.

"Not yet. Not until you learn a few more lessons from me. You're a good lover, baby, but you need to respect my wants and needs before your own. Then you'll be perfect. . . . Or as perfect as you can be, since you're Puerto Rican and not Italian."

"You told me I was perfect an hour ago. Puerto Rican or not, you told me I was the best you've ever had."

"Now, there's always room for improvement, honey. You stick with me, and I'll teach you a lot."

"Untie me now. My wrists are starting to hurt."

"Not yet, lover. Not yet."

"Carlo, untie me now. Please!"

"Oh, that's good, Elisa. I like to hear you beg. Beg me, baby!"

"Please stop. It was fun for a while, but I'm tired of this game now."

All of a sudden Carlo's face clouded up, and he yelled at the top of his lungs. "Shut up, bitch! I'll say when the game is over. I'm the one in control here!"

Carlo walked around for a few minutes, flexing his muscles.

I realized that he was admiring himself in the mirror. He posed and turned, observing himself from every angle. He smiled approvingly at his image in the mirror. Then he turned and displayed himself tauntingly to Elisa.

"Come on, Carlo. I want you, baby."

"How bad?"

"Real bad."

"Tell me."

"I'll do anything for you."

"Anything?"

"Anything. You know I will. I've already shown you, Carlo."

"You've got to work harder at showing me. You've got to convince me."

"I will. I'd do anything for you. I can't live without you now. You're like a drug. I know you're not good for me, but I've gotta have you."

Carlo laughed maniacally and ran his fingers over the curves and contours of her body.

Then he reached down and pulled something out from under the bed. It was a long, black bullwhip. He cracked it over her head.

Elisa screamed, and my blood ran cold.

He cracked the whip again. This time it hit the side of the bed. She screamed and began sobbing hysterically. He dropped the whip and tossed it onto the floor. He untied her arms and her feet. He lay down next to her and roughly turned her face toward him.

"Look at me, bitch!" he shouted as she continued to cry hard.

"Why do you want to hurt me, Carlo? I love you!"

"Love? Who needs it? Who wants it? I need fun! Thrills! Excitement! You're no fun anymore. You're just like all the others. Bitches, all of you!" Angrily he got up and began putting on his clothes as Elisa lay on the bed crying softly.

Totally disgusted and nauseated, I moved away from the

door and headed straight back the way I had come. I walked as fast as I could, and once I got outside, I started running. I had gone about a mile when my stomach cramped up, and I had to stop. Up came the great lunch Genesis had prepared for me. I walked slowly for a few minutes and then sat down on the beach to try and steady myself. I had never felt so deeply repulsed in my life. What in the hell was I going to do now?

I sat there for about thirty minutes, just looking at the incredibly blue ocean and the gentle waves lapping lightly at the shore. I could see nothing but ocean and sky. But then I remembered the scene I had just witnessed, and I shuddered. The day was balmy, but I felt cold inside and out. I wished that I had someone to talk to. Someone to help me figure out this mess I was in. The mess that Nikki was in. What should I do? The fresh air and the sun slowly began to warm me. I decided to go back to the main house and see how Nikki was.

When I returned to the house, I came up the steps and onto the terrace. I hurried into the house. I needed to take a shower. I felt dirty.

As usual, my room was in perfect order. I'm a neat person, but I could smell the scent of lemon oil and see that a fresh bouquet of bright pink and yellow flowers graced my bedside table. Quickly I locked the door to the hall, shed my clothes, and went into the bathroom. I stood under the warm water letting it flow over my body. Too bad the water couldn't wash away the scenes that kept replaying over and over in my mind. I dressed quickly, putting on a light blue sundress and sandals. My hair was still damp, but I didn't want to waste time drying it, so I fluffed it a few times with the towel and decided it would have to do. I ran a powder puff across my nose and dashed out the door toward Nikki's room. Now knowing what I did about Carlo, I felt more compelled than ever to be a good friend to Nikki. When I reached her room, I tapped lightly on the door. To my surprise, a Hispanic woman wearing a nurse's uniform opened the door.

As soon as she had a glimpse of me, she clasped her hand over her mouth as though she had seen a ghost.

"Who . . . who . . . are you?" she gasped. She couldn't take her eyes off of me.

"I'm a very good friend of Mrs. Cappelli's. I know, I look just like her."

She breathed a sigh of relief. She appeared to be a pleasant woman, about fifty, average in size and looks.

"I came to see how Nikki is doing." I tried to see around the door and into the room, but the nurse held her ground.

"Oh, she's much better. I got here about an hour ago. Mr. Cappelli called Dr. Laurenza, and he sent me with some more medication immediately. I can already see a change in her condition."

"Really? That's good. I've been sick with worry. Could I come in for a few minutes? I promise not to disturb her. It's just that I stayed with her when she was so violently ill, and I need to see for myself that she's okay."

The nurse looked worried.

"Well, I'm not supposed to let anyone in, except Mr. Cappelli."

"Mr. Cappelli is tied up in a conference right now, so it will be quite a while before he gets away. He told me that I could stop by."

"Well, I don't know. . . ." She was weakening. It must have been my honest face. If she only knew how truly deceiving looks can be.

"I promise you won't get in trouble. I won't be able to rest without seeing her for myself."

Finally she gave in.

"Well, okay . . . but only for a few minutes. I don't want to get fired for disobeying orders."

"Don't be silly. You're not doing anything wrong."

Worriedly she stepped aside, and I entered the room. She followed two steps behind me.

Nikki did look better. She was sleeping peacefully. Her face looked serene. Someone had changed the bed linens and her nightgown, and her face was washed and her hair combed. She looked comfortable.

"The doctor ordered intravenous drugs, I see."

"Yes, he's treating the nausea and vomiting and also replenishing her fluids."

"Good. Well, she certainly looks better. Will you be staying with her around the clock?"

"Yes. I will be checking in with Dr. Laurenza every few hours to keep him up-to-date on her progress."

"Will someone need to relieve you?"

"Oh, no, that won't be necessary. Inez will bring in a cot for me. I'm a very light sleeper. Don't worry, I'll take good care of your friend."

"I'm greatly relieved. Thank you for letting me see her. I'll be able to relax a little now." I turned to go, but as an afterthought, I went back over to Nikki and smiling down at her, gently laid my hand on her cheek.

"Sleep well, little twin," I whispered.

I walked over to the door to leave, the nurse two steps behind me again.

"Nurse, if Nikki should ask for me, will you have someone come and get me? Or better yet, just punch 'six'. I'm in guest room six according to the house phone in my room. I'd really appreciate it."

"Of course. And your name is?"

"Catherine. Catherine Hanson. Thanks again. Oh, Nurse, one more thing. What does Dr. Laurenza think is causing Mrs. Cappelli to be so ill?"

"He believes she has contracted a tenacious viral infection."

"I see."

I left and headed back to my room. I felt like hiding. I was certainly not up to another dazzling dinner with our adulterous host. After I reached the main hall, I saw Inez arranging the large bouquet of flowers on the central table.

She looked down to avoid my glance, but I spoke to her just to annoy her.

"Good evening, Inez," I said sweetly.

"Good evening, Mrs. Hanson."

I retreated to my room. There, I kicked off my sandals and threw myself across the bed. I was emotionally exhausted. Too many things swimming around in my head. I thought I was too tired to sleep, but I drifted off.

It was dark, when a persistent knock at my door woke me up. Turning on the bedside lamp, I squinted at my watch. It was eight o'clock. I had been out for hours. The knocking continued at my door. I managed to get myself up and went to the door. My head felt like it was stuffed with cotton.

"Who is it?" I called out.

"It's me. Jeremiah. Can I talk to you?"

I opened the door.

He was dressed to perfection in a white sports jacket and light blue slacks. His aftershave exuded a pleasing citrus scent.

"I'm sorry to disturb you, Catherine. We were worried when you didn't show up for dinner. I was afraid maybe you had come down with that nasty virus Nikki has. I wanted to make sure you were all right."

"Jeremiah, come and sit down." I led him to the two comfortable wing chairs in front of the French doors.

"It's very kind of you to be concerned. I'm fine, really, just tired. I was so worried about Nikki that it just took all the fizz out of me. After I went to her room and learned she was much better and that a nurse was with her, I was able to relax, and I just fell asleep. I'm sorry you worried about me."

"Oh, my dear, I'm just glad you're all right. We certainly missed you at dinner, though. Carlo sent his apologies and so did Laura. So it was just Luca, Alberto, Richard, and me. Rather dull, actually."

"Why wasn't Carlo there?"

"Oh, he wanted to spend some time with Nikki."

"I see. May I ask you something that probably isn't any of my business, Jeremiah?"

"Of course."

"Is it proper to assume that you and Richard are here on business?"

"Yes, that's correct. Richard and I have been waiting for the go-ahead on the hotel. Carlo needs some more financing, and we wanted to see how that's going."

"And?"

"Well, Carlo said it will be taken care of very shortly. Probably within the next couple of weeks. I hope that's correct, because once I start a project I like to keep on working through to its completion. This is a big job for me and should be very lucrative. Why do you ask?"

"Oh, Nikki had mentioned something to me about the financing, and I was curious to know if things were working out."

"Yes, everything seems to be under control according to Carlo."

"That's good. Jeremiah, have you ever worked for Carlo before?"

"Just a few small things in New York. Richard, on the other hand, has known him for years. Why so many questions?"

"Just curious. I hope I don't sound too nosy. It's just that a lot of people seem to be depending on the completion of this hotel, especially Nikki."

"You're right about that. At any rate, our business is finished here for the time being, so we're going back to New York in the morning. I'll probably return in a couple of weeks, as soon as this financing thing is cleared up. I'll look forward to seeing you then." He stood and shook my hand.

"Thanks for coming by, Jeremiah. I'll see you in a couple of weeks."

"You can count on it. Maybe next time I can talk you into some tennis. Of course, Nikki will be fine by then, and including Richard, we can play some doubles."

"Sounds like fun. Have a safe trip home."

"Take care of Nikki, Catherine. I went to her room to say good-bye, but the nurse said she was too ill for visitors. There's a wistful quality about Nikki. Some deep sadness underneath her sweet smile that puzzles me."

Jeremiah's round face looked very sympathetic.

"Nikki is the kind of person that we all want to protect. I felt that way even back in college. I understand how you feel."

He smiled.

"Yes, you really do. Good night, Catherine."

"Good night."

He left. I decided to go and see Genesis. Maybe he could answer some of my questions. I wanted to avoid being seen by anyone else, but I wasn't sure about how to do that. Every big house has a set of back stairs, and I hoped to find them.

I walked down to the end of the hall, and there was a door that had SERVICE on it. I opened it, went down, and then outside. It was dark and a little spooky.

I got my bearings and managed to find my way to Genesis's house. I was pleased that I hadn't run into anyone. The moon was full, but little clouds kept racing in front of it from time to time.

His house was just as Genesis had described it. A neat, small, white, one-story cottage set back from the beach. There was a beautiful flower garden in the front that looked well tended.

The house had a covered porch that extended around its entire perimeter. A collection of white wicker furniture occupied the front porch: a supersize rocker, two chairs, and a table. In the rocker sat Genesis.

He seemed surprised but stood to greet me as I reached the porch.

"Can we talk?" I asked.

Instead of directly answering my question, he smiled and opened the screen door, gesturing for me to come in.

"Thank you."

We went inside. The interior was as charming as the exterior. It was decorated simply but tastefully in bright tropical prints. All of the chairs including the sofa were supersize to accommodate Genesis's extra-large frame. Solid-looking but comfortable, like the man himself.

"Please sit down, Mrs. Hanson," Genesis said politely.

I sat on the huge, overstuffed couch. He took a matching armchair directly to my left.

"I'm sorry to bother you. I need to talk to you, and I thought it would be more private here."

"Does anyone know you were coming here?"

"Oh, no, I'm sure they don't. I didn't tell anyone anything. Why?"

He sat quietly for a few moments, studying my face.

"I don't want to frighten you, Mrs. Hanson, but it would be better if no one saw you come here."

"Why?"

"First, please tell me why you came here tonight."

"I came, because there are some odd things going on at that house, and I'm especially worried about Nikki."

"Before we begin, would you like a glass of iced tea?"

"I'd love some."

Genesis went through a large arched door into the kitchen. In a few minutes, he returned with a frosty pitcher of iced tea, some sugar, fresh lemon, two tall glasses with ice in them, and a plate of assorted homemade cookies.

This had not been a good day for me foodwise, considering that the one meal I had eaten hadn't stayed down. I was hungry again.

"Thank you. These cookies look delicious," I said, accepting a glass of tea with lemon and a handful of fat cookies.

Genesis's eyes widened, and he chuckled. He sat down and took a long sip of his iced tea.

"Nothing comes close to iced tea in the summer," he remarked.

I nodded, my mouth full of delectable sugar cookie.

We sat quietly for a few minutes, sipping our tea. I was a bit embarrassed because I had literally gobbled the cookies down.

"I was starving."

"I can see that," he said, chuckling once more.

He offered me the plate of cookies again.

"No thanks. I missed dinner, and I was . . . Never mind. It's a long story."

His face turned serious again.

"Now, what do you want to know, Mrs. Hanson?"

"Catherine. Please call me Catherine, Genesis."

"Okay, in private anyway. Not at the main house, though. It wouldn't be proper."

"I understand. Well, it's hard to begin. I feel very uncomfortable talking about any of this. But you seem like a genuinely caring person, and I thought you might have some answers for me."

"Go ahead," he said.

"As you know, I arrived here only a few days ago as a guest of Nikki's. Since that time, several things have happened that have caused me to feel uneasy."

"Like what?"

"Well, Nikki's illness for one thing. Is this Dr. Laurenza a legitimate doctor?"

"As far as I know, he is. Keep in mind that I've only been here myself for about nine months. The doctor visited the island once, but at the time, no one appeared to be ill. I didn't see much of him really. He was only here a short time."

"But do you think he is a legitimate doctor?"

"I guess so. I know he gave Nikki a prescription for her stomach. I don't know what the medication was though. Remember, I'm only the chef so I don't have many meaningful conversations with anyone else here on the island, except for other staff members. And you, that is." He laughed his hearty laugh.

"I suppose you're right. Genesis, I'm very concerned about

Nikki. All I'm interested in is whether or not she's getting good medical treatment. I wanted to talk to Carlo, but he was . . . unavailable. I talked with the nurse in charge of Nikki's care, but . . . I need some answers. I'm worried that Carlo might not be taking her illness seriously enough."

"Catherine, I suppose you talked to the nurse, and you also saw for yourself that Nikki looked much better. Isn't that right?"

"Well, yes, but there are other complicating factors in this whole thing."

"I'm sure there are. Maybe you can talk to Mr. Cappelli when you go back tonight."

"Somehow I have the feeling that he may be unavailable all evening."

"I see."

"I don't want to overstep my boundaries as a guest, but I am a good friend of Nikki's, and I'm especially concerned about her since she became ill. I've discovered some . . . well . . . certain things by accident that cause me to be doubtful about Carlo's commitment to her."

"Hmmm."

"Genesis, this place is one big puzzle. Things are not what they appear to be. Some things make very little sense. I'd like to ask you a personal question that may be out of line. Please tell me if it is."

"Go ahead, ask."

"Jeremiah tells me that you were the top chef at a very elite restaurant in Miami. Why would you give all that up to come here to this isolated island to cook for a handful of people?"

"Excellent question. I can answer you, Catherine, but what I'm about to tell you could get you and me and other people in a lot of trouble. If I tell you my story, will you keep it a secret?"

"Of course. This sounds serious."

"It is. And I mean it when I say that your keeping this information to yourself is a life-and-death situation. Understand?"

I felt a chill go down my spine.

CHAPTER 10

Genesis got up and went to the front screen door. He peered out then closed and locked the solid wood door. He returned to his chair, sighing.

"Okay, Catherine. This is kind of a long story, but I need to start from the beginning so you'll get the complete picture. Bear with me, okay?" His voice was low and secretive.

"Okay, Genesis."

"As I told you earlier today, I used to be a singer. That's how I made my living. Those were great years for me. I loved to sing, and I loved performing, too. I started singing in church when I was only three. Started singing professionally at sixteen. I was lucky enough to get hooked up with a gospel group, and we traveled the country, first performing at revival meetings, then at county fairs, and eventually, we even cut some records. Those were the days, all right. Well, after ten years of that, the group sorta broke up, and I drifted into black musical theater in Georgia. Mostly regional stuff, nothing high-powered, but pretty damned good, really, by anyone's standards. I loved it, and I got paid for doing it.

"I met a beautiful young woman named Samantha. She was the prettiest and sweetest woman I had ever known. Drove me crazy. She sang soprano, and she was really special. We fell in love and got married. We continued to do shows, all regional stuff in the South. Didn't make much money, but we didn't need much back then. We were part of a traveling troupe, and the theater company paid our expenses. So we lived on tomato soup and love." His eyes had a faraway look.

"Anyway, we were performing in Atlanta. It was a big night for us. We were performing *Oklahoma!* I played Curly. That night, a New York agent heard me and Samantha sing, and after the performance offered us a contract with an all-black company in New York City. We were still young and wanted to reach for the stars. We signed up and left the troupe, all our friends, and the South, our home. Life in New York was a lot different from what we were used to.

"The company was very successful. It was the top-rated group for black theater in the entire country. In our world, Sam and I were celebrities of a sort. After a few years, our daughter, Sally, was born, and we were very happy. Sam dropped out of the company to stay home with the baby. The years flew by, and Sally went to nursery school, and Sam went back to work. Soon after Sally's fourth birthday, Sam became very ill. After tests and more tests, she was diagnosed with a rare type of lymphoma for which there was no cure. She . . . uh . . . she only lived two more months."

"What a tragedy for you, Genesis." I reached over and touched his hand, remembering my husband's sudden death at a young age.

He sighed, tears welling up in his eyes.

"I thought my life was over. But I still had little Sally. I had to make some tough decisions. I decided to take Sally out of the city and try to give her a sense of family. With her mother gone, I wasn't much good by myself. She needed nurturing from a woman, and so I took her home to live for a while with my own mama in Alabama. Alone, I returned to New York City, back to our old apartment with all its memories, and tried to put the pieces of my life back together again.

"It was awful. Everything reminded me of Samantha. I was a mess. Couldn't sleep or eat and sure as hell couldn't sing, which was how I made my living. I was totally devastated. I resigned for the good of the musical company, packed up, and went home to my mama's.

"It was real fine being there for a while with my mama and my little girl. I did the hard part of my grieving. After a couple of months, my sweet little mama took me aside and looked me straight in the eye.

" 'Genesis,' she said, 'it's time, my son, to go to work and build a life for you and Sally.'

"I knew she was right. It's just that I had this big empty place where my heart used to be, and it still hurt a lot. I didn't think I could go back to singing, and I didn't know what else I could do. Once again, it was my mama who came through and saved me. One morning I was sitting on the front porch reading the employment section of the newspaper, and Mama took the paper out of my hands and said, 'Cookin'.'"

" 'Cooking'?" I asked.

" 'Cookin'," she said, and folded her arms. So I spent some time working with a great Cajun chef in Mobile (a friend of my mother's cousin), then took a French cooking course in New Orleans, and worked in one of the finest restaurants in the city. I worked hard, and the early days of cooking in my mama's kitchen came flooding back to me. I had become a damned good cook! Got a fine job in Memphis and moved my little girl up there with me. It was hard working in the restaurant and trying to be a good daddy. Both of us missed my mama's taking care of us. I worked odd hours, nights, and weekends. We did okay, though, Sally and me. We were real close, and it was good. For a while, life had meaning and made sense again."

The memories of that time seemed to bring a smile to his face.

"But things didn't stay that way," I interjected.

The smile was gone.

"No, they didn't. Sally became a teenager. It seemed to happen overnight. The sparks started to fly. We argued about everything and nothing at all. The housekeeper I had hired years ago, who had always gotten along well with Sally, was no longer interested in being around a smart-mouthed fourteen-year-old brat, so she quit. And then there was no one at home to supervise Sally when I couldn't be there.

"The reality was that I had to work. Besides, I was home every minute I wasn't working, but that didn't help either. Sally would hole up in her room, lock the door, and play that awful, violent rap stuff so loud I thought my head would burst. I needed help desperately. By this time, my poor mama was fighting her own tough battle with crippling arthritis. She was being cared for in a good nursing home near one of my older brothers. She couldn't save me from this one. Things got worse. Sally took up with a group determined to destroy themselves. I had strong suspicions that they took drugs and drank and were sexually promiscuous. Sally knew how I felt about all those things, but she was too busy trying to defy every value I had ever taught her.

"I tried to get her to see a family therapist with me, but she laughed at me and refused. I was out of my head with worry. I wanted to save her from destroying herself, but I had tried everything, and I was losing the battle."

"Did things get even worse?" I asked.

"About that time, I got an offer from a big, fancy Miami restaurant. This place had a reputation for being one of the top ten restaurants in the world. They wanted me, Genesis Revelations Jefferson, to be their top chef! They offered me a great salary, terrific health benefits, the works. It was a once-in-a-lifetime opportunity."

"Sometimes," I said, speaking from personal experience, "when it looks like nothing good can ever happen again, something like a miracle comes along and surprises you."

"This looked like an honest-to-goodness miracle all right. I decided to take the job, thinking it would help to get Sally away from the wild bunch she was running around with. And, with the added income, we could buy ourselves a really nice house. I broke the news to her as gently as I could. She was outraged. She yelled and hollered and cried and said she wouldn't go. I said she had to. She complained for days and stomped around the house, slamming doors and giving me dirty looks. I let her rant and rave, hoping she would work it all out of her system."

"Did she finally accept the fact that you two were going to move?"

"Well, all of a sudden, her attitude appeared to change. The moving date was set and everything. She became very quiet. She was not outwardly hostile to me anymore. When I asked her to clean out her closet, she did it with no argument. Her sudden switch in attitude worried me, but I kept hoping that maybe she was beginning to see that I was right after all. For about a week, she behaved like that. She didn't go out with her friends. She didn't go out at all. Several days before the movers came, she helped me finish packing. Stood right beside me and helped me. She was very cooperative and unusually quiet. I remember the night before the movers came to load our stuff. It was ten o'clock, early by Sally's standards. Her door was closed, and her light was off, but I knocked softly anyway. She didn't answer, so I peeked in and saw that she was sound asleep. As I saw her lying there so peacefully, I thought to myself: Maybe things will work out in Miami. Maybe we can start over and be friends again. I wanted it with all my heart, Catherine."

"You wanted your loving daughter back again."

"Oh yes, I did! Well, I had set my alarm clock for six o'clock the next morning. I wanted to be all ready for the movers. They were due to come about seven. I showered and dressed quickly and drove up the street to a great little bakery. Sally loved their Danish rolls, so I bought several and some milk and hurried home. I went to her door and knocked softly. There was no answer. I hated to wake her so early, but I knew she would want to be dressed before the movers came. I knocked again. Still no answer. I opened the door. The drapes were pulled shut, and it was dark in the room so I turned on the light. I walked over to her bed and saw two pillows stuffed underneath the covers. I went all over the house looking for her, but I didn't find her. I realized that I must have been the stupidest man in the world. She had planned to run away all along."

"My God, what a nightmare!"

"I searched her room, but even her makeup was still sitting on her dressing table. I spent the rest of the day calling everybody in her book of phone numbers, trying to track her down. No one knew anything, supposedly.

"Finally I called my new employer and told him the situation. He was very kind, and even though it put him in a bind, he agreed to let me have as much as two more weeks before I reported to work. The next two weeks were pure hell. Of course, I called the police, but there seemed to be no trace of her. I hired a private detective to continue looking while I went on to Miami. I was heartsick."

He was silent for a few moments, lost in his nightmarish past.

"Genesis?" I said softly. "What happened then?"

"A year went by and still no word. I felt like a robot. I went to work every day and and pretended to be enthusiastic. I went to bed every night feeling like someone who was being hit by a big Mack truck on a daily basis. I had no life outside of the restaurant, but I was determined to be successful at my profession, because it was all I had left. The private detective finally told me that it was foolish to keep looking for someone who did not want to be found. Over the past year, he had followed up on a number of false leads that took us nowhere. We were no closer to finding her than we were the day she left. Everything led to a big fat zero. With a heavy heart, I gave him the okay to give up, and I felt the emptiness closing in on me."

"And then what?" I asked, urging him on.

"About six months after I had given up on the investigation, I received a phone call one night at the restaurant. The man calling had a heavy Italian accent. He said he had news about my daughter, and if I wanted to hear it, I should meet him at midnight at an all-night diner two blocks away. I was to come alone and on foot. Naturally I agreed.

"The restaurant I worked at closed around eleven-thirty, so I finished up and walked the two blocks to the meeting place. I noticed a silver Rolls-Royce parked almost directly in front of the diner. A large Italian man got out of the car and asked me if I was Genesis Jefferson. He said there was someone in the car who wanted to talk to me. I was scared, but I was so desperate for information about my Sally that I would have done anything. I climbed in and met Mr. Cappelli."

Genesis paused. I guess to see what my reaction was. I was stunned. He got up and walked around the room restlessly for a few minutes. At last he went back to his chair and sat down. He took a long drink of his iced tea.

"Yes, Catherine. The same Mr. Cappelli that I work for. The same Mr. Cappelli who's married to your friend Nikki. He was dressed immaculately and expensively and seemed very much in control, which he was. He shook my hand and offered me a drink, which I politely refused. All I wanted was to find out about Sally. He took a drink of his Chivas Regal and began to talk. He told me that he was a businessman and that he owned a hotel and casino called The Black Pearl in Las Vegas. Four months before, he had received a phone call from his house detective who had informed him that one of the employees there, a room-service waiter, had gone to deliver a meal, when he noticed that unusually loud music was coming from the room right next door. The waiter knocked on the door because the music was blaring so loud. When no one answered, he turned the knob and opened the door. What he saw was shocking. A young woman on the bed, totally nude and unconscious, and a man lying next to her, who was obviously dead from two gunshot wounds, one to the head and one to the heart. The gun was clasped in the hand of the unconscious girl. Quickly the waiter closed the door behind him and turned the music off. Mr. Cappelli told me how proud he was of the young man because he had followed the instructions that all his employees had had drummed into their heads. If anything looked wrong, they were told to call the house detective first."

I found it hard to sit still. An eerie feeling of intense dread threatened to overwhelm me.

Genesis stood up and nervously ran his hands over his shaved head. He looked miserable, too.

"Go on, Genesis, tell me what happened."

He sat down again. "The house detective's instructions from Mr. Cappelli were to eliminate the possibility of any 'messy problems' with the law. To get to the point, the detective, using extra available manpower, removed the man and the girl from the room by secretive means making very sure that there were no other witnesses. The dead man turned out to be a policeman, which made matters even worse. The girl was taken to another room and interviewed by the house detective. He said she was totally out of it. By the looks of the veins on her arms, he knew she was a heavy drug user. The house doctor was called in and concluded that in the shape she was in, she wouldn't make any sense and should sleep it off. She slept in the guarded room. The next day, the detective talked to her again. He described her as young, shapely, pretty, and scared out of her mind. She was edgy and needed a fix. She couldn't remember anything that had happened the previous night. She reluctantly admitted that she was sixteen and a hooker." Genesis choked on the last word.

"Are you okay, Genesis?" I asked.

He cleared his throat vigorously and nodded.

"I've got to finish telling you, Catherine. I've gone too far to quit now." He sat for a few minutes in an effort to pull himself together.

"Okay," I said with renewed fear in my heart.

"The house detective sent for Mr. Cappelli. Mr. Cappelli met the girl and said she seemed to be bright, definitely worth saving. He explained to her the conditions under which she had been found, and that she had two choices: to go out of the country for rehab, or return to the streets. She was scared stiff, he said, and didn't give him an answer. He told her that he was good at making decisions for other people, and that he was putting her into drug rehab and she had no other choice but to go along with it. He asked her if she had parents or family who were living, but she said she had none. So, he sent her to San Juan to a drug-treatment center for ninety days. She came through it okay, and he went to see her as soon as her treatment was over. He asked her again if she had any family. She finally admitted she did, and that was why he called me. . . . It was my Sally." Genesis covered his face with his hands and sobbed hard.

I went over and put my arm around his shoulders.

"Genesis, I'm so sorry. I'm so very sorry."

He clutched my hand and squeezed it. Then he took a handkerchief out of his pocket and dried the tears from his face and blew his nose. He stood up, walked around the couch, came back, and sat down again.

"At our meeting that night, Mr. Cappelli offered to fly me out the very next day to see Sally. I accepted. Sally had finished the drug rehabilitation, and Mr. Cappelli had placed her in a Catholic private school there in San Juan. He arranged for her to meet us in private in a house he owned there. Sally didn't want to see me, but Mr. Cappelli insisted on it. She didn't say much. In fact, she would hardly look at me. I was crushed. I tried to talk her into coming back to Miami with me, but she refused. She said she liked it where she was, and that she was actually happy there. Mr. Cappelli suggested a compromise. He said I should come and work for him here. That way I could see Sally frequently, and her secret would be safe from the world forever. She could continue school where she was happy, and I would be paid handsomely."

"Or else what?"

"Well, he didn't put it to me that way. He had saved my daughter's life twice. He had saved her from being convicted of murder and remember, it was a cop she would have been tried for killing. She was a druggie, a hooker, and she was black. She would have been convicted for sure and sent away for life. Next, he had rescued her from killing herself with drugs. This man had saved my daughter's life. If I wanted a chance to ever be part of her life again, the only way I could hope to do it would be on his terms."

He got up again and paced around the room. Then, as before, he returned to his seat.

"I told him I wanted to repay him for all he had done for me and my daughter. He said he didn't want my money, and besides, he said the price tag on what he had done was too high for me to pay. And, of course, he was right. Then he looked me square in the eye and said, 'Repay me the only way you can, Genesis. With your loyalty.' I knew what he meant, and no matter what I thought, I knew he had me by the balls."

He sighed deeply. "Sorry to put it so crudely, but it's true. I sold my soul that day, Catherine. I sold it to hang onto the one person in my life who means everything to me."

I was overwhelmed. None of this seemed real. It was like some bizarre story out of a movie. Finally I found my voice.

"How are you and Sally getting along now, Genesis?"

He brightened up instantly.

"Very well. I go see her most Sundays and spend the day with her. She's so different. Almost like another person. We've been getting acquainted all over again. The last month has been really good for us. The last few Sundays that I was there she made a big fuss over me and seemed genuinely glad to see me. She hugged me real tight and started calling me 'Pop' again. That's what she used to call me, before she ran away. Sally likes the school there and her friends, and she seems happy and peaceful."

"How does she feel about the prostitution, the drugs . . . ?"

"She's been seeing a woman psychologist several times a week, since she's been at the school. Sally says it's helped her a lot. She feels terrible about all the awful things she did. She's glad to have a fresh start, a chance to begin again. My little girl is back, Catherine."

Tears glistened in his eyes.

"That's quite a story, Genesis. Thanks for sharing it with me. I won't betray your secret. You can count on me."

"Thank you, Catherine. Because if Mr. Cappelli ever found out that I've told you about this, I don't know what he would do. I'm in a difficult situation already. I don't want to do anything to make things worse."

"I understand."

"For your sake, that's all you need to know. You'd better get back now."

I felt numb and electrified all at the same time. I was frightened and confused. Had I asked the questions I needed to ask?

"Thank you, Genesis. You're right, I'd better be getting back." I started to shake hands, but then it seemed ridiculous in light of all he had revealed to me, and so we hugged.

I hurried back to the house, thankful for the moonlight, and was careful not to trip over vines or rocks. Thankfully, the servants' door was still unlocked, and I hurried inside and went straight to my room. It was dark when I entered the room, but the moonlight pouring in through the French doors startled me as it revealed the silhouette of someone sitting in a wing chair next to the glass doors. My throat went dry.

"Hello, Catherine," said a husky voice. I recognized it as Luca's.

I jumped. "You?" I shrieked, switching on a bedside lamp. "What are you doing here?" I picked up a high-heeled shoe and hurled it at his head. Still seated, he ducked, and the shoe missed him.

Unruffled, he stayed where he was and observed me with an amused grin on his face.

I threw open the door. "Get out! I mean it! Now!"

"You do get angry, don't you? There's no reason to get so upset. I just came by for a friendly visit."

"I don't want your friendship, and I don't want to hear

another lie either about why you're in my room. Now get out! I'm going to tell Carlo tomorrow about your coming in and out of my room whenever you feel like it. I'll have him put a special lock on my door if that's what it takes."

"You'll need to talk to the head of security about that, Catherine."

"Fine! Then that's what I'll do! Now, get out, damn it!"

Slowly he got up from the chair and sauntered casually to the door, as I moved away to put distance between the two of us.

"There's just one slight problem, Catherine."

"What's that?" I yelled.

"I'm the head of security. Sleep well."

He left.

Furious, I slammed the door behind him and locked it.

CHAPTER 11

I had a great deal of trouble falling asleep. All that emotion before bedtime does not prepare one for a restful night. I tossed and turned for the better part of the night. Sometime in the early morning hours, I must have dozed off because I woke myself up snoring. It happens to the best of us at times when we become totally exhausted and end up sleeping in an unusual position. When I awoke, I was clutching two pillows over my head, hence the snoring. The sheets lay tangled in a heap underneath me. Another day in the House of Lies. I couldn't wait to see what fresh, shocking revelation this new morning would bring.

Okay, so I was in a bad mood. I had every right to be. I forced myself to look at the little gold clock by the bed. It was nine A.M. I told myself to get up and get with it. The hot water in the shower helped to revive me, and by the time I was blow-drying my hair, I felt my attitude had markedly improved. I quickly applied my makeup, put on a cool blue-and-white floral sundress and white sandals, and headed for the dining room. There was no one in sight. I poured myself a glass of fresh orange juice and ate a delicious cinnamon roll while standing up. I had no time for the niceties of life this morning. I had a goal, and that was to find out how Nikki was. Stacking my dishes on the sideboard, I set off for her room.

When I arrived, the door was standing wide open. This was very odd. I looked inside and was surprised to see that the king-size bed was fully made up, ornate bedspread and all. I entered the room, but there was no sign of Nikki, or the nurse, or the thingamabob that held the intravenous medications. I looked in the bathroom, but she wasn't there either. Something was wrong.

I set off down the hall filled with trepidation, looking for some signs of activity. I spotted Elisa going into another room. She was carrying a stack of fresh bed linens.

"*Buenos días,*" I said to her.

"*Buenos días,*" she answered with a curious smile.

"Would you happen to know where Mrs. Cappelli is?"

"Oh yes, señora."

"Where is she?"

"She is gone," she said, and went into the room carrying the linens.

Fear gripped my stomach.

"What do you mean, she's gone?"

Elisa began to strip the bed linens from the bed.

"I mean, señora, that she is gone," she repeated patiently.

Oh good, at the rate this game of Twenty Questions was going, I would be here all day.

"Gone where?" I asked, trying to appear politely patient.

"Gone to the *hospital*," she said, accenting the last syllable as she would do in her native language of Spanish.

"When? When did she go to the hospital?"

"Very early this morning."

"Why?"

"She became *muy enferma*, I mean, very sick in the night. The doctor says to bring her quick." She continued to make up the bed.

"Where is the hospital?"

"In San Juan, señora."

"Okay, thank you." I turned to go, but all kinds of thoughts were spinning around in my head. I knew I had to speak to Carlo immediately.

"Would you happen to know if Mr. Cappelli went with his wife?"

"Oh, yes. He went with her," she said, and then added, "but he will return tonight." She had a big smile on her face.

"Oh, I see. Do you know where I can find Inez?"

"Yes, she is in the library."

And that is where I went.

My favorite housekeeper was busy dusting the spines of several thousand books with a large lamb's-wool duster.

"Excuse me, Inez. Could I speak with you a moment?"

"Of course, Mrs. Hanson." She left her position in the corner and came and stood in front of me. We were back on her turf again. Same game. She had the answers and all the power, and I had nothing but the tenacity of a pit bull. "Inez, I understand that Mrs. Cappelli has been taken to the hospital in San Juan, and that Mr. Cappelli accompanied her. Could you tell me what her condition is now?"

"I will tell you what I know, Mrs. Hanson. In the night, Señora Cappelli's condition worsened. Nurse Moreno and Señor Cappelli flew with her to San Juan. There was to be an ambulance waiting at the airport to take Señora Cappelli to the hospital where Dr. Laurenza would be waiting to examine her immediately."

Well. Inez had certainly outdone herself by being so complete and up-front with her answers.

"Thank you, Inez. Could you give me the name and phone number of the hospital so I can call and check on her condition?"

"There's no need for that, Mrs. Hanson. Señor Cappelli said he would call as soon as he had any information." She gave me her milk-of-magnesia smile and returned to her dusting.

I stood there for a moment thinking about the situation. Clearly I was stymied again.

"Would you care to select a book, Mrs. Hanson? It would help to pass the time. It's a large library as you can see."

I sighed. No. I wanted a simple answer to my question. "I suppose so. Is there a section for mysteries and suspense?"

"Yes." She pointed to a block of shelves that probably contained several hundred books.

The system was simple, organized by the author's last name. I looked for one of my favorite authors and chose a book. A new Dick Francis.

"Thanks, Inez. And if you hear anything from Mr. Cappelli, would you please let me know immediately? I'm really worried about Mrs. Capelli."

She nodded and continued her dusting.

Fat chance of her seeking me out to give me any information about Nikki. I would just have to remain diligent in bugging the hell out of her.

Taking the book, I decided to read outside. The fresh air and sunshine would do me good. I walked to the patio, selected a comfortable chair, and put on my sunglasses. I was really too edgy to read. I opened the book, but I couldn't get into it. All I could think about was Nikki. Besides, there wasn't much sun. The bright, cloudless skies that had seemed to be ever present were replaced today with big, dark clouds. They looked like they were full of rain. I took my book and went inside. Just in time. A fork of jagged lightning lashed out over the ocean, and then soon afterward came a deep rumble of thunder. The monstrous clouds opened up, and big raindrops began pouring down. The wind had picked up, too, and began to whip harshly at the fronds of the tall palm trees. Two of the young Puerto Rican men I had met in the kitchen rushed out of the house in rain gear and hurried to quickly roll down the umbrellas that were attached to the patio tables. The rain was coming down in sheets accented with frequent bursts of flashing lightning and crashing thunder. The two men finished their job quickly and disappeared down the main steps and out of sight.

Being from Kansas, I was accustomed to rainstorms and thunder and lightning. But this was my first tropical storm, and it displayed an intensity that seemed somehow different from the ones I had experienced at home. All of a sudden, I felt very vulnerable and exposed. I shuddered and moved away from the French doors. Looking for a friendly face, I went into the kitchen. The lights were off, and all the gleaming appliances, counters, and cabinets had a clinical look in the dim light.

"Genesis?" I called, absolutely certain that no one would answer. I turned to go back through the swinging door and into the dining room when a familiar baritone voice boomed out.

"Mrs. Hanson? Catherine?"

It startled me, and I jumped.

"Genesis?" I called out. I peered around the large central cabinets and saw him sitting at the table with a cup of coffee in front of him. He was grinning at me.

"Should I turn on the lights?" I asked.

"Naw, I kind of like it this way."

I walked over to the table and sat down next to him.

"Would you like some coffee?" he asked me.

"No thanks, Genesis. I'm jittery enough already. This storm isn't helping me any either. Do you think it's unwise for anyone to see us talking?"

"I think it's okay, Catherine. I'm not expecting any kitchen help for another hour, and everybody else stays out unless they're authorized to be here. There's a small kitchen down in the basement that's always open to the staff. But this, this is my office, and they know it's off-limits unless it's time to cook or serve a meal."

His eyes twinkled mischievously.

"I have a reputation for being something of a tyrant around here."

"Really?"

"Really."

"Aye, aye, sir."

"I know it sounds ridiculous to you, but it works. Keeps people like Inez out of my way."

"Now that's real power. I didn't think there was any place in this house that was off-limits to her."

"Well, she's slightly in awe of me on my own territory. Remember, I'm the famous chef. I'm allowed to be temperamental and demanding . . . about certain things, that is."

"Hmmm. Genesis, they took Nikki to the hospital before dawn."

His dark eyes opened wide, and I told him what Inez had told me.

"It doesn't sound good, does it, Catherine?"

"No. I wanted to call the hospital, but Inez said Carlo would call here as soon as he knew anything more about her condition."

"But that's not good enough for you, is it?"

"No. I don't trust Carlo, and after what you told me yesterday, I'm really concerned for her safety. After I got back here last night, I realized that I hadn't asked you all the questions I wanted to ask. I was so overwhelmed by the story about your daughter that I forgot what I had really come to find out."

"Go ahead, but keep your voice down. You never know if Inez has her ear pressed to the door."

The storm was still pounding rain against the windows, and the thunder and lightning continued on. To be safe, I leaned closer to his face so he could hear me better.

"Genesis, by mistake I saw Carlo with Elisa in a very compromising situation."

He looked down and nodded sadly.

"I'm not surprised, Catherine. I try to look the other way as much as possible. As you know, I'm stuck between a rock and a hard place myself. When I came to work here, I decided to keep to myself as much as possible. I don't want to know anything I'm not supposed to know. The less I know, the better off I am. I'm not in a position to help anyone anyway. The only thing I have to live for is seeing my daughter, and I don't want to do anything that might jeopardize her situation."

"I understand, Genesis. All I want is a few answers. I promise I won't involve you in anything that might cause you or your daughter a problem."

"Ask away."

"Laura Masters is pregnant. Who is the father of her baby?"

"I honestly don't know, Catherine. I hear a lot of gossip from the staff, but I don't know what's true and what isn't."

"Is it possible that Carlo is the father?"

"I suppose it could be true, but there are other possibilities. Almost everyone goes to the main island over the weekend. The father could be someone living in Puerto Rico."

"What do you think?"

He sighed. "I don't know. Carlo has a reputation for being a ladies' man, but he's a shrewd guy. He's too smart to get caught, if he doesn't want to be."

We sat in silence thinking for a few minutes. The rain was still pouring down.

"Genesis, would you know which hospital Nikki is in?"

"No, and there're lots of hospitals in San Juan. I take it Inez wouldn't tell you."

"Of course not. How can I find out?"

"Why not try asking Laura Masters or Alberto or Luca?"

"Do you think they'd tell me?"

"Why not? It doesn't hurt to try. If that doesn't work, I could sneak a peek at a list of frequently used phone numbers that Inez keeps posted on a bulletin board in the basement kitchen."

"Could you do that for me?"

"Yeah, I guess I could. They're not secret or anything. I didn't think of it before. In fact, I'll go right now."

"Thanks, Genesis. Should I wait here?"

"No, someone might think we're getting too chummy. Wait for me in the dining room."

"Okay."

He left, and I went into the dining room. As I sat waiting for Genesis to return, I shivered and wondered why in the world I had ever left Kansas where I could have spent a long, boring, uneventful summer. At least there I wouldn't have been privy to all kinds of disturbing, worrisome information about other people's lives. Here I was quickly becoming involved in things that were certainly none of my business.

The rain continued to pour down making everything outside look like a big blurry watercolor. I glanced at my watch. Genesis had only been gone five minutes. I sat and listened to the rain and tried to stop myself from thinking about how sick Nikki might be.

I could hear heavy footsteps—tennis shoes squishing against the hard marble floor—approaching me. Turning in my chair, I saw Genesis. He had a smug look on his face as he stopped at my chair.

"Here you are, Mrs. Hanson. Here's that recipe for coconut-cream pie you wanted. I'm sure it will get you lots of compliments back home in Kansas."

"I'm sure it will, Mr. Jefferson. Thank you very much. I appreciate your giving it to me."

"My pleasure, ma'am. Oh, also, ma'am, I have a tasty lunch planned for today. Seafood salad, clam chowder, and my own freshly baked sourdough rolls."

"Sounds lovely."

He smiled gratuitously and went into the kitchen.

Thank you, Genesis. I glanced at the small piece of paper he had handed me and slipped it into one of my front skirt pockets. As I stood up to leave, three young housemaids, led by Inez, came in carrying a load of cleaning supplies. As I left the room, I could hear her barking out orders in Spanish in a no-nonsense, authoritative tone. From my point of view, she had missed her calling. She would have been an excellent drill sergeant.

Entering my room, I noticed that it had already been cleaned, scrubbed, and polished. This was good since I did not want to be disturbed. I locked the door from the inside and hurried over to the phone, which was situated on the mahogany bedside table next to the little gold clock. I wasn't sure if I could make a direct call, but I decided to try. On the slip of paper Genesis had given me, he had written Hospital del Sol,

San Juan, and then the phone number. I dialed for an outside line and punched in the numbers. About ten seconds elapsed before I could tell that the phone was ringing somewhere. At least it was ringing.

On the fourth ring, a woman's voice with a Hispanic accent answered.

"Hospital del Sol."

"Hello, can you speak English?"

"Yes. Go ahead, please."

"I'm calling because a dear friend of mine was admitted to your hospital today in the early morning hours. I'm very worried about her. Could you please tell me the status of her condition?"

"The patient's name, please."

"Nikki Cappelli, Mrs. Carlo Cappelli. Shall I spell it for you?"

"No, ma'am, that won't be necessary. One moment, please."

I waited as I imagined her consulting a central computer.

"Hello, ma'am. You said the patient's name is Nikki Cappelli?"

"Yes, that's correct."

There was a pause.

"I'm sorry, ma'am, but there's no patient here under that name."

"Are you sure? Could there be some mistake? Could she be in intensive care or something like that?"

"I'm sorry, ma'am. I have access to all of that information, but no one of that name has been treated here at this hospital in the last twenty-four hours."

"Could you please double-check that?"

The patient, efficient voice was becoming perturbed.

"I have, ma'am. I'm sorry. Good-bye."

"No, wait, please. Do you have a Dr. Laurenza on your staff?"

"I'll check that for you. . . . No, ma'am, we do not. Good-bye."

She hung up.

Now what? I put the receiver down and stared at the phone as if it could give me an answer.

The nightstand had a storage compartment underneath. I opened its drawer and found a San Juan telephone directory. Turning to the listing for hospitals, I discovered that there were six other hospitals besides the one I had already called. I began dialing them systematically. None of them had a patient named Cappelli, and none of them had a Dr. Laurenza on staff. Just as I was saying thank you to the last hospital employee, someone picked up another phone in the house. They said nothing, but I could hear breathing. I hung up.

My worst fears were becoming a reality. Where was Nikki? Who was Dr. Laurenza? Who could answer any of these questions? Carlo. I checked my watch. It was noon now, time to eat again. What I needed desperately was not food, but answers. Well, if no one was going to give them to me, I was going to have to dig them out myself. I glanced out the French doors. The rain had finally slowed down to a simple, steady downpour.

This time when I arrived at the dining room, I found Laura and Alberto. Lunch was another serve-yourself kind of setup. I filled a bowl with the delicious-smelling clam chowder and took a warm sourdough roll. Decanters of water and wine and pots of coffee and tea sat in the middle of the table. I noticed that Laura and Alberto, seated opposite one another, were hungrily putting away the food. Laura was drinking milk, and Alberto was indulging in white wine. They greeted me amicably, and I sat down next to Laura. I poured myself a cup of hot tea. The chowder was undoubtedly the best I had ever eaten. One thing was certain: Genesis was a very talented chef.

We exchanged pleasantries, talked about the storm, the delicious lunch, and so on. When I felt they were comfortable with my presence, I decided to do a little digging.

"Laura, I'm sure you know that Nikki became very ill in the night and was taken to San Juan."

"Yes. I was sound asleep when all of that was going on, but Carlo called Alberto before they left. Carlo sounded upset, and rightfully so."

"I'm very worried myself. Alberto, do you know what hospital they took Nikki to?"

"I'm not certain, Catherine. It was probably Hospital del Sol."

"I see. Inez says that Carlo will call when he has news of her condition. Have either of you heard anything?"

Both of them shook their heads.

"I know Carlo will call us as soon as he can," Alberto said. He poured himself another glass of wine and helped himself to another roll.

"Yes, I'm sure he will," Laura echoed. She took another helping of the seafood salad. I could tell how concerned they were by their lack of appetite.

"I'm sorry to make such a pig of myself, Catherine. Since I've been pregnant I've had this insatiable hunger. Alberto has been so understanding. He wants our baby to be healthy, and he says it's important that I eat and not be skinny like some of the young pregnant women of today."

Alberto smiled a bit uncomfortably and bit into his roll.

"It must be a comfort to have such an understanding husband," I said.

Laura looked slightly distressed.

"Oh, no, we're not married. Marriage is such an important step. We want to make sure we're really right for each other."

"Well, I wish you both the best. I'm sure your baby will be a blessing." I was becoming very adept at spewing this kind of blarney.

Laura and Alberto smiled and nodded.

I excused myself and headed back to my room.

It was time for me to start doing something, so I decided to slip down the back stairs and find the servants' kitchen.

I went down the stairs. The outside door was directly in front of me. Or I could turn right and go through another door. I took a right turn and found myself in a hallway. There were four doors from which to choose. I opened the first one. It was a storage room full of outdoor furniture and odds and ends. I opened the second one, and it was the servants' kitchen. It was a large rectangular room with a small kitchen at one end, complete with a long table and at least a dozen chairs. The bulk of the room was a kind of lounge area with comfortable couches and chairs and a large television area. At the present time, there were about ten people in the room. I saw Elisa and the three young maids in the kitchen area, and six men in the lounge area watching television and eating. Everyone seemed surprised and unsettled that I was there.

Elisa came over to me and smiled. She made me feel uncomfortable because all I could think of was seeing her and Carlo together.

"Mrs. Hanson, are you lost? This is the servants' kitchen."

"Actually, I needed to ask you something. How does one get to Puerto Rico from here besides by plane or helicopter?"

She seemed relieved at my question.

"Oh, that's easy. There is a large boat that comes every morning and leaves every evening. That is how we get supplies. Also, most of the servants live in San Juan, and that is how they travel back and forth."

"Okay. What happens when there's a big storm like today?"

"Well, the people who live in San Juan will have to spend the night if the weather doesn't improve."

"What time does the boat usually come in the morning, and what times does it leave in the evening?"

"It takes about an hour and a half to come here from San Juan. The boat usually leaves there about six-thirty and gets here at eight. In the evening, the boat leaves here around seven-thirty. Are you wishing to take the boat to San Juan, Mrs. Hanson?"

"Oh, no, I was just curious. I wondered how so many

people could be transported quickly. Thanks, Elisa. I hope I didn't interrupt your lunch."

"No problem, Mrs. Hanson. Do you know how to get back to the main floor?"

"Yes, thank you." I left and decided to see what was behind the remaining two doors. The third door was locked, so I went on to the fourth. It opened easily.

I went in and closed the door quietly behind me.

I was in a very large room with no windows. Like the servants' kitchen, it was cooled by central air-conditioning. The room looked like a large loft with the different living areas separated by shelves or tables or the arrangement of the furniture.

"Hello?" I said. I didn't want to come upon the occupant of this place by surprise.

"Hello, is anybody here?"

No one answered, and since they didn't, I decided to do a very unwise thing and snoop around. I had no idea what I would say if someone walked in on me. Since I had determined to be a person of action, I put that thought out of my mind.

The entire room was decorated attractively in white wicker. The cushions on the sofa and chair were bright yellow, and the king-size bed was covered with a cheery yellow-and-white checked comforter. Everywhere there were accents of yellow and white. There appeared to be four main living areas: the kitchen, the dining area, the living room, and the bedroom.

The walls and the eight-foot ceiling were white, and the recessed lighting gave the overall effect of airiness and spaciousness even though there were no windows. A nice apartment by anyone's standards. There was a desk in the bedroom area, and I decided to start with that. A small, elegant wooden box bearing the intricately carved name of Inez sat atop the desk. So! This was Inez's quarters. I took a deep breath and decided to look through a large stack of papers that were anchored by a heavy lead-crystal paperweight. The top paper was a birth certificate. Mother: Inez Castillo. Infant: Elisa Castillo.

Really? I read it again. So Inez had slapped her own daughter. Why? I read further.

Very interesting. Father: Pablo Castillo. My eyes swept down the page. The next paper was a letter from an attorney. I heard a noise. Frantically I looked around for a place to hide. Oh, God, if Inez caught me in here, there was no telling what she might do to me. I restacked the papers quickly. My hands were shaking, and adrenaline was shooting through my veins like crazy. *Hide, quick!* I saw three doors to the left of me. Like a nightmare version of the old TV show, *Let's Make a Deal*, I chose door number two and dived in. It was dark inside and full of shoes. Hundreds of pairs of shoes. Inez and Imelda Marcos had a lot in common. I moved carefully into a corner and prayed that she wouldn't be needing a change of shoes. I could hear her walking around outside the door. Then I heard another door open. It sounded like it was right next to me. Soon I heard a familiar sound. It was the sound of running water. Perhaps she was washing her hands. Maybe, just maybe, this was my chance. I was sweating heavily now. Slowly I turned the knob and opened the door. No squeaks. Carefully I peered out. So far, so good. My heart started to pound harder. Go! Now! Run! I felt like a little kid playing hide-and-seek. Only this time the stakes were much higher. I was afraid. Actually I was terrified. Taking a deep breath, I quickly sped across the room thankful that my sandals were rubber-soled. I reached the door to the outside hall and carefully slipped outside, remembering to release the door knob slowly. Didn't see anyone. Hurry! I turned down the hall and did not slow down until I reached my own room, where I collapsed exhausted on my bed. I lay there, trying to calm down. I still felt a little shaky in my limbs, but the rush of adrenaline was beginning to dissipate.

It was late afternoon, and it was still raining. I tried to focus on the rain in an effort to stop my mind from being bombarded with a million unanswered questions and fears. I was just beginning to feel somewhat normal again, when there was a sharp rapping on the door.

I sat up and went to the door to answer it. My God! It was Inez! My heart began to pound furiously again. Did she know?

"Hello, Inez." *Stay cool, Catherine.*

"Mrs. Hanson, you have a call on the main house line. It is Mr. Cappelli."

"Mr. Cappelli?"

"Yes. Just pick up your receiver." She turned on her heels and left before I could say another word. I closed the door and raced over to pick up the phone.

"Hello, Carlo. This is Catherine."

"Yes, hello, Catherine. I wanted to talk with you because I knew that you would be upset and worried about Nikki."

That was an understatement.

"Yes, I am worried, Carlo. How is Nikki?"

Some static crackled across the line.

"Carlo, are you still there?"

"Yes, Catherine. We seem to be getting the brunt of the storm here right now. Nikki is going to be fine. We reached the hospital in good time, and after Dr. Laurenza ran some tests, he determined that she needed a completely different type of medication. She is gradually improving, and the doctor says she's out of danger now."

Out of danger. Interesting choice of words.

"That's good news, Carlo. What does Dr. Laurenza think caused her to be so violently ill?"

"He says the tests confirmed an extremely virulent type of bug that was resistant to the previous medications he had tried. She is showing marked improvement hourly on this new medication, and he is very confident that she will have a full recovery."

"Well, that's wonderful news. How long will she need to stay in the hospital?" I was still hoping with all my heart that what he said was true, and that somehow I had missed something.

"Even though Dr. Laurenza is very happy with Nikki's response to the new drug, he wants to keep her here in the hospital for a while so he can keep a close eye on her. He doesn't want to take any chances with a relapse. He said the most difficult part of her recovery is being patient with herself while she regains her strength. It will take time. He wants to keep her here for at least another two weeks."

"Two weeks is a long time, Carlo."

"Yes, it is, but I want my Nikki to have the finest medical care possible and fully regain her health. She's been through a hell of an ordeal. Dr. Laurenza has her best interests at heart, and I've hired two private nurses to be with her around the clock."

"Yes, what we want is for Nikki to get completely well and be her old self again." I felt a catch in my throat. I was forcing the words out and trying to disguise my true feelings.

"That's right, Catherine. I spoke with her a few minutes ago, and as sick as she still is, she's worried about the fact that you'll be in our home without her for a couple of weeks. You know how she is."

"Yes, I do, Carlo. Tell her not to worry. I'll be fine. Of course, I could come to San Juan and visit her every day. I would really like to do that."

"Oh, Catherine, I know you would, but that's inadvisable right now. She's terribly weak, of course, and Dr. Laurenza wants her to sleep as much as possible and regain her strength. He says it is critical to her full recovery that she remain as quiet as possible, at least for the first week. He's given strict orders: Absolutely no visitors for one week. Including me. Very extreme, I think, but he's adamant about that point. If she's doing well after a week, we could fly you here for a day to visit her here in the hospital. Right now, though, it's imperative that we adhere to Dr. Laurenza's strict orders and let the health-care professionals do their job. I'm sure you understand."

"Oh, yes, Carlo. I understand much more than you think I do." I just couldn't resist saying that.

Static crackled again.

"What's that, Catherine? What did you say? The storm is really playing havoc with these phone lines."

"I simply said that I understand, Carlo."

"Oh. Oh, yes, of course. I'm glad you do. Well, Catherine, I'll be home tomorrow afternoon, and I'll update you on Nikki's condition. There're some contracts that absolutely must be signed as soon as possible."

"Thank you for calling, Carlo. Please tell Nikki I'm thinking of her and to get well soon. . . . Oh, wait, one more thing."

"What's that, Catherine?"

"What hospital is she staying in? I'd like to be able to call her tomorrow."

"That's a thoughtful idea, Catherine, but Dr. Laurenza also insists that her phone stay disconnected at least for another week to insure complete peace and quiet for her. I promise I'll keep you informed by talking to Dr. Laurenza every day. Hospital del Sol is the most modern hospital in San Juan. She couldn't be in a better place."

"I see."

"Good-bye, Catherine. See you late tomorrow afternoon."

He hung up, and so did I.

Dear God, what had he done with her?

CHAPTER 12

I was baffled. My options were definitely limited. I needed to find out where Nikki was. Maybe she really was at Hospital del Sol, and the person answering the phones had simply made a mistake. After all, people make mistakes all the time. Honest people. Intelligent people. I retrieved the slip of paper from my purse and punched the numbers in for Hospital del Sol. It took about ten or fifteen seconds before the line began to ring.

On the second ring, a man's voice answered. Good, this was an entirely different person—an even better way to test for accuracy.

"Hospital del Sol," said a very American male voice.

"Yes, can you please tell me the condition of a friend of mine? She was admitted in the early morning hours today. Her name is Nikki Cappelli or Mrs. Carlo Cappelli."

"Please spell that name."

"C-a-p-p-e-l-l-i."

"Thank you. One moment, please."

Several minutes passed, and I became hopeful.

"Hello, ma'am. I'm sorry it took so long, but I wanted to be absolutely certain. There is no patient of that name in this hospital. No one of that name has been treated or admitted and released here in the last twenty-four hours."

"Thank you," I said dully, and hung up.

The rain had stopped, but dark clouds threatened to renew their assault later in the evening. The little gold bedside clock said it was six P.M. Too early to try to talk to Genesis. He would be busy preparing the evening meal. I didn't think I could fake my way through another meal with Little Red Riding Hood and Alberto, Laura's wolf in grandma's clothing. On my phone, there was a button marked HOUSEKEEPING. Perhaps I could have a meal brought to my room. It was worth a try.

I punched the number, and it rang twice before a young female voice answered. I asked if it would be possible to have my dinner sent to my room. The woman said it would, and that it would be approximately twenty minutes before it would be delivered. I thanked her and hung up.

Although I was not in the mood, I took out some stationery that I had brought along and wrote another short letter to Bob and Millie. As I tried to sound upbeat and lighthearted, I longed for home. I wished I were there now, bored stiff and painting the house, instead of stuck here in a frustrating situation where I was totally helpless. Loyalty to Nikki was turning out to be extremely complicated. A firm knock at the door brought me out of my reverie into the sharp reality of the moment.

I opened the door. It was Luca, smiling. He was carrying a tray full of food. I started to close the door in his face.

Gripping the door with one large hand, he held it open.

I gave him a warning look.

His face looked sad, as if I had genuinely hurt his feelings. I glared back at him.

"Wait a minute, Catherine. I was in the kitchen, and they were filling up your tray. I asked if I could deliver it to you. Can we call a truce?"

"I don't know. Can we?" I snapped.

He looked contrite, an emotion I was sure he had never truly experienced.

"I never meant to make you angry," he said softly.

"I don't understand you, Luca, but it really doesn't matter because I don't intend to have anything to do with you anyway. Thanks for the tray. Now go away."

"Sure." His eyes looked like those of a wounded deer, as he shrugged and turned to go down the hall.

That guy was a real enigma. He showed up twice uninvited in my room and had no clue as to why I would be upset with him. I set the tray down on a small round corner table. Just to be sure, I went back and locked the door. Raising the stainless-steel food covers, I found that Genesis had created another culinary masterpiece. Poached salmon with dill sauce, luscious garden salad, straight-from-the-oven Italian bread, fresh asparagus, and *crème brûlée* for dessert. I unfolded my napkin and laid it on my lap. At the moment, the rest of my life was shot to hell, but I was damned sure going to enjoy this gourmet meal. I sighed. The foul mood I had started out with early this morning had returned as the day became increasingly sour.

I did enjoy the meal and made a mental note to compliment Genesis when I talked to him later that evening. After eating, I stacked my dinner things neatly and set the tray outside my door, hoping that that was proper household etiquette. Realizing I had time to kill, I picked up the Lawrence Sanders book I had brought with me, made myself comfortable in a wing chair by the window, and forced myself to read.

As usual, Lawrence Sanders had written another compelling novel, and I was able to lose track of the time. I glanced at my watch. It was eight o'clock. I decided to call the kitchen and see if Genesis had gone home for the day.

No one answered, so I assumed he had left.

Luckily I had packed a trench coat. In her letter, Nikki had suggested that I bring one. I changed into jeans and a black sweatshirt and sneakers. I didn't want to carry an umbrella since I wanted to move quickly through the trees. I dug out an old plastic rain cap for my head and tied it under my chin. Next, I put on the black trench coat, buttoned it, and fastened the belt. Looking out the window, I could see that the cloudy sky was very dark with no help from the moon and stars, so I put a small flashlight in my pocket. Glancing in the mirror over the dresser, I was glad to note that I didn't look like Catherine Hanson at all. Switching off the light, I slipped out the door, down the servants' stairs, and out into the night.

It was pitch-black outside, so I was grateful for the flashlight. It wasn't very large, but at least it would keep me from stepping in some big hole. The ground was wet, and my tennis shoes were going to be soaked by the time I reached Genesis's house. I walked slowly trying to avoid any major mud holes. Finally I reached his house. I could see lights on inside.

I knocked on his door. No one came. I knocked again. It was spooky standing out there. At last I heard his heavy footsteps approaching the door. He opened the door and squinched up his eyes at me. He chuckled.

"Catherine? Is that you in there?"

"Okay, stop laughing. I know I look like somebody's maiden aunt, but it has been raining all day, you know."

"Come on in."

As soon as I entered, I sat down on the tile floor and peeled off my wet shoes and socks. Genesis hung up my trench coat.

"I'll get you some dry socks," he volunteered, taking my wet ones with him.

He came back and handed me a pair of white socks that looked like pillowcases they were so large. We laughed as I put them on, and they flapped like flippers as I followed him into his living room.

I brought him up-to-date on all of my phone conversations with the various hospitals, as well as my talk with Carlo and my second call to Hospital del Sol.

He poured a welcome cup of hot tea and handed it to me.

"What are you going to do now, Catherine?"

"I don't know, Genesis. I wish I could just pack up and go home and forget any of this ever happened. But I can't do that, at least not yet. I owe it to Nikki to find out where she is and what's going on."

He nodded. "I understand. I wish I could be more helpful."

"Oh, you already are, Genesis. Since Nikki became ill, I

had no one to trust, no one to confide in, until I met you. You have helped. As far as I'm concerned, you're the only other sane person on this island."

"Why did you come to see me tonight?" Genesis asked.

"I don't know. Moral support, I guess. You have a sympathetic ear." Then I told him about going into Inez's room and what I had discovered about her.

He looked surprised.

"I had no idea that Inez was Elisa's mother. Pretty interesting stuff, I'd say. So what now?"

"I suppose I'll have to confront Carlo when he comes back tomorrow. I'll ask him why Hospital del Sol has no record of Nikki's being a patient there. I have no choice."

A worried look settled over Genesis's face.

"Catherine, I told you before, you never know how he's going to react to things. He's a dangerous, violent man. Please don't do anything to jeopardize your own safety."

I reached across and patted his big ham of a hand.

"I'm touched that you're concerned, Genesis. Don't worry. I'll be very careful not to upset him."

"And what if you don't find out anything? I don't think that you will. He's very shrewd, Catherine, and I'm not sure how far you can push him. If you accuse him of foul play, there's no telling what he might do. You don't know what you're dealing with here."

"Genesis, you talk like a person who knows something he's not telling. What is it?"

He grimaced and set down his cup of tea.

"All I know is that he's definitely capable of violence."

"What do you mean exactly?"

"You know who Eduardo is, don't you?"

"Of course. He came to Miami to escort me here on Carlo's private plane. And he works here as a servant."

"Exactly. Well, you must have wondered why he never speaks."

"Yes. I wanted to ask Nikki about it, but I never got a chance."

"Eduardo doesn't speak because ten years ago, Carlo cut Eduardo's tongue out."

CHAPTER 13

"It's true. When I first came here, Inez took me aside and told me to keep my mouth shut about any conversations that I might overhear in the house. She said that Carlo had cut Eduardo's tongue out years ago when Carlo lived in New York, as a lesson to the other employees."

"Genesis, are you sure she wasn't just trying to scare you to death?"

"Oh, she scared me all right. But one of the gardeners who has been with Carlo for over ten years told me it is the truth, because he witnessed it."

"I still can't believe it. How could Carlo get away with doing something so cruel? There are laws against mutilating other human beings."

"Catherine, did Nikki tell you that Carlo was raised by a Mafia family in New York?"

"Yes, she did."

"Have you ever considered the fact that his upbringing was not like yours?"

"I really hadn't given it much thought."

"Catherine, you can't be naive about this. Carlo has lived a life where power and money run everything. His rules for living probably come straight out of the pages of *The Godfather*. Think about it."

"Nikki gave me the impression that he was running legitimate businesses."

"Maybe she didn't want to know one way or another. Or

maybe she didn't want you to know that his business is a little on the shady side."

"You could be right, Genesis."

"Well, we know he has his own set of morals and values, Catherine. And they're nowhere close to yours and mine. Inez said that Carlo cut Eduardo's tongue out in front of the staff. Carlo actually had pictures taken of the whole ugly process. Eduardo had repeated to the other servants a piece of information that he had overheard from Carlo. The boss was furious and demonstrated that he was willing to use violence to discipline those who disobeyed his orders."

"That's horrible! It's so barbaric. Cheating on his wife is nothing short of despicable, but cutting out a man's tongue for gossiping is quite another matter." I shuddered at the thought.

"Please, Catherine, believe it. The man is dangerous, and I wouldn't have told you any of this except that you must be very careful not to make him angry. In fact, I think it would be best for you to go home as soon as possible. If he has done something to Nikki, then there's nothing you can do about it. For God's sake, don't risk your own safety. I know Nikki wouldn't want you to get hurt. This is out of your league. You're dealing with a madman." His intensity frightened me.

"Genesis, I appreciate your concern, really I do."

Genesis shook his head. "Catherine, look, I'm leaving tomorrow morning to visit my daughter for the weekend. Pack up your things tonight, and we'll go to San Juan together. From there, you can book a flight to Miami. You can leave Carlo a note about some emergency at home and how you had to leave immediately without waiting to see him to explain in person."

"Even if I were to consider it, Genesis, it wouldn't work. Carlo's returning late tomorrow afternoon. Elisa said the morning boat arrives here about eight A.M. and doesn't return to San Juan until evening."

"That's true, most of the time. I happen to know that tomorrow the boat will dock here at eight A.M., refuel, and return to

San Juan immediately. There's some special furniture delivery that won't be ready in San Juan until later in the morning. So the boat will make its usual run to bring employees here, and then head back to pick up the delivery."

"Thanks, Genesis. I'm strongly tempted, but I can't. I owe it to Nikki to stick around and make sure she's all right. I'd go with you to San Juan if I had a clue as to where to begin looking. I can't go to the police. I don't have any evidence that a crime has been committed. I have nothing but my gut feeling and my suspicions. I don't like it, but all I can do is sit tight for a while and see if I can squeeze more information out of Carlo when he gets home."

Genesis sighed.

"Catherine, I admire your loyalty to your friend, but it's time for you to go home. Now."

"No can do right now, Genesis."

We sipped the rest of our tea in silence.

The sharp ringing of the telephone disrupted the quiet. It startled both of us.

Genesis answered the phone that sat on a corner table.

"Hello?" he said in his deep baritone voice.

I watched his face as he listened carefully. I could see why he had been successful in the theater; his face was very expressive.

He frowned.

"I don't understand. Is she sick?"

He listened.

"I'm sorry, Sister Consuela, but that doesn't make any sense. I saw her last weekend, as you know, and everything was fine. What's happened this week to change things?"

He listened again.

"None of this is logical, Sister. Will she speak to me on the phone?" He paused. "Well, it just doesn't make any sense. I'm coming there anyway. Even if Sally won't see me, maybe some of her teachers or classmates can explain this abrupt change in her behavior. Sister, what about her psychologist, Dr. Hernandez? Have you spoken with her?"

He listened again.

"She missed her last appointment? That sounds mighty suspicious to me. I've got to find out what's wrong. She seemed perfectly normal last weekend. We had fun together. We laughed and joked. We took a picnic lunch and went to the beach. She and I had a great time. She was happy and relaxed. Are you certain that she . . . uh . . . has not been using drugs again?"

He nodded.

"Okay, well that's good news. There has to be a logical explanation for all of this. I'll come up in the morning. Maybe she'll have changed her mind by then and will want to see me. Could you please tell Dr. Hernandez that I'll need to talk to her?"

He listened.

"Something's really wrong here. We've come a long way together, she and I. I've got to find out what has caused this sudden change of heart. I'll come by and see you as soon as I arrive. Thank you for calling, Sister. Good-bye."

He hung up the phone and came back to the couch and sat down. He was a beaten man.

"What's wrong, Genesis?"

"My daughter, Sally, went to Sister Consuela, the head of her school, and asked her to call me and tell me not to come this weekend. The sister said Sally was very upset. She said Sally didn't want to see me, and that she would refuse to see me if I came. Sister Consuela said she tried to talk with Sally, but Sally became almost hysterical and kept bursting into tears. She asked Sally if she felt sick or if anything else was bothering her, but she said no. Sally missed her last appointment with Dr. Hernandez. That doesn't sound good to me. Catherine, I don't understand what could have happened to change her attitude toward me so quickly."

"Maybe it will turn out to be something simple."

"I don't think so, Catherine. I have a bad feeling about all of this. I'm going to go ahead tomorrow as planned. Maybe I can find out what's going on while I'm there."

"I think you should do what feels right to you."

"The sister said Sally continues to do well in school, has lots of friends, and doesn't appear to be ill. She also said Sally has been passing her regular urine tests for drugs. She's clean. I'll talk to her friends and teachers as well as the psychologist. Maybe someone can tell me something."

"Sounds like a good plan."

"I've got a bad feeling about this, Catherine."

With good reason, he looked horribly depressed. I squeezed his hand. "I understand. It's hard being a parent under any circumstances, but you two have had some major things to deal with. Well, I guess I'd better get going. Thanks for being here for me, Genesis. I appreciate your advice, the hot tea, and the dry socks."

"I'll go get your socks," he said, leaving the room to retrieve mine from the clothes dryer.

They felt warm and toasty as I put them on. I hated going back out into the wet, dark night to the main house. Genesis's house felt safe and serene and sane.

I told him that, and he was genuinely pleased.

"I'm glad you feel that way, Catherine. You know it's nice having you as a friend. Even if we have to sneak around about it. I've had to lead a very solitary life here. Except for the weekends, when I see Sally, my life consists of work and nothing else. I'm like an old hermit. It helps to have someone to talk to."

"I agree. Well, we both have busy days tomorrow, Genesis."

"Yes, we both have missions to accomplish. Please be careful in that house and especially around Carlo. I wouldn't want anything to happen to you."

I laughed nervously.

"I don't either. Okay, my friend, have a good trip tomorrow. I hope with all my heart that everything works out between you and Sally. I'll be thinking about you. We'll talk when you get back."

"Thanks, Catherine." He helped me with my coat and chuckled again as I tied on my ridiculous rain hat.

"Better get your flashlight out. It's awfully dark out there, so be extra careful. I wish I could walk you back."

"Thanks, big guy. See you Sunday night."

He started to wave and then changed his mind and gave me a big brotherly bear hug.

"If you change your mind about going to San Juan, call me. I'm number ten on your phone. I hope you'll really think about what I've said, Catherine. Carlo is dangerous. It's time for you to go home. You're in over your head."

"You never give up, do you? Good luck tomorrow, Genesis."

He waved and went into his house.

I shivered. I wasn't cold, but all that talk about Eduardo's tongue or lack of it gave me the willies. I steeled myself and with the help of the small flashlight began to pick my way back to the main building. I felt relieved when I reached the house. Taking off my muddy shoes outside the door, I carried them inside and tiptoed up the servants' stairs to my room.

Quickly I took off my damp things and put them in the bathroom. I slipped into a nightgown and decided to get in bed and read until I fell asleep. First, though, I brushed my teeth and even flossed.

It wasn't long before I fell into a deep sleep. I woke up a few minutes later when the book fell out of my hands and onto the floor.

I snapped off the light and slid back into sleep. It was not a restful sleep though because I kept having nightmares. Carlo and Luca took turns cutting off people's ears and noses. Very gruesome stuff. Luca was just about to cut off my nose, when

I woke myself up moaning. I turned on the light and looked at the little gold clock. It was only midnight. It was going to be a long night.

CHAPTER 14

About four A.M., something awakened me. I didn't know if it was a noise in my room or something in the hall. I sat up in bed, snapped on the bedside lamp, and looked around. I listened but heard nothing unusual. I got up and went into the bathroom. Nothing there either. The French doors to the outside were closed and locked. I moved a curtain aside slightly and looked out into the night. It was still dark, but it was not raining.

Irritated with myself, I climbed back into bed. I tried to relax and go back to sleep, but I had that antsy feeling that generally proves to be irreversible. I tried mind-over-matter psychology on myself, but my brain wasn't buying any of it.

Okay. I gave up. I decided to get up. Something kept nagging at the back of my mind. An idea that wouldn't leave me alone. It had occurred to me that I might learn something more about Nikki's abrupt departure if I looked around her room. I had no idea what to look for, but it seemed like a logical thing to do. Also, if I was going to do any serious poking around, it would be best to do it at a time when everyone else was asleep. At four A.M., even the omnipresent Inez had to be sleeping.

I dressed quickly, putting on a light gray T-shirt and sweatpants. I knew it was silly, but since I couldn't lock my door from the outside, I hurriedly arranged some pillows underneath the covers to make it appear that I was still in bed asleep.

I went into the bathroom and, fishing in my trench coat pocket, retrieved the small flashlight I had carried to Genesis's house.

Quietly, I went out into the hall and closed the door behind me. I moved swiftly to the main staircase. Seeing no one, I continued to cross above the main entry hall into another hall where Nikki's room was located. As I expected, the door was closed. I hoped it wasn't locked. Turning the knob gently, it opened, and I entered the completely dark room. It felt creepy. I took the flashlight out of my pocket and directed its beam around the room. As far as I could tell, everything looked the same.

Since the dressing table was immediately to my left, I decided to look through the drawers. There were two on each side and a single one in the center.

The middle drawer contained nothing but makeup items: eyeliner, eyelash curler, mascara, foundation, loose powder, blush, and lipstick. The top left-hand drawer contained creams and lotions. The bottom left-hand drawer held different kinds of hair rollers: brush, magnetic, and Velcro. I put my hand in and felt for the bottom of the drawer. I touched something made of metal. Pulling it out, I discovered it was a small silver flask. I screwed the top off and sniffed. Bourbon. Nikki's secret stash. I sighed and put it back where I had found it. Opening the bottom right-hand drawer, I saw envelopes and monogrammed stationery in blue, yellow, and white. Again, I put my hand underneath the paper, trying to touch the bottom of the drawer. At the very back, underneath a stack of envelopes, my fingers touched a smooth object. Clasping it, I pulled it out and held it under the flashlight's beam. It was a small red-leather book. A diary. Laying it on top of the dressing table, I opened the book to the first page. I recognized Nikki's handwriting. The entry was undated.

> Carlo has found out that I cannot have children. He is furious with me for not telling him that before we were married, which makes no sense since I was into my forties

when he married me. He never mentioned wanting to have children before. He says he would never consider adopting a child, because adopted children are nothing more than "mongrels." I don't understand this attitude since Carlo was adopted himself. He is obsessed with having a child of his own. I'm afraid of losing him, but I don't know what to do.

I thumbed through the rest of the book, noting that none of the entries were dated. I turned to one of the later pages.

My stomach has been giving me fits over the last few weeks. I'm suspicious of Laura. She watches Carlo like a hawk. She's the worst kind of predator, very sly but equally determined. All sweetness on the outside, but hard as steel inside. One evening at dinner when I had to excuse myself because of stomach pain, she laughingly said, "Better be more careful about what you eat, Nikki." I told Carlo, but he laughed it off and said I was imagining things. I'm not imagining things. She's a snake. I don't believe that Alberto is the father of her baby either. She runs off to San Juan every weekend. With the morals of an alley cat, she probably has no idea who the real father is. Still, I'll bet she'd like to see me out of the way. Then she might have a chance at being lady of the manor. It must have passed through her mind. I've been thinking that maybe someone . . . maybe Laura has been trying to poison me.

Poison? Could that have been what caused Nikki's mysterious illness? Did Laura do it?

I closed the book and stuck it into the front waistband of my pants. Surely, nobody would miss it for a while. They probably didn't even know of its existence. I might find the answers to my questions somewhere in this little leather book. I shone the light on my watch. It was five o'clock. Time for me to get out of here. I was just closing the drawer, when the next events happened so fast and without warning that I'm not sure what really took place. The door flew open and a voice I knew as Inez's shrieked, "You nosy bitch! You just couldn't mind your own business, could you? Well, this time you've gone too far. Go ahead, shut her up!"

I don't remember much except strong hands snatching the diary away from me and then pinning my arms behind me. I recall feeling faint and thinking I might wet my pants, and having a rag saturated with chloroform held tightly over my nose and mouth. Everything went dark inside my brain.

This is where my story began. I awoke to find myself bound and gagged in a dark closet, totally disoriented, my lip split, and my nose bleeding. My head was throbbing, and I was panicked. I was scared to death. I heard footsteps and then heard Carlo's voice. The door opened. I was blinded by the light, so I couldn't focus very well. Someone untied my arms and legs and took the gag out of my mouth. Then I heard Carlo tell Luca to carry me to the bed. I wanted to kick and scream and fight, but I was still groggy from the chloroform and possibly some other drug. I was in no shape to struggle. The room was spinning around, and my vision was all messed up. The harder I tried to focus my eyes, the dizzier I became. I was afraid and totally at the mercy of Carlo and Luca. Carlo offered me some water, but I spilled most of it trying to swallow, a task I found practically impossible. A voice inside me kept telling me to stay awake, stay awake, but I could not. I had no control over what was happening to me. I sank into a deep chasm of drugged sleep.

As I mentioned at the beginning of my story, I awoke to find myself bruised and battered, woozy and weak, but not permanently damaged. I was more afraid than anything else. By looking at the bedside clock, I found that it was almost five A.M. I had lost twenty-four hours. An entire day. I was back in my own guest room, and I did not remember how I had gotten there. I recalled going to Nikki's room, finding the diary, and then hearing Inez shrieking at me. I did not see who was with her, but it had to have been Luca, my constant nemesis, because he appeared later with Carlo. After assessing the physical damage done to me—split lip, sore but unbroken nose, aching body, and trembling legs—I positioned myself as comfortably as possible on my bed and did a complete mental replay of all of the events that had taken place since I had arrived. I was more confused than ever about what was going on around here. Why would I be attacked for reading Nikki's diary? Evidently it contained damaging information to someone. Who? Carlo? Laura? Inez? Whatever it was, it would remain a mystery to me. The book was gone.

I knew I had to keep my wits about me. I couldn't afford to get hysterical. Somehow I had to make sense out of all of this and let everyone know I couldn't be pushed around. Ha! Who was I kidding? They had already done that and very effectively, too. But why wasn't there someone guarding me now, either inside this room or outside in the hall, if I were such a threat? I thought hard. I could remember what Carlo had said when they took me out of the closet. He said, "This was all a terrible mistake. I'm very sorry. Truly sorry." Okay, so I had to talk to Carlo as soon as possible. Let him do the explaining. Right now, however, it was very early morning. I still felt thickheaded, and I hoped a shower would help.

I locked the door to the hall, which was probably stupid, since I'm sure they had master keys to every room in this house. Not to mention the fact that Luca was the head of security. I locked it anyway. I would have to muster all the courage I had to deal with this entire nightmarish situation.

I hobbled to the bathroom, on the way collecting bra and panties and a hanger supporting a pink slacks outfit. I wanted clothing to be as close as possible. As soon as I undressed, I felt very vulnerable. I shivered but got on with the business of showering. Thankfully, no monsters or people attacked me, but I toweled dry and dressed hurriedly. My clothing was the only armor I had. I used a hair dryer to get the job done quickly and then sat down to tackle the problem of makeup.

My split lip was tender and swollen and so was my nose. Gingerly I applied foundation and all the other stuff. I didn't look great, but at least I felt more normal, a little more like myself. I was operating under the untested theory that if I looked halfway decent, I would, in turn, feel better. So much for theories.

I still had a throbbing headache. Returning to the bathroom, I dug around in my small travel bag of medications until I found a bottle of Tylenol. I swallowed two pills and chased it with a full glass of water. I needed shoes. I sat on the side of the bed and put on a pair of sandals I had left close to the edge of the bed. I still felt really odd in the head. Okay, food was needed next. I don't know how many meals I had missed, but I was starving. I've always believed that it is a pathetic statement on the frailty of humanity that people can be in the midst of life-threatening disasters and still our bodies demand sustenance. I, too, was human and at this moment feeling very frail.

I slowly crossed the room and bravely opened the door. Everything was quiet. I walked down the hall, down the stairs, and crossed the large entry hall. When I reached the kitchen door, I paused.

What I would have given to push through that door and find my friend Genesis inside with a big warm smile! A tear rolled down my cheek. Angrily I brushed it away. I might be a bowl of mush on the inside, but I had to be tough on the outside.

Pushing through the swinging door, I went to one of the large refrigerators and took out a decanter of fresh orange juice. I spotted some ham and Swiss cheese. A sandwich would be fortifying. Locating rye bread, I built myself a substantial sandwich in no time at all. I carried my juice and sandwich over to the table on the far side of the kitchen. As I began eating, I realized I had never asked Genesis who substituted for him as chef on the weekends that he was gone. I would find out soon enough. The windows in the kitchen were high, but I could see that the sun was up already. Having finished my orange juice and sandwich, I took the dishes to one of the large sinks, rinsed them, and stacked them on the counter. At least my stomach was full, and my headache was beginning to fade away. I left the kitchen by way of the side door and decided to walk down to the ocean.

It was going to be a beautiful day. The sun was already warm, and the sky was a deep blue. The ocean looked majestic and powerful, purposefully sending its waves up onto the shore in a rhythmical, orderly fashion. Standing out here in the company of nature, it seemed that I was the only one who was out of sync, powerless, and confused. I walked down the beach for about a mile. The salty air and the waves rolling in made me feel stronger. I wished I could walk and keep walking, away from this mess I was in, away from these people. After more than an hour, I decided to go back to the house and confront Carlo. Sea gulls flew high above my head, gliding and turning and heading out to sea again. I envied them their freedom.

I came up the main steps of the raised balcony. And there he sat. "The Man." Carlo. Immaculately dressed in sports attire, his dark skin in direct contrast to his tennis whites, adding to the overall effect of the handsome, wealthy, Italian entrepreneur ready for a morning of tennis.

He was not alone. Alberto and Luca appeared to be having a cozy little breakfast with all the trimmings. Carlo stood and smiled as soon as he saw me and pulled out a chair gesturing for me to come and sit next to him.

My heart beat furiously, and my knees felt weak. *Buck up, old girl, and stand tall* I told myself. I had to meet this head on. *Hold on to your cool. Don't lose it, or you'll be easy pickings.* I was a wounded sparrow in the presence of circling vultures.

I sat down next to him.

I poured coffee into an empty cup. Caffeine would help. I took a sip. It was hot and strong. I took another. They sat there and watched me, waiting.

I raised my eyes and met Carlo's with a steady glance I had thought myself incapable of based on the circumstances.

He smiled. I did not return the gesture.

"Carlo, what in the hell is going on around here?" I asked.

CHAPTER 15

He sighed and shook his head. Reaching out, he took my hand in his. His touch was repellent, and I pulled my hand away. He looked deeply hurt.

"Catherine, I'm very sorry. I can't apologize enough for what happened to you yesterday. You have every right to be angry with all of us. I wish there were some way to make it up to you. All I can say is that I sincerely hope we can put the entire episode behind us. It was all a terrible mistake."

I had decided that I would keep my anger under control as much as possible. If I showed my anger, I would be at a definite disadvantage.

"Carlo, why don't you tell me your version of what happened?" I said.

"Of course. Inez had gone to the kitchen in the middle of the night to get a glass of milk because she couldn't sleep. She has insomnia, so she is often up and about at night. She heard a noise coming from Nikki's bedroom. There has been a bad pilferage problem lately from some of the help, but Inez was frightened and went to get Milo's help. They overreacted, of course, by not finding out first who was actually in the room. Inez has a tendency to take her position here a little too seriously sometimes. Without stopping to ask questions, she gave Milo an order, and he followed it. I'm very sorry, Catherine. I've spoken with Inez and Milo, and they wish to apologize for their actions."

"As soon as they realized it was me, Carlo, don't you think

the logical thing was to let me go? Instead, they bound and gagged me and threw me into a closet for God knows how many hours like a common criminal and kept me there until your return. It's obvious that this incident is more than just a trivial mistake."

"I assure you that it was a major mistake, and they have been reprimanded severely. I don't know what else I can say. I hope that you can forgive all of us, because no harm was intended."

I studied his face. He looked repentant but righteous at the same time.

You could try telling the truth, you bastard, I thought.

"Carlo, how is Nikki?"

He looked relieved that we had changed the subject.

"She's very weak, but the antibiotic is definitely working, and she isn't having any more gastrointestinal problems. The doctor says it will take time to regain her strength."

"I'm glad to hear that she's improving." Carlo, you are a liar! Where is she?

I had been caged like an animal, and now he was giving me some flimsy excuse that even a child wouldn't accept. A chill went down my spine, as I wondered seriously if I really were the only sane person present.

I looked at Alberto. He was looking down at his coffee, stirring some sugar into it. Luca appeared to be completely detached from the conversation that was taking place. He gazed calmly out at the seascape.

"Carlo, please be sure and thank Milo and Inez for my split lip, my headache, various bumps and bruises, sore muscles, and an enchanting time spent tied up in a stuffy closet. You people certainly know how to show a girl a good time!" So much for my good intentions of containing my anger.

"Catherine, wait . . ." Carlo stood up to stop me.

"Wait for what, Carlo? It's dangerous being a guest in your home. If this is the way you treat guests, I don't want to be one anymore. Please get your pilot lined up to take me to San Juan in one hour. I'm going home. Do I make myself clear?"

"I can understand why you're so upset, Catherine, but it truly was an awful mistake. Please wait until tomorrow, and if you still feel the same way about going home, of course I'll arrange it."

"No, Carlo. I want to go home today, while I'm still in one piece. I wanted to be here when Nikki returned, but your inability to give me a reasonable explanation for my unpleasant treatment and confinement leaves me no choice."

Carlo smiled his little irritating smile. The one where it looks as though the cat has just eaten the canary and is ready for a second helping.

"Catherine, I would like to do that for you, but I'm afraid there is a slight problem. The maintenance crew will be working all day on the jet. And there's some major repair work to be done on the helicopter, which is in San Juan at the present time. I'm afraid you'll have to wait until tomorrow."

My frustration was so great I thought I would explode. I wanted to punch his lights out. Instead, I arose from the table, rushed into the main house, and up to my room. The bastard! I was tired of his cocky arrogance and his little island kingdom where everything operated according to his own set of rules.

I suddenly felt tired, sick and tired of the lies and deception. I decided to lay down for awhile to calm my nerves. Miraculously, I dozed off again. When I awoke, I was still angry. I sat on the bed and tried to control my rage. I looked around the room. For a week, this room had at least represented a certain degree of relief from the insanity outside its doors. It had served as a welcome refuge. But not now. I felt confined and exposed at the same time. I could not stay here another moment. I knew that Genesis was not due back yet, but I thought I could at least sit on his front porch and escape from this house and its feeling of oppression. I jumped up and took the servants' stairs.

The balmy midday breeze felt good on my face. Walking

briskly, I felt stronger with every step. Maybe Genesis hadn't even bothered to lock his doors, or maybe he had hidden a key in an obvious place. At any rate, his porch and his garden represented a safe haven for me. I knew he wouldn't mind my going there. I walked faster.

Just seeing his house in the afternoon sun gave me a feeling of comfort. His beautiful flower garden looked fresh and cheerful and seemed to have survived the storm with no damage. I walked up the steps and decided to try the knob. I didn't really expect it to be unlocked, because Genesis was such a private man. When it opened, I felt a welcome sense of relief. Now I wouldn't have to hunt for a hidden key.

I entered the front door and closed it softly behind me. The living room looked neat and orderly as usual. I sat down on the couch. I did feel safe and removed from the craziness of Carlo's house. After a while, I realized I was thirsty and decided to see if Genesis had any soft drinks in the refrigerator. I went into the kitchen and stopped as soon as I entered. I screamed.

Dear God in heaven! Nothing could have prepared me for what I saw. In the center of the kitchen was a large light fixture made of brass. From the base of the light fixture was a heavy rope tied in a hangman's noose. Genesis's head hung in the noose, his neck at an odd angle and obviously broken, and his feet dangling, lifeless. His face was a ghastly purple, his features swollen and his eyes bulging. Horrified, I ran over to him and felt for his pulse. There was none. No evidence of life. I let go of his wrist. A wave of intense nausea swept over me, and I fainted.

I was in that dark pit again where there was no time or space or reality. Someone was holding smelling salts up to my nose. I came to and jerked my head back to avoid the strong smell. Opening my eyes, I realized that I was lying on Genesis's couch in his living room. As my eyes focused, I saw Luca's face anxiously watching mine.

"What happened? I . . . What am I doing here? What are you doing here?" I shrieked at him while trying to sit up.

"Please lie back, Catherine. You've had a major shock. Please lie back and rest for a few minutes. I was really worried that you weren't going to come around. You were out cold for several minutes."

I lay back. Light-headed and woozy, I felt as though I might faint again. My stomach was doing major flip-flops.

"Okay," I agreed. I didn't have the strength to argue or run or do anything, even if I didn't have any use at all for Luca.

"Would you like some water?" he asked softly.

"No, not now. I just need to lie here for a few minutes."

"Take your time."

I turned my head slowly in order to see him. He was sitting on the floor by the couch watching me. Why did he act so concerned?

All at once, I remembered what had happened. It wasn't a nightmare I had had. It was real. Genesis was dead. My friend Genesis was dead. Dear God, how could it be true? A wave of deep sadness engulfed me, and I began to sob.

"Catherine, are you all right?" he asked. His eyes were dark brown and very expressive. I had never noticed before. He took my hand in his. His hands were warm. Mine were cold. I felt like ice inside. I shivered. Quickly he arose and disappeared into the bedroom. He returned carrying a heavy, navy blue blanket and covered me up, gently placing my arms underneath the covers and tucking the blanket up under my chin.

"I . . . I feel so cold."

"We must keep you warm. We don't want you going into shock."

"Could I have that drink now?"

"Of course." He smiled at me and went back into the kitchen, returning with a glass of water.

"Sit up slowly," he advised, gently assisting me.

I sat up. Then I took the glass from him and sipped the

water. I handed the glass back to him and scooted down under the blanket again.

"How do you feel now?" he asked.

"Awful . . . is it true? About Genesis? Is he really dead?"

"Yes. It's true."

"My God! What did you . . . uh, where is Genesis's body?"

"I just called the main house. Milo and some of the gardeners are coming over to take the body back with them. They'll be here soon. There's something I have to do. I'll be right back."

He went into the kitchen. I could hear him walking around on the tile floor. In a few minutes, he returned with a grim look on his face. He sat on the floor next to the couch.

"Why are you here, Luca?" I asked. I was suspicious of his motives about everything.

"This morning, I got a call from the captain of the ferry. He told me that Genesis was scheduled to take the eight A.M. ferry, but he never showed up. I called here, but Genesis didn't answer, so I came to see what was going on. You arrived minutes before I did, and the rest you know."

I decided to sit up. Slowly. I felt too vulnerable lying down. Besides, Luca was on the side of the enemy. I wanted to be in more control of the situation.

"He didn't kill himself," I said. "He did not kill himself," I repeated adamantly.

"How do you know it wasn't a suicide?" he asked. He got up from the floor and sat in the easy chair next to the couch.

"I'm not sure I want to talk to you about this."

He looked at me sadly.

"I understand. You don't trust me. Why should you? Our personal encounters have all been irritating to you at best. You have no reason to believe me or anything that I might say."

"That's right. I couldn't have said it better myself. Don't take this personally, but I don't trust anyone around here now. I did trust Genesis. He was my friend."

"I know."

"How did you now that?" I snapped. "Oh, wait, let me guess. Since I am obviously such a dangerous threat to Carlo's kingdom, you've been observing me and watching me ever since I arrived here."

"That's right."

I knew I was becoming my old self again because uncontrollable anger welled up inside of me. On impulse, I jumped up, charged at him, and slugged him right in the nose. As soon as I'd hit him, I was sorry I'd done it. It seemed odd that he hadn't tried to move out of the way, or block my punch, or defend himself in some way. He was most definitely superior to me in physical adeptness. This guy was no wimp. In fact, he was the epitome of macho.

He looked surprised but not angry. My hand hurt terribly. It felt like it was broken. I moved back to see how he would respond, but he simply pulled a handkerchief out of his pants pocket and held it to his bleeding nose. I held my injured hand up against my chest. The pain was unbelievable.

"I . . . I'm sorry. I've never done anything like that before. Even if you are the monster I suspect you to be, you don't deserve a broken nose. I'll get you some ice or something. I guess it's in the kitchen. I'll . . ."

He interrupted me. "It's okay, it's not broken. Your hand might be, though. I'll take care of this." He went back to the kitchen leaving me standing there like an idiot. My hand was throbbing terribly. I sat down again on the couch. Here came the nausea again. How could I have been so stupid? Being unconscious twice in two days was turning me into a fool who lashed out first and asked questions later.

Luca returned with two plastic bags filled with ice.

"One for you and one for me," he said softly, handing me one and returning to his chair. He closed his eyes and draped the bag around his nose. We sat there for a few minutes without saying a word. The cold helped to numb the pain in my hand. With his eyes closed, I could observe him. He was a tall, large-boned man. Very muscular and in good condition for a man in his forties. His hair was thick and dark and his skin was olive toned. He was nice looking with strong features. I hadn't noticed before. Realizing his size now, I was appalled that I had actually struck him. A man of his stature could have easily knocked me down with just one well-directed blow. I was like an ant trying to fell a bear.

"Uh, do you . . . do you think it's broken?"

His eyes opened.

"Which? Your hand or my nose or both?" I noticed that his nose had stopped bleeding.

"Your nose. Do you think it's broken?"

"No, I don't think so. I'm something of an expert. It's been broken twice before."

"Oh, that's awful. As I said before, I'm really sorry. I . . . I shouldn't have hit you."

"You pack quite a punch. Have you ever had any martial arts training?" I detected a twinkle in his eyes.

"No."

"I think you'd be good at it. If you can harness your temper, you can turn your intensity into a powerful tool."

"Hmm, well, that's the least of my worries right now."

"How's your hand? Mind if I examine it?"

"I guess not, but be careful. Do you have medical training, or did you just acquire the knowledge as a result of being a bully?"

"Ouch. You deliver some hefty verbal punches as well as physical ones. For your information, I was a medic in the Marine Corps, so I do have a fairly decent working knowledge of certain types of injuries."

"I see."

"Do I have your permission to advance and carefully examine your injury, or are you going to throw another wild punch at me?" His amused smile disappeared, and he replaced it with a serious expression.

"Permission granted, Sergeant."

"Captain. Captain Romano," he said.

He came over to the couch and sat down next to me. Gently he took my injured right hand in his and carefully felt the bones in my hand and fingers. Although his hands looked large and powerful, his fingers were long and sensitive. He concentrated on the delicate task and took several minutes to examine my hand. I was afraid that it would hurt, but other than some tenderness, the examination was not painful.

"What's the diagnosis, Captain?"

"It's my medical opinion that no bones are broken. Of course we can't be sure without X rays, but I believe I'm safe in concluding that you have badly bruised your fingers and hand but that you have sustained no fractures. In other words, it's going to hurt like hell for a while, and there'll be swelling and tenderness, but it will heal gradually. It would be best if we could have a doctor examine it, of course."

"Thank you. I hope your diagnosis is correct."

He grinned. "So do I, because I don't have any malpractice insurance."

I laughed. It surprised me that I could after all that had happened.

"Your face lights up when you laugh," he said softly. "Now, put this ice pack back on your hand. Doctor's orders."

"Okay. Better put yours back on, too."

"Right." He went back to his chair and placed the ice pack back over his nose.

I checked myself. He is the enemy, remember? He works for Carlo, remember? Don't be sucked into trusting him just because he's attractive and appears to be nice. Appearances are often deceiving.

Suddenly I heard voices outside, and footsteps coming up the porch steps. It had to be Milo and the gardeners. Luca jumped up to intercept them and stopped them outside the door. For a few minutes, I heard them talking in low voices. Then Luca came back inside, alone.

"They've come to get Genesis. They'll use the back door," he said solemnly.

I could hear Milo and the other men in the kitchen. Occasionally, I heard Milo laugh, a response I found loathsome under the circumstances. Then the back door slammed shut, and they were gone.

Tears ran freely down my face. My friend Genesis was dead. Gone forever. I shuddered, as cold, hard reality hammered its way into my brain with piercing intensity.

I had to figure out what to do. My friend Nikki was missing or dead. And now the only other person I could trust on this island was dead. It occurred to me that it was deadly to be a friend of mine. I was in a terrible mess, and I was concerned for my own life. I had to figure out how to get out of here in one piece.

Luca stood up and went over to the telephone. He took the receiver apart and removed a little thing that looked like the bugging devices I had seen in television mysteries. He put it into his pocket and continued around the room collecting other similar pieces. Then he went into the kitchen. After a few minutes, he emerged and went into the bedroom and finally the bathroom. He returned to the living area and took one of the little devices out and showed it to me.

"Do you know what this is?" he asked.

"I think so. Is it a bugging device?"

"Yes."

"So you had Genesis's phone bugged and his whole house, too?"

"Yes, according to Carlo's orders."

Fear began to creep back into my head. I was in no shape to run, but if I had to, I would. Adrenaline was beginning to shoot through my system again, and my heart began to pound.

"Why are you telling me this?" I asked, frightened of the answer.

"Because you need to know the truth, or you're not going to be able to stay alive," he said in a matter-of-fact tone.

I gasped. "What do you mean?"

"Catherine, I have to tell you the truth about certain things."

"I don't understand what you're getting at, Luca. You're not making any sense. Besides, I don't want to know any more about Carlo. As far as Carlo is concerned, I already know too much and knowing more is only going to further jeopardize my safety. I want to remain ignorant of all of this long enough to get off this damned island alive. Now look, I don't have much money, but if you'll help me get off this island safely, I promise you I'll pay you what I can. It won't be much, but I'll borrow money if that's what I need to do. Please help me. I don't understand this, but either you're a great actor or someplace down deep you really are a decent guy. I know you work for Carlo, but surely you don't want to see any more people hurt. Please help me, Luca. I just want to go home."

"Catherine, you don't understand."

"No, I don't."

"I'm trying to tell you that I really am a good guy."

"By whose definition?"

"No, I mean it, Catherine. I'm not what I seem."

"What are you trying to say, Luca? I hope you're not trying to confess to previous acts of violence. I told you I don't want to know anything. I just want to get out of here."

He came over to the couch and sat down next to me. By reflex, I pulled away. I wanted to trust him, but I knew better than to trust my intuition, which seemed to be totally confused.

He moved closer to me anyway and put his index finger up to his lips. When he spoke, his voice was low.

"Catherine, as I told you, I am not what I seem to be. What I am about to tell you is not known by anyone else on this island. If you divulge this information, they'll kill me."

"For heaven's sake, what are you trying to tell me? Who'll kill you?"

He brought his finger up to his lips once again.

"Catherine, you have to trust me, and I have to trust you. Quite literally, our lives depend on trusting each other."

"Go on."

"I'm an undercover FBI agent. I've been working undercover as a bodyguard, security man, etcetera, for Carlo Cappelli for two years."

I regarded him with skepticism.

"Go on."

"Carlo Cappelli is guilty of committing a variety of crimes: racketeering, larceny, extortion, fraud against the government, mail fraud, drug trafficking, arson, prostitution, and last but not least, murder. The FBI has been after him for years, but the slimy bastard has managed to slither out of their hands like a disgusting snake. Two years ago, the bureau decided to take drastic actions and assign some patriotic slob in their employ to stick to this guy like a leech and pin something on him once and for all. I am the aforementioned patriotic slob, and it is up to me to nail him. I've been this creep's bodyguard and confidant for what seems to me like a lifetime. The last two years of my life have been infinitely miserable and frustrating, but they will have been worth it if I can finally catch this piece of shit and put him away for the rest of his life. I'm very close to doing that now, Catherine, but I need your help."

Exhausted from his lengthy confession, Luca leaned back against the couch, folded his arms, and sighed deeply.

I sat there shocked, trying to absorb everything he had said. I knew that all of the color had drained away from my face. I felt woozy again.

"I need to lie down," I said weakly, not waiting for him to move down. I laid my head on the arm of the couch and stretched out my legs. He did manage to move down a bit, ending up with my feet practically in his lap.

"I'm having trouble digesting all of this. Too many shocks in one day," I muttered.

A few minutes passed, and I began to feel a little better.

"Luca?" I said.

"Yeah?"

"How do I know you're telling me the truth?"

"Why would I make up such an elaborate story?"

"Don't ask me that question. At this point, I'm completely

incapable of making any judgments, coming to any decisions, or arriving at any logical conclusions. I'm numb, completely numb to everything."

The phone rang. I jumped.

"It's okay, I'll handle it," he said, going to the phone.

My heart was pounding again. Fear, frustration, anger, and mental anguish were becoming automatic reactions for me. My adrenaline response was on overload now, and I wondered how long I could remain rational under these conditions. I listened to Luca talk on the phone.

"Yeah, Carlo, everything's under control here. She was hysterical for a while, but I handled that."

Luca listened to Carlo.

"Right, right. Yeah, she's really scared right now. Uh-huh. Just like you said, Carlo."

Luca listened again.

"Let's go ahead with the plan we agreed on."

Carlo spoke.

"I'll keep her here tonight. Everything's cool, under control. I've got everything I need.

"Yeah, I'll use the drugs if I need 'em. I can handle her easy. She's a psychological wreck right now, and physically and emotionally she'll be easy to intimidate.

"Okay, gotcha, Boss. This Genesis suicide thing works in our favor, too. She's scared to death. Everything's cool over here. I'll call you in the morning, and let you know how things are going."

Something Carlo said made Luca leer and made me tremble.

"You're right about that. She's got a cute little ass on her, that's for sure. I'll play that by ear. Could be fun. It might make her more submissive and more willing to do what we want."

Carlo made another comment that made Luca laugh lasciviously. I shuddered.

"You know I always like to mix business with pleasure.

We're exactly alike, *compadre*. Haven't had anything this good in a long time. Just leave everything to me. You know my methods.

"Talk to you tomorrow, Boss. Don't worry, she's in good hands. Right?"

He laughed again. It was disgusting.

CHAPTER 16

Luca hung up the phone.

"Wait, slugger. Before you wind up for a big left-handed punch directed at some other vital part of my anatomy, give me a chance to explain what just transpired over the phone."

I sat up again. I had to be poised for flight.

"Okay, start explaining! Now! Because I didn't like what I was hearing from your side of the conversation."

"Bearing in mind what you and I were discussing before the phone rang, remember that I am a good guy. I'm playing a role around Carlo. To him, I am his employee and his friend. Lean, mean, loyal, tough, womanizing Luca. That's who he thinks I am. I have a job to do, Catherine, and I have to play the part to the fullest because this is for big stakes. It's for real. It's life-and-death stuff. Now, are we clear on that?"

He was still standing by the phone, watching me to see how I reacted.

I sighed.

"I suppose so, Luca, but it's very hard for me to trust you. I don't know who or what to believe anymore. I feel like a character in *Alice in Wonderland* where nothing is what it seems to be. Everything is topsy-turvy, backwards, inside out, and upside down. And frankly, that is an accurate description of my mental state right now. I'm an emotional wreck. I feel as though I'm on some irreversible collision course, and that there's very little I can do to save myself."

Unfortunately, my nerves were shot, and I began to cry

again. I couldn't help myself, and I hated feeling out of control. By nature, I'm not a whiner or complainer. At the moment, I felt powerless.

Luca crossed the room and sat down on the couch beside me. He pulled a tissue from a box on the coffee table and handed it to me. I wiped my eyes, but the tears continued to flow. Gently he drew me to him in a comforting embrace. I hated to admit it to myself, but it felt good. We stayed that way for several minutes, with me sobbing into his shoulder and him holding me. The tears were cleansing for me. I cried for my old friend Nikki, sick or dead; I cried for Genesis, a good and decent man, now dead; and I cried for myself and the impossible situation I now found myself in. Finally the tears stopped.

"I feel better now. Thanks for the shoulder to cry on." I managed a small smile.

"Any time, Catherine," he said, as we released each other simultaneously.

I wiped my eyes again with the tissue.

"Luca, specifically, what did Carlo say over the phone?"

"I'll tell you later, Catherine. We'll talk about it when you're more rested. Right now, try to relax. You don't have to worry about dealing with Carlo or anyone else for now."

"But I need to . . . okay? Did Carlo have Genesis murdered? Did somebody else murder him?"

Luca ignored my questions.

"As a matter of fact, do you think you could sleep for a while? It would do you some good. You've had an exhausting couple of days. Today's been awful for you, physically and emotionally."

"I couldn't sleep now. I couldn't. I'm too geared up. Exhausted, but really wound up."

"Well, how about something to eat? Could you handle that?"

"I don't know. Maybe." Sadly I remembered my theory

about crisis situations and the ever-present need for sustenance to fuel the human body.

Luca looked at his watch. "I know you didn't have any lunch. You must be starved."

"True," I admitted.

"Luca, do you want me to help you put something together?" I asked with no enthusiasm.

He smiled.

"No thanks. Just lie back and let me take care of it."

The thought of going back into that kitchen where Genesis was hanged gave me a panicky feeling inside.

"Good. I don't think I can face the kitchen yet."

"I understand. Try to let your mind go blank. Maybe you'll drift off to sleep. Under normal conditions, I could whip up a delicious, authentic Italian meal. But today, I'll see what's available and fix something quick and easy." He turned and went into the kitchen.

My mind began flying off in all different directions again. *Stop it!* I said to myself. *Get hold of yourself.*

All at once, I realized that I must look awful. Crying and fainting are not conducive to one's appearance. Even though I was emotionally exhausted, I still cared about how I looked. It sounded ridiculous, but I did care. It wasn't an ego thing. Really. It had to do with survival, holding onto myself as I perceived myself to be. Holding onto my sanity, to some semblance of normalcy in a situation of chaos. Holding onto what made me Catherine. I felt dirty all over. Tainted somehow by the horrible memory of seeing Genesis hanging from the kitchen ceiling, dead. What a horrible day!

I decided to take a shower, hoping for some renewal of mind and body. I knew that only a lobotomy could erase the horrid images from my mind, but a shower was the only choice I had. I longed for makeup, clean underwear, a fresh change of clothes, and deodorant, but the soap and hot water would have to do.

I passed the kitchen on the way to the bathroom. Luca's

back was to me. He was whistling cheerfully as he worked. Obviously he was enjoying himself.

Genesis's bathroom was immaculate. Just what I would have expected from him. The room was large and attractive. A tropical, printed wallpaper depicted a lush jungle with giant flowering plants in bright greens, reds, yellows, and oranges.

I opened a small window at one end of the room to let the steam out and the fresh air in. The shower was vast. It was designed of clear glass and looked like it could easily accommodate a small party. I glanced nervously at the lock on the bathroom door. I started to lock it and then decided against it. I had to trust someone, I thought. So throwing all caution to the wind, I shed my clothes and hung them on a hook on the door.

The warm water felt great, and so I stood under the shower stream for a while before soaping down. By the end of the shower, I felt refreshed and somewhat renewed. Opening the shower door, I reached out for a thick yellow bath towel. A light tapping at the door got my attention.

"Yes, what is it?" I called apprehensively through the door.

"Catherine, dinner in five. Okay?"

"Fine."

I smiled. He had knocked after all. It was a small but welcome triumph toward the building of trust. I toweled dry.

Somberly I studied myself in the mirror over the lavatory. A pale ghost of myself stared back. The signs of exhaustion and emotional trauma were written all over my face. Taking up the towel again, I fluffed my hair a bit to get it to the damp stage. My hand began to throb again, my nose was sore, and my lip was tender. I looked like a poster girl for the walking wounded. Foraging in a drawer, I found toothpaste and, squeezing some onto my left index finger, I used it as a makeshift toothbrush. I sighed. The best I could say for myself was that I was clean.

I opened the door and, as I passed the kitchen, called out to Luca.

"Can I help with anything?"

"No. Wait for me in the living room."

I chose a chair next to a round corner table and sat down. Luca came out of the kitchen carrying a tray loaded with two plates of food and two glasses of white wine. He brought the tray to the table and then set a plate full of food, a filled wine-glass, some utensils, and a yellow cloth napkin in front of me. Next he set his place and sat down opposite me.

I looked down at the plate. Actually, the meal appeared very appetizing. It was a ham-and-cheese omelette, a small green salad, and rye toast.

"It looks good, Luca."

He seemed pleased. "You look great. The shower did wonders for you."

We chewed in silence for a few minutes. The omelette was quite good, and it needed to be eaten hot.

"It's delicious. Especially the omelette. Where did you learn how to cook one so expertly?"

"Genesis. I used to eat very early in the morning during the week. Nobody else was around, and we'd have coffee together. He was a nice guy and offered to teach me a few things about cooking."

"Yes, he was a good person. Then you were friends with him, too?"

"Well, we didn't have any deep discussions or anything, but I considered him a friend. In his position, he didn't have many social opportunities here on the island, so I think he enjoyed having somebody to shoot the breeze with in the morning. We talked about little things: the weather, food, fishing, his daughter sometimes. He was good company."

"I see. I didn't know that you knew him."

"I feel terrible about his death. He was totally devoted to his daughter, living for the weekends when he could see her."

"Luca, he didn't kill himself. I know he didn't. Genesis was a survivor, not a quitter. He would never have even considered suicide. Besides, he was determined to go see his daughter. He told me that last night. He did not kill himself."

"You're right, Catherine. He didn't."

His quick answer startled me.

"What do you know?"

"I just found out what happened. Milo was bragging about killing Genesis just a few minutes ago. He came back to deliver Carlo's 'persuasive' drugs. He said Carlo ordered him to kill Genesis. Carlo, the murdering son of a bitch!"

"My God! Why did Carlo have Genesis killed?"

"I don't know why. Carlo has his own set of rules and priorities. He's a raging psychopath."

"Did you . . . did you know anything about Carlo's plan to murder Genesis?"

"Good God, no! Believe me, I would have done everything I could to stop him!"

"Luca, why would Carlo want Genesis dead?"

"God only knows what goes on in Carlo's twisted excuse for a mind."

"Can't we go to the police on this?"

He shook his head sadly.

"Not yet. I'm adding this to his endless file of despicable crimes. Genesis didn't hang himself. I have proof. Anybody knowledgeable about hanging knows the difference between a suicide and a murder. You can tell by the way it was rigged. I've got it all on film right here," he said, pulling a tiny Minolta camera out of his pocket.

"I thought you were Carlo's right-hand man. Why wouldn't he include you in this?"

"Milo is Carlo's hatchet man. Carlo is a shrewd SOB who never lets the right hand know what the left hand is doing. That's the way he operates. Carlo has a lot of secrets. He covers his tracks and never lets anyone get too close to him. I've been building a case against him for a long time." His eyes looked hard and cold and frightening. I shuddered.

"You have no idea how many times I've stopped myself from shooting him in cold blood and ending his miserable life forever. God! I've wanted to do it so many times," he said through clenched teeth.

We sat in silence for several minutes.

Luca stared at his empty wineglass. His expression was one of disgust. After a few minutes, he came out of his dreamlike state. He retrieved the wine bottle from the kitchen and poured us each another glass.

"Oh, I shouldn't. It makes me sleepy."

"Sleep is just what you need."

I didn't feel like arguing. Besides, he was right.

"Luca, what about Nikki? I'm so worried about her. Do you know anything about her disappearance?"

He took a sip of his wine. "Yes."

"Well, what? What do you know?"

"I know that you've been calling hospitals all over San Juan trying to track her down. Right?"

"Yes, that's right. Is she still sick?"

"She's being cared for in a private home in San Juan."

My heart beat wildly again. I was afraid to ask the next question. "Is she . . . is she alive?"

"She's supposed to be."

I sat upright. "What does that mean?"

"That was Carlo's plan for her."

"Come on, Luca, tell me what you know."

"As far as I know, Nikki is sedated and being cared for by a private nurse and the lovely Nina, with the shady Dr. Laurenza close by to monitor things."

"Luca, I don't get it. Why don't you explain this so I'll understand?"

He took a big swallow of his wine and nodded.

"Okay, I'll do the best I can. It's pretty complicated, but I'll try to give you the basics. About a year ago, Carlo needed money to build his small luxury hotel here on the island. No legitimate banks would have anything to do with him, so he went back to his roots: the Mafia. Massiliano 'Gentleman Johnny' Mancuso is the head of one of the big crime families that's still very active. Most of what the Mancuso family does is legitimate because Mancuso is a godfather with a conscience, so to speak. Anyway, Mancuso is sixtyish, very successful, and enormously wealthy. He knew Carlo from the days when Carlo's adoptive mafioso father was alive. Mancuso and Carlo's adoptive father were friends.

"Carlo invited Mancuso to come out and visit his glorious pleasure island and discuss the loan. Mancuso came and literally fell in love with your friend Nikki. Not in a romantic way, but a father-daughter type of relationship. The two of them actually hit it off—he's a suave, gentlemanly type—and they became fast friends over the week that he was here. Mancuso, being a shrewd businessman and a devotee of Nikki's, made a deal with Carlo. He would loan Carlo the money he needed with one nonnegotiable stipulation: that Carlo stay married to Nikki, not cheat on her, and treat her well. He made the loan in both Carlo's and Nikki's names."

"Ha! So far he's broken nearly every one of those conditions."

"Yeah, but that's not all. In Carlo's grand scheme to build this magnificent hotel, he underbudgeted. The bottom line is he needs more money to finish it. He's invited Mancuso to return and talk money again. Not only that, but Carlo is in deep shit because some of his other businesses are in trouble, too. The investors for those companies are not exactly the kind of guys you'd invite over to meet your grandmother. He's got some big debts to pay off, and his only hope is Mancuso." He paused.

"But the most important thing of all is the mega drug deal coming up. Carlo needs big bucks to pay for the drugs. Then he plans to turn right around and sell the 'merchandise' for twice the money he paid for it. Unfortunately for Carlo, the FBI will be on hand to arrest him before he gets the chance."

"Sounds like Carlo needs Nikki's help to carry this off."

"Right."

"Then I don't get it. Why would he take her to San Juan and keep her sedated? Why wouldn't he have her here?"

"Two reasons. First, Nikki was becoming more and more suspicious of Carlo's philanderings. Second, her drinking had become such a problem that Carlo couldn't count on her to stay sober enough to convince Mancuso to give Carlo more money."

"The puzzle pieces still don't fit together."

"Things were going from bad to worse, until a short while ago when Nikki received a letter from you with a snapshot of you and your son. Bingo!"

My mind was beginning to put things together, and I was horrified at the final picture.

"Me? But . . ."

"When Carlo discovered that Nikki had a friend who looked like Nikki's identical twin, he began actively promoting your visit. Nikki thought he was just trying to be nice to her by bringing you out here for a reunion of two old college friends."

My mouth fell open, and I could only sit there, frozen, trying to comprehend the whole scenario and how I fit into it.

Minutes passed by, and I was still trying to make sense out of the whole elaborate plot. Oh, yes . . . I could see it all now.

Finally Luca spoke. "Catherine, are you okay?"

His voice brought me back to the present.

"I . . . I guess so . . . No, no, I'm not!" I stood up and walked a few steps away from the table. I ran my fingers through my hair. I wanted to smash something, hit something, run, scream, lie on the floor, and pound my fists. But I didn't, because I was all out of steam. My emotions were spent, and my body was tired and sore and exhausted. For the time being, I had nothing left inside. I felt empty and violated. I stopped walking and sat down on the floor, drew my knees up to my chest, and covered my head with my hands.

Luca came over to me and touched one of my hands.

"Catherine? Catherine?"

I said nothing for a few minutes. I just sat there on the floor, doubled over, not moving. Sensing my need for space, Luca moved away and sat down on the couch.

Everything was quiet again.

My ubiquitous tears had returned. I despised them. Before they had been cleansing. Now they were a sign of weakness and vulnerability.

Minutes passed. Then Luca came back over to me and took my hand in his. "Let me help you, Catherine."

"I don't think anyone can, Luca."

"Yes, I can. I know what to do, and I'll do it. Just trust me, Catherine."

I stood up, his arms opened to me, and we embraced. I looked up into his eyes and saw compassion and tenderness and integrity.

"I want to trust you, Luca. God knows I want to."

CHAPTER 17

Nikki had the nightmare again. She was lost in a deep, dark cavern with hundreds of bats flapping and squeaking around her. Running as fast as she could, she headed toward the illusive sliver of bright light. If there was light, she thought, there must be a way out of the cave. There must be. She ran toward the light as fast as she could, stumbling and falling on the damp, slippery floor but getting up once again. She was totally exhausted, but she knew that she had to keep running or she would surely die. At last she reached the place where the sliver of light was flickering. Her spirits lifted. She was going to get out of this awful place of endless darkness and shadows. She leaned toward the light, and it disappeared. Vanished into nowhere. She collapsed and began to sob. Her hopeless sobs were so intense that they wracked her body.

Nikki woke herself up crying.

When she became aware of her weeping, she stopped and looked around. She remembered where she was, and the weight of her despair felt physically heavy. Her depth of depression deepened with every day that passed.

She was in a small, darkened room in a tiny house in San Juan. The room itself was coldly impersonal in appearance. The floor was laid with green tile, and there were no curtains on the windows, only green miniblinds tightly closed. The walls were the same shade of hospital green. The only furniture in the room consisted of the hospital bed she lay in, a metal chest of drawers, a green metal nightstand with a small lamp, and a folding chair with green vinyl padding.

"Nurse, Nurse!" Nikki called out.

After several minutes, the nurse entered the room. Short and fat, dressed in a dingy, white uniform, she waddled in slowly. She was half Puerto Rican and half Caucasian, about fifty years old, with short, dark hair.

"What do you want?" she asked. "I'm trying to watch my show, so hurry it up, will you?"

"I want to know if you've heard from my husband."

"I told you he called last night to see how you are. That's all. I haven't heard anything since then, and I don't expect to. Now I'm going back to my program."

"Wait, I need to talk to you."

The nurse stopped, sighed impatiently, and folded her heavy arms beneath her large, pendulous breasts.

She frowned. "Make it fast, lady. I ain't got all day."

"I need to use the telephone. Please, I need to call my friend and tell her I'm okay."

The nurse laughed, snorting through her piglike nose. "I follow orders, lady. One of them is no phone calls for you. So don't get no crazy ideas, entiende*?"*

"I'm sure my husband would want me to call my friend. He just forgot to tell you that it would be okay."

"Uh-uh. Mr. Cappelli, he don't forget nothin'. He said no phone calls, so don't be askin' me again. I might decide to give you a big dose of that drug you don't like. You know, the one that gives you nightmares about bugs crawlin' all over your body!"

Nikki shuddered and pulled the covers up under her chin.

"No, no! Don't do that again. Please, don't give me that stuff." Her eyes reflected the fear she felt.

The nurse smiled unpleasantly. She had regained control of her charge. "Don't be bringing up the subject of the phone again, missy. You do, and I'll fix you up good with that mean old shot." She giggled. Then, all at once, her expression and tone became nasty.

"Now shut your face, you spoiled bitch!" She turned to leave.

"Wait . . . please."

"What is it now?" growled the nurse.

"Let me talk to Nina."

The nurse made a face at Nikki and yelled out into the living room. "Nina, Nina! Her royal highness wants to talk to you."

Nina waddled just inside the bedroom door. She was so large that it was difficult to fit through the door. The nurse was fat, but Nina beat her weight by a good hundred pounds. Arrayed in a flowing, full-length, bright red-and-gold muumuu, she resembled a circus tent. In one hand, she held a heaping bowl of popcorn, in the other, a jumbo plastic tumbler filled with red wine.

"Whassup, crybaby?" she asked, leaning up against the door frame for balance. Then she hiccuped. "Sheep wine'll do that to you," she said, slurring her words.

"Nina, please let me call Catherine and tell her I'm okay. Please."

In her drunken stupor, Nina smiled and shook her head from side to side.

"No, no, no, no! Papa said no phone calls. Have to do what Papa says so I get money to buy booze 'n' stuff. Gotta go now, bye-bye. C'mon, Nurse, lessgo watch the tube."

"Wait, Nurse, wait," cried Nikki.

The ponderous Nina stopped and, frowning, looked at Nikki.

"You're driving me crazy with your constant whining and complaining," snapped the nurse. "I can't believe I took this crappy job anyways. Easy, they said. A piece of cake. This job stinks, lady, and so do you! So what the hell's eatin' you now?" yelled the nurse.

"I . . . I need to go to the bathroom."

"Well, ain't that just too friggin' bad. Should have asked

me before. You'll just have to wait, Miss Priss, or should I call you Miss Piss?" Her crude joke sent both Nina and the nurse into loud peals of laughter. "I'm missing my show! You'll just have to wait till I have the time."

Nina hiccuped, giggled, and then staggered out of the room. The nurse paused at the doorway and turned back to face Nikki.

"Don't make no mistakes now, missy, or I'll make you lie in your own filth," the nurse said in an ugly, threatening tone. She left the room, slamming the door behind her.

Tears ran down Nikki's cheeks. This was what she had come to in her life. She was reduced to begging two ignorant, vulgar, lazy women to help her. If the drugs didn't kill her, the humiliation and degradation surely would. She was losing her grip on sanity. That was what Carlo wanted to happen. That was what Nikki feared would happen.

Her bladder felt like it would burst. Something they were giving her made her thirsty all the time. The thirst was unquenchable. It didn't matter how much she drank or what she drank, she was still thirsty. In turn, she needed to urinate frequently, which only served to aggravate the nurse who wanted to be left alone to gorge herself on junk food and watch endless hours of television. It was a vicious cycle, and that's how Nikki spent her days and nights. She wished they would just knock her out so she could sleep all the time. More and more, she wanted to die. Nothing and no one could help her now. She longed for an end to her interminable physical and mental anguish.

The drugs caused her to be so weak and dizzy that it was impossible for her to stand and walk alone. She had tried several times, but she had always fallen. She was terrified that she would fall and break her leg or maybe her neck.

The pressure on her bladder was increasing. She had to try to get up alone. Slowly she sat up and tried to slide out of the bed and onto the floor. The room was spinning around. Block it out, she told herself. Get control of yourself. Her stomach rolled, and she felt as though she might vomit. Nevertheless, she steeled herself and eased out of the bed headfirst and lowered herself to the floor, supporting herself on all fours. Inch by inch, she began to move herself across the room to the bathroom. She was sweating profusely now, but she focused on the bathroom door and kept crawling.

Through the closed door, Nikki could hear the muffled sounds of a television rerun of Green Acres. *Nina and the nurse were laughing hysterically. Occasionally, they punctuated their enjoyment by slapping their pillarlike legs or clapping their pudgy hands together.*

CHAPTER 18

I helped Luca stack the dishes on the tray, and he carried them to the kitchen to put them in the dishwasher. I felt guilty about not helping, but I still couldn't face that kitchen.

I walked over to one of the large front windows and looked out. I hoped that nobody had been spying on us. That would really be dangerous. Luca had assured me that Carlo trusted him implicitly and that he would not waste his time having us watched. Luca also told me that that trust was built on two years of being Carlo's right-hand man. The real proof of this trust was going to be demonstrated in only a few days when the big drug deal took place at Carlo's house. That meeting represented the successful culmination of two long and difficult years for Luca as a special undercover agent of the FBI assigned to Carlo Cappelli.

The palms were gently swaying in the breeze. Such a shame that all of the island's beauty was wasted by a violent, immoral con man.

I continued to gaze wistfully out the window at the sand, the surf, and the deep blue tropical sky. I wished that things were normal. I wished that I really were on vacation and that I could walk barefoot along the ocean's edge with not a worry in the world, feeling the warm sand beneath my feet.

"Catherine?" I turned to see Luca standing behind me. "You were lost in your thoughts."

"I was thinking that I wish all of this cloak-and-dagger stuff was a bad dream. And that this really was a vacation, and we could just enjoy ourselves and this incredible island paradise."

"Ditto."

"Reality stinks."

"Agreed."

"Luca, when do we have to go back to Carlo's house?"

He shrugged. "Sometime tomorrow. It can be afternoon, if you like. Carlo believes that I'm using this time to make sure that you agree to masquerade as Nikki when Mancuso comes. I'm supposed to use drugs, force, intimidation—whatever methods are necessary—to convince you to play along with this very important charade."

"How charming . . . Luca, I wish we never had to go back there again."

"Me, too."

His face clouded over for a few minutes. Suddenly a smile lit up his face, and he took my uninjured hand, the left one, in his.

"Catherine, I know this sounds crazy, but why don't we pretend, just for a few hours, that none of this mess exists. We'll act like we're on vacation. Just for tonight." His eyebrows were raised waiting for my answer.

"I don't know if I can put all of this horrible stuff out of my mind, but I'm willing to try. It's better than rehashing this situation over and over again."

"Good." He seemed genuinely pleased.

I looked at his handsome face smiling at me. A few hours ago, I had hated and feared him. And now I saw him through new eyes. He was ruggedly attractive, virile, well muscled, and deeply tanned. He was what we used to call a "hunk" in college. But more than that, he was a man of integrity and sensitivity. I had had him pegged all wrong.

"Okay, so we've just finished a delicious dinner. Now what?" I asked.

"What would you like to do?"

"I'd like to walk down the beach barefoot and watch the sun setting. Under the circumstances, that's a bad idea."

"You're right. We'll move to Plan B."

"And what would that be?"

"Plan B is to pour a little more wine and play some soft, romantic music."

"All right." My heart began to beat faster. How could it be that in the midst of all this violence and death my hormones were still able to race around madly in my body? I couldn't answer that question, so I decided not to think about it at all and, as my son Mark would say, "Go with the flow."

Luca went to the kitchen and returned with a new bottle of white wine. He opened it and poured the wine into two crystal wineglasses. Handing me mine, he raised his glass for a toast.

"To a beautiful evening. And to a permanent truce and lasting friendship . . . and whatever else might follow."

Our eyes met as we clinked glasses and then sipped the mellow wine.

Next Luca went over to the large entertainment center that occupied one entire wall of the room. It was an elaborate sound system. Being a music lover, Genesis had insisted on the best. Remembering the circumstances of his tragic death threatened to ruin the moment, so I channeled my thoughts to the present. Even so, I fought back stinging tears.

Luca searched through some drawers and looked among a large selection of CDs before settling on one. He placed the compact disc in the disc player and turned it on. Then he took my glass and set it next to his on a nearby coffee table.

The lush, romantic sound of a full orchestra flowed out into the room. It was Johnny Mathis singing "Misty." One of my favorites, and evidently one of Luca's.

"I know you're a great dancer. I watched you the second night you were here," he said.

"Oh, I remember now. It seems like a million years ago."

"It was. But remember, focus on the present. Shall we?" he asked, holding out his arms to dance. There he stood in white

Levi's Dockers slacks, navy blue knit shirt, and sneakers, but he looked just as dashing as he would have had he been wearing a tux.

"I'd love to."

"I promise to be careful of your hand," he said seriously.

"And I will be careful of your nose," I agreed in a solemn tone.

At first, he held me at a respectable distance, as if he were dancing with somebody's great-grandmother. But after we had danced beautifully through "Misty" and then "Chances Are," he pulled me gently but firmly closer to him.

My heart was beating so loud that I could hardly hear the music. I felt like a teenager at my first prom. Every nerve in my body was on fire, and I felt very much alive. When Johnny began singing "Come to Me," Luca stopped dancing, and still holding me very close, looked down at me. His face had taken on a distinctly different aura. I saw warmth, tenderness . . . and desire. Framing my face with his large hands, he kissed me long and hard.

"Are you going to hit me?" he asked in a husky voice.

"Not if you shut up and kiss me again," I whispered.

He did. And then we held each other close for a long time. I was tingling all over. I hadn't felt this way since my husband and I had been together. It was nothing short of wonderful.

CHAPTER 19

"Catherine, I'm reluctant to say good night, but I . . . uh . . . I know that you're exhausted, and tomorrow is going to be tough for both of us." He was stammering and stuttering, something I had not heard him do before.

I sighed.

"You're right. You must be worn out, too. We need some rest so we can cope with tomorrow's problems." The familiar feelings of doom and gloom were returning to roost in my brain. For a short time, I had shoved it all to the back of my mind.

"You take Genesis's bedroom, and I'll sleep out here on the extra-long couch. No problem for me. I'll lock everything up tight first and take a quick shower. Sleep in as late as you want. I'll call Carlo in the morning to let him know we'll be back after lunch. You and I can have a civilized breakfast, and then I'll fill you in on what you need to know."

"Okay," I agreed. "Luca?"

"Yes?"

"I enjoyed our evening together."

"I did, too, Catherine. You're a beautiful lady in every way."

"Good night, then."

"Good night."

He kissed me lightly on the cheek. "Is your hand hurting?"

"It's not bad. How about your nose?"

"I'll survive. Well, good night." He went to the front door to begin the locking-up process.

I made a quick trip to the bathroom and then went to the bedroom. I flicked on the light switch just inside the door, turning on a pretty crystal ceiling fan and light. I left the fan on low to move the air in the room.

Genesis's room was papered in a companion pattern to that of the bath. It had the same jungle motif, but there were animals in this rendition. Brightly colored parrots, lions, tigers, zebras, monkeys, and elephants. The furniture was of high quality, constructed of teakwood. The bed was a beautiful, massive piece of furniture, featuring elaborately carved animal shapes.

I swallowed the lump in my throat. I felt as though I were invading Genesis's private space, even though I knew it was a stupid thought in light of the situation. I stared at the bed. I couldn't sleep there, I just couldn't. Across the room, there was a contemporary, white-leather couch. On closer examination, I realized it was a sleeper sofa. I pulled it open, revealing a full-size bed already made up with fresh navy-blue-and-white checked sheets. With a throw pillow for my head, it would make a comfortable bed.

Next I decided to look for something to wear to bed. After opening a few drawers, I found a pair of handsome red-silk pajamas, king-size, of course. Fortunately, the top was short-sleeved so the mammoth sleeves hit me only at the wrists, and the hem hung down to my knees. It would work, so I undressed and laid my clothes and underwear neatly across a wicker chair. The window was open several inches, giving me an adequate amount of air. Since it was a warm night, I folded down the light blanket on the sofa bed. Turning out the light, I slid between the cool sheets.

The house was still. The only sound I could hear was the muffled sound of the shower running in the bathroom across the hall.

I tried to relax and go to sleep. First, I counted backward

from one hundred. Next, I tried thinking pastoral, peaceful thoughts. All the usual stuff. I tossed, I turned, I kicked the top sheet off. All I could see were the faces of people I cared about: my husband, Mark, Nikki, Genesis . . . Luca. My mind was filled with images. I looked at the bedside clock. It was ten o'clock. I stared at the ceiling. I watched the fan blades turn in a rhythmic fashion. I knew I wasn't going to be able to sleep. And I knew the real reason why.

I heard the shower shut off. A few minutes later, I listened as the bathroom door opened. I got up and opened the bedroom door. The hall light was on. Clad only in white boxer shorts, Luca was already halfway down the short hall toward the living room.

I stood in the dimly lit hallway.

"Luca?" I called softly.

He stopped immediately and turned around.

"What's wrong, Catherine? Is something the matter?"

"Yes," I said.

"What is it?" he asked. Wearing a concerned look, he moved quickly down the hall toward me. He moved me aside protectively and stuck his head in the bedroom.

"What is it? What's wrong?" he asked again.

I stood beside him in the doorway. He had the clean, fresh scent of bath soap. His hair was still damp from the shower, and he was barefoot.

"Did you hear a noise outside?" he asked, leaving the ceiling light off and crossing the softly moonlit room to check the large bedroom window.

"Um, it's nothing like that."

He looked puzzled.

"Then, what's the matter?"

I stepped into the bedroom and went over to where he was standing next to the open window. He looked down at me from his six-foot vantage point. Arms folded, he stood there trying to ascertain the problem. Obviously, I was having trouble communicating.

"I need . . . you," I said softly, reaching up to put my arms around his neck. He responded by kissing me full and hard on the lips. His kiss left me breathless.

Luca was a gentle, warm, and passionate lover. When we made love, all the barriers came down. A kaleidoscope of emotions washed over me. Sensitivity and tenderness intertwined with exhilaration, sensuality, and a depth of caring that ran deep below the surface. Our lovemaking was not merely a physical coupling of two first-time lovers, but a conjoining of souls as well.

Afterward, I felt the warm glow that comes with the culmination of the most intimate expression of love between two people. We lay very still on our sides facing each other. He caressed my cheek lightly.

"Luca, I haven't felt like this in a long, long time."

I could see his face clearly because of the moonlight streaming through the window.

He smiled and gently traced the outline of my lips with his fingers.

"I've never felt this way before, Catherine. Not like this." He paused for several minutes. There was something else he wanted to say.

"I've never married. Brief relationships, yes, but I've never met anyone like you. I've known you for such a short while, and yet, I feel like I've known you for a lifetime."

I reached out and touched his cheek. I felt oddly comfortable in sharing my true feelings with him. "Since my husband's death eleven years ago, I've dated different men, but there was never any romantic relationship, never any deep feelings, never any true connection. I was just going through the motions, because I thought it was the 'right' thing to do. Tonight, you've reawakened feelings in me that I thought had died eleven years ago. I feel alive again, Luca."

"Oh yes, Catherine, you're very much alive." He reached out and drew me even closer so that our faces were only inches apart. "I never knew what a paltry life I was leading, what I was missing, until you came here."

He held me close and whispered, "I care for you a lot, Catherine."

I answered him with a kiss.

We stayed close in an embrace for a long while, enjoying the intimate bond we now shared. Finally Luca spoke. "Can you sleep now?"

"I think so. If you stay, I can." We found a comfortable position lying on our sides, in tandem, fitting together as snugly as spoons. I was worried that I wouldn't be able to sleep, but I felt safe and relaxed in his arms. He fell asleep almost instantly, and soon I drifted to sleep as well.

The next morning I realized that I had slept soundly the rest of the night, because when I looked at the clock, it was eight o'clock. The warm tropical sun was spilling in through the open window. Luca was gone. I sat up and yawned. I felt amazingly rested. I realized that it was the first good night's sleep I had had since I had arrived on the island.

"Good morning, sleepyhead!" Luca appeared at the door with a tray of food. He was dressed in the same clothes he'd worn the day before, but he smelled fresh and clean from a morning shower and shave.

"Are you always this cheerful in the morning?" I asked, stretching and trying to wake myself up.

"Always," he said, smiling.

"I must look awful," I said, imagining the worst.

"Uh, uh. You're cute with your hair all tousled."

I wrinkled my nose. "Really?"

"Well, actually, that's not true."

"Are you retracting your statement about my being cute?" I asked in mock anger.

"Yes. Actually, you're beautiful."

"Even with my swollen lip?"

"Even with your swollen lip. It's very sensual. It makes you look pouty, like the famous models."

"I like your saying that, even if it is a bunch of blarney. Is there a wee bit of the Irish in your background? But you're Italian, so that's not possible, is it?"

He grinned. "Actually, I'm Irish-Italian. My mother is Italian, and my father is Irish."

We laughed together.

"Stay put, and we'll have breakfast," he said, fluffing some pillows behind my back and placing the large wicker tray across my lap. There were two steaming cups of black coffee, two glasses of freshly squeezed orange juice, and a big stack of buttered whole-wheat toast with several choices of jams. I moved over a bit, so he could sit on the edge of the bed and share the tray with me.

As we ate our breakfast, we asked questions about each other's background. He was born and raised in New York City by his Irish cop father and his beautiful Italian mother. They had met at a church social and were immediately smitten with one another. His father was a good, hard-working man who had given thirty years to the force and was happily retired. His parents still lived in New York City. Luca was the youngest, with three older sisters. He had wanted to grow up to be a policeman like his dad. First, though, he had finished four years of college. After a year in the Marines and five years on the force, he became interested in the FBI. He had been with the FBI now for fifteen years. And his real name was Luca Patrick O'Brien, the result of a major compromise between his parents.

Starting on his second piece of toast, Luca asked me to tell him a little about myself as a child. I told him I was born in a small town in southern Kansas. My mother had been a housewife, and my father had been the principal of the only high school in town. I had had one sister who was a year older than I. I didn't remember much about my father, because he and my sister had been killed in a car wreck when I was a child. From then on, it was just me and my mother. She had gone to work cleaning other people's houses and managed to save enough money to send me through college with my working part-time.

We finished our breakfast, and Luca picked up the tray and started off toward the kitchen.

"Thanks, Luca. As soon as I shower and dress, I'll be able to face the difficulties of this day."

He smiled sadly.

"Catherine, being with you is wonderful. I wish we could leave this island and all of the mess with it. But we can't." He hesitated a few minutes and then added, "Go ahead, and get dressed. When you're ready, we can talk about some things you'll need to know."

I got up and quickly showered and dressed, and wished again that I had some makeup with me. It's a theory of mine that a woman has less credibility without her eye makeup—just a dumb, personal hang-up.

I made the bed and folded everything neatly back inside the sofa. I couldn't help thinking ruefully that the only good reason to return to the main house was for a clean change of underwear.

Luca was on the phone in the living room when I entered the room. His back was to me.

"We'll be back right after lunch, Carlo. Everything has gone according to plan here. I think you'll be happy with her attitude. She's ready to do what we want."

He listened to Carlo talk.

"Right. See you later. *Ciao*." He hung up the phone, looking deep in thought. As soon as he saw me, he brightened up. "Do I rate a kiss today?"

"Of course." We kissed, and he held me tight.

"Is everything okay, Luca?"

"Yeah. Come and sit beside me on the couch," he said.

We sat close to each other. He put his arm around me.

"Catherine, we have some important things to talk about."

"Of course. I know we have to face things as they are."

"First, I want to tell you some things that I found out when

Carlo had me check out your background before you even arrived here. Remember, it was Carlo who told me to do the digging. I think it's your right to know what I found out. Obviously, Carlo doesn't know I'm telling you this."

"Found out? What was there to find out that I don't already know about myself?"

"Some rather important details about your life. Just listen, please." He squeezed my hand. My heart began to pound in dreaded anticipation.

"Catherine, your father had an affair with a young math teacher at the high school. When your mother found out, she was devastated. She gave your father an ultimatum: give up the other woman or give up your mother and you and your sister. He refused to make a decision. Your mother threw him out. A few weeks later, without telling your mother, he picked Melissa up after school one day. Evidently, the young female teacher was in the car, too, because the three of them were never seen again."

I swallowed hard. "But my mother told me . . ."

"I know it's hard to accept, Catherine. I did my homework. It's all true."

"But why wouldn't my mother tell me the truth?"

"You were only a child, Catherine. Your mother was devastated. Back then, they didn't put pictures of kidnapped children on milk cartons, you know. Your mother hired a private detective, but there were no leads. Soon her money ran out, and she had to give up the investigation. Your father and the teacher and your sister had managed to disappear without a trace. Your father grew a beard, the teacher bleached her hair, and he got their names changed. They virtually became new people with new identities. Your sister, Melissa, was gone. And your mother had to accept the fact that she might never see Melissa again."

"I don't . . . I just don't know. . . ."

"Remember, Melissa was very young, too. Her father told her that you and your mother had been killed in a fire at home and that everything had been destroyed. She was only five, and she was easily brainwashed. She believed what her father told her."

"I . . . it's so difficult to accept. My sister, Melissa . . . is she . . . is she alive?"

"Yes, I followed up on that. She's happily married and living in Jacksonville, Florida."

I began weeping, and Luca put his arms around me and held me tight.

Finally I stopped crying. He handed me a tissue, and I wiped my eyes and blew my nose.

"Catherine, maybe this wasn't the right time to tell you, but I knew you had to know the truth. I'm sorry you're so hurt."

"My God! Why didn't my mother tell me? I thought we were close. I just wish that she had told me. . . . All those years . . . why?"

"I'm sure she had her reasons for not telling you. She probably thought she was protecting you. And besides, the truth was too painful. She was in denial herself. . . . Suddenly she was on her own, had to find a job, had to support you. The bottom dropped out of her world." He paused a moment. "Catherine, did your mother ever see Nikki?"

"Yes. She did, just once. I brought Nikki home with me for the weekend, soon after we became roommates. Now that I look back on it, I remember Mother's reaction well. When we first walked in together, she burst into tears. She excused herself, said she wasn't feeling well. Said she had a terrible migraine headache. When I took her a supper tray later, she asked me all kinds of questions about Nikki's background. She seemed oddly relieved when she saw a photo of Nikki's parents and learned they were dead. It was eerie really, but I just chalked it up to her bad headache. She was often very emotional when one hit. When Nikki and I left the next day, she hugged Nikki, and there were tears in her eyes. I never brought Nikki home with me again. I just thought our resemblance made Mother uncomfortable. Do you think that . . .

is it possible that Mother thought at first that Nikki was Melissa?"

"It's very possible." Luca watched my face carefully. "It's a big shock, isn't it?"

"Dear God, yes! It's going to take a long time for me to get used to the idea. How could my father do that to all of us? All of these years, I thought he was a good and loving father who was the victim of a tragic accident. Now . . . now, I don't know what to think."

"Your parents are dead, but you do have a sister, Catherine. When this is all over, you can go and see her. But right now, we've got to try and save your best friend, Nikki."

I quickly pulled myself out of the depths of self-pity. I had no time for that now.

"Yes, we've got to save Nikki. But how?"

Luca explained to me that I had to pretend to go along with Carlo's plan. When Mancuso came, I was to be Nikki. Mancuso was bringing millions of dollars in cash to the island. I was to act like a happy and loving wife, and Mancuso, believing that all was well with the marriage, would lend Carlo the money. Mancuso would then leave, thinking the money was for the building of the hotel. Instead, Carlo was going to use the money to pay for the drug deal he was planning to consummate on the island. The FBI would arrive in force by boat in time to arrest Carlo and the drug dealers. Then Carlo would be put away for good.

"Luca, what is Carlo's plan for Nikki and me?"

His face was grim. "His plan is to kill you both as soon as the drug deal is completed."

My face went white.

"That won't happen, Catherine. I promise. But we've got to play along with Carlo and make him think that you'll cooperate fully in order to save your own life and Nikki's, too. I'll tell you exactly what to do. We'll get through it."

CHAPTER 20

Luca spent the next three hours preparing me for the return to the main house. I found him to be extremely thorough and well organized. He explained in detail how I should act and what I should say when I was with Mancuso. We talked about knowledge that Mancuso and Nikki would have in common. He told me about their relationship, and the personality attributes that Mancuso seemed to admire about Nikki. Then we did some role-playing in which he played the part of Mancuso, and I played the part of Nikki. We rehearsed a variety of possible dialogues, and how I could hedge successfully without arousing Mancuso's suspicions. We talked about mannerisms that Nikki had and specific likes and dislikes that were distinctly hers. Most of them I knew about. By the end of the three hours, I felt as though I had been cramming for final exams. It was exhausting work.

Luca was relentless in his efforts to teach me. At last, he declared me ready to impersonate Nikki very effectively. He suggested we eat a quick lunch before we returned to Carlo's. It was a welcome suggestion. Together we created a delicious salad. As we worked, we laughed and talked about a variety of things from favorite flavors of ice cream to a love of classic movies. He was fun to be with and easy to talk to. We enjoyed eating the salad and sharing bits and pieces of our lives. Being with him seemed natural and effortless and . . . wonderful.

As we cleaned up the kitchen, reality began to settle heavily upon me. I wanted to take his hand, escape from the island,

and never look back. I knew I couldn't do that. Nikki's life was hanging in the balance. And for that matter, so were Luca's and mine.

When we had put the last dish away, Luca drew me close to him. "Catherine, I'm sorry you're involved in this god-awful mess. But you are, and Nikki's life is depending on us and what we do. It's going to be difficult, but if you follow my instructions, we can get out of this thing alive and manage to put Carlo away for the rest of his miserable life."

"I'm really scared, Luca. I'm not a professional at this like you are."

"I know you're scared, and I understand. Believe me, fear is as much a part of my life as breathing. The most difficult thing for both of us is to behave as though there is nothing between you and me. Whatever you do, don't let anyone see even a glimmer of affection between us. It's a tough thing to do, but our lives depend on it."

"I won't do anything to put you in danger, Luca. I promise."

"Don't worry about me, Catherine. It's you I'm concerned about. Concentrate on your goal: to get out of this thing alive. Keep your emotions hidden deep inside. It's a necessity that you function not on an emotional level but on a goal-oriented one. I've been living that kind of life for fifteen years now. It's been a daily requirement of my profession. This is my last assignment with the bureau, and one thing I won't miss is disguising my true feelings on a regular basis."

"You're retiring after this is over?"

"Damn right. I've been living a double life for most of the fifteen years that I've been with the bureau. I'm not saying that I haven't had some good years, because I have. Now it's time for me to stop being somebody else and start being myself. I've been compensated well financially and professionally, but I've had my fill of role-playing. I want to be Luca O'Brien all of the time, not just inside my own head."

"Sounds like you've made up your mind for good."

"I have. I told them two years ago that this was my last

hurrah, so there are no surprises there. I want to go out with pride, knowing that I gave my all to this project just as I've done with all the others. This is the most involved and the longest undercover I've ever done. And this time, there's also more at stake from a personal standpoint: your life and Nikki's, too."

"I understand, Luca. Just promise me that you'll be careful yourself. I want you to come out of this thing in one piece."

"I'll be careful. A lot of people are counting on me. Remember this above everything, Catherine: Don't provoke Carlo. We already know the violence and cruelty that he's capable of. He's like a hand grenade with the pin already pulled. Ready to detonate at any time in all directions. Please don't push his buttons. He's a dangerous, explosive man. Once we walk out this door, I can't do much to outwardly defend or protect you. I become his soldier again, so you've got to be smart and control your tongue and your temper. I care for you deeply. Please be careful and don't set him off. It won't be long before this is all over. Keep your emotions under control, and you'll stay out of trouble."

"Okay, I'll do my best to pull this off."

"I know you can do it."

I felt like a lamb going to the slaughter. My fate was in the hands of a vile, money-hungry maniac, Carlo. My heart was filled with loathing for him as I thought of Nikki, Genesis, Genesis's daughter, Luca, myself, and countless other people who had been hurt by Carlo Cappelli. I was a novice in this business of masquerade with the stakes so high that I dared not make even the smallest mistake—it might prove to be fatal.

All of a sudden, Luca smiled at me. Then he pulled me close to him, embraced me, and kissed me. He was a great kisser.

"Okay, slugger, are you ready?" he asked.

"Yes, I'm ready."

As we left the house, closing the door behind us, my heart sank. I had lied. I was not ready for this. Nothing I had ever lived through or read about or experienced had prepared me for this. I was scared to the core. I felt like a prisoner being marched to the electric chair.

We had walked in silence for several minutes because it was dangerous to talk. Someone might be listening. Besides, we were both trying to prepare ourselves mentally and get into character. I was startled when Luca broke the silence and said, as though he could read my mind, "It's natural to be afraid, Catherine. Use your fear as a tool, not as a stumbling block."

I nodded and straightened my back. We walked on toward the main house. The lamb to the slaughter.

CHAPTER 21

We arrived back at the main house without incident. As usual, it was another beautiful day in paradise—or purgatory, depending on one's point of view. The sun shone brilliantly in the bright blue, cloudless sky, scattering its splendid rays like dazzling diamonds across the surface of the Caribbean. The weather was in direct contradiction to the dark drama that would soon unfold inside the huge mansion.

As we walked up the back terrace steps toward the house, I reminded myself that I had to keep my emotions in check. I had too much at stake to lose control of my temper. No one was sitting on the terrace, and no one was in the dining room. Inez and several young Puerto Rican women, including her daughter, Elisa, were busy polishing and dusting in the living room. Inez stopped her work and quickly bustled over to speak to us.

"Luca, Mr. Cappelli wants to see you in his office immediately." Turning to me, she flashed a supercilious smile and said, "Mrs. Hanson, your room is ready. The one you've been staying in since your arrival."

I nodded with a deadpan expression.

Luca turned to me. "Go ahead to your room and freshen up. I'm sure Carlo will want to see you shortly."

He left, and so did I.

My room was clean and shining as usual. I felt like it had been months instead of just one night since I had been there. I looked around the room dispassionately. Opening a few drawers, I determined that everything looked undisturbed. The dirty-laundry bag in the closet was empty. I assumed that Inez had taken care of that for me. I looked through the hanging clothes to find something suitable for my discussion with Carlo. I decided on a white cotton sundress. It wasn't low cut, and it wasn't anything spectacular. Rather plain. Totally neutral.

The idea of clean underwear and access to makeup brought a brief smile to my lips. Naturally I changed my underwear, and then I used deodorant and a little dusting powder. I decided against perfume. The last thing I wanted to do was turn Carlo on. I brushed my teeth and spent time carefully applying my makeup. Fine, I was ready. Luca knew what he was doing, and I was going to do my best to help him. Focus on the goal!

Having nothing to do but stew, I reluctantly sat down in a comfortable wing chair next to the open French doors. A warm breeze was gently blowing, and the heavy scent of tropical flowers from the garden below wafted into my room. I picked up the Lawrence Sanders novel that lay on a small table next to the chair and opened it to the place I had marked the last time I had tried to read. Only a few minutes passed before I heard a sharp tapping at my door. I opened it. It was Inez.

"Mr. Cappelli wants you to go to his office now. You know where that is, don't you, Mrs. Hanson?"

I nodded expressionlessly. I refused to give her the satisfaction of observing any kind of emotion on my face. She glided off down the hall, and I followed at a slow pace.

I walked to the adjacent building. The door to Carlo's office was open, and I could hear him talking.

"Soon, very soon we'll have time to celebrate again, my friend. All of our hard work will be rewarded. It's been too boring around here lately, Luca. As you know, I'm a man who demands excitement in his life. We need to get back to Miami. This island is like a damned nursing home! Peace and quiet and sun and no nightlife. Shit! I'm growing old and senile just thinking about it. What we need are gorgeous, sexy women. Lots of them. All strutting around in string bikinis. And booze and cards and hot music. Hell, I'm getting a hard-on just thinking about it." Carlo laughed aloud, and Luca did, too.

I had reached the door, and I took a deep breath as I stood in the doorway.

Carlo was dressed in tennis whites, seated in a large leather chair behind his massive, mahogany desk. His feet were propped up on the desk, and he was puffing like a smokestack on a big Cuban cigar. Luca sat in a black-leather armchair facing Carlo. Evidently, they had not heard me come to the door.

Carlo was busy studying brochures of some kind and was showing Luca a picture of something.

"Damn, I'd like to have a piece of that!" He laughed again.

"Carlo, you wanted to see me," I said in an even voice.

Carlo looked up, surprised. He was thrown off guard temporarily. One of his customary wanton grins lit up his face.

"Catherine. Good! Now we can begin. Come in, come in and sit down." He stood and gestured to a chair. My eyes made quick contact with Luca. No emotion registered on Luca's face. He was a cool professional in complete control of himself.

I sat down in the chair.

Carlo seemed to wear the same consistently cocky look on his face I had seen before. It appeared to be his favorite facial expression. I found it annoying, but I couldn't afford to let it get to me.

"So, Catherine, I trust that Luca *convinced* you to take part in our little plan." His emphasis on the word "convinced" made it sound lewd and lascivious. He watched my face carefully.

"Yes, I understand that I'm supposed to pretend to be Nikki so that Mancuso gives you the money you need."

"That's right. And you understand the consequences of failing to comply with my demands?"

"I think so. But why don't you tell me yourself, Carlo."

"Of course, Catherine." He got up from his chair and walked around the desk so that he was looking down at me.

"Really it's very simple. You act like my dear and loving wife, Nikki. You persuade Mancuso that our marriage is very much intact and that I have been treating you like a queen. He gives me the money and is on his way. You and Nikki get to L-I-V-E! Basic. Simple. Uncomplicated."

He took a big puff on his cigar and turned his head to blow the smoke away from my face.

"How can I be sure that you'll live up to your side of the bargain, Carlo?" Oh, God, why had I said that?

He laughed softly.

"You're a smart lady, Catherine. I like that in a woman. Up to a point, that is. Don't be a smart ass, honey. The answer to your question is 'You can't be sure.' But I'm holding all the cards, darlin', so don't cross me. I can take you out at any time. Hell, I could do it now."

Casually, he reached across the desk to a leather box, opened it, and pulled out a handgun. Standing in front of me, he leaned down close and pointed the gun to my forehead. Adrenaline began pumping wildly through my veins, and I broke into a sweat. The gun made a clicking sound. There was no bullet.

I licked my lips and swallowed hard. I could hardly breathe.

Carlo took the gun away from my head and tossed it on the desk.

"Gotcha!" he said, and laughed maniacally.

I felt totally numb, as abject fear held me in its viselike grip. He was pleased with his little joke. Big man. He had a gun, and I didn't.

"Okay, Catherine. You get the idea. Don't cross me, don't even think about it. One phone call and Nikki is dead, just like that. Plus, you're dead, too. Easy as one, two, three. I say the word, and you're history. Luca, my right-hand man, is packing a piece, too, not to mention Alberto, etcetera , etcetera.

There's no escape, no one to tell, no place to run, no place to hide. Do we understand each other?"

"Yes, but . . ."

"Yes, but *what*, Catherine?" Carlo was beginning to look irritated.

"How can I be sure that Nikki is still alive?" I regretted having said it the moment the words slipped out of my mouth.

"I thought you said her attitude was right," he said to Luca in a very nasty, flat tone. "I don't like being questioned, Luca. I don't like it, and I won't tolerate it. Especially from a broad." He was standing in front of me but still looking at Luca. It all happened so fast that I didn't know exactly what had occurred. Like a flash of lightning, Carlo leaned down and slapped me so hard across the side of the face that I almost fell out of the chair. Tears were streaming down my face as I tried to recover from the blow. It hurt terribly, and the shock of being hit magnified my trauma. My face was throbbing, and I was struggling to stop my tears. *For heaven's sake, Catherine, stop sniffling!*

Calmly Carlo went around the desk and sat down again. He scooted a box of tissues across the desk at me.

"Okay, honey, now shut off the tears. God! You bitches turn on the waterfall at the least provocation. Do you understand now how very serious I am?" Agitated, he snubbed out his cigar in a big brass ashtray.

"Yes."

"Okay, then. Listen up. We don't have a lot of time, doll. In fact, we're down to the wire. Mancuso is arriving here in the morning, according to the plan. Right, Luca?"

I couldn't look at Luca. I stared at Carlo, while I fought hard to hold back the tears. My cheek was stinging.

"Right, Boss. Tomorrow. On schedule."

"Sweetie, I want you to get a good night's sleep and look absolutely gorgeous tomorrow. Nikki was gorgeous the last time Mancuso was here. I had such high hopes for her. Too bad the booze got to her brain and chewed it up. Well, the important thing is that you've got to look perfect, act perfect, and be perfect. I'm counting on you, doll. Don't let me down. You've had your last warning."

"I . . . I understand, Carlo."

"Good! 'Cause I don't want to take you out, sweetie. You're too good lookin' to die young."

"Carlo, I'll rehearse Catherine one more time tonight to make sure she's got all the details straight," said Luca.

"Right. She's a smart bitch. Just let her know who's in control. Know what I mean, Luca?"

"You bet, Boss. I'm surprised she mouthed off at you like that. I used some of our less-than-pleasant methods to convince her last night, and she was totally submissive. She's still emotional over the cook's death, I think. Women are like that."

"You've got that right, my friend. Women! They've got all of this magnificent equipment—big tits, great asses—then they go and pull all this emotional crap on you. Go figure! Just make sure she remembers without a doubt who the boss is, Luca!"

"Right," responded Luca.

Carlo turned his attention back to me. "Sweetie, I've got all kinds of fun, slow, painful ways of executing people. That's what I do in my spare time: dream up excruciating methods for murder. It's kind of like my hobby, and I'm just aching to get another chance to be creative. Especially with Nikki. The bitch! Just look at all the trouble she's caused me."

He was a madman. Suddenly he clapped his hands together. "Okay, now be a good girl, Catherine, and come through for me. Enough of this torture talk. I'd rather talk about love any day. I'm a lover. Did you know that, darlin'?"

I felt sick all over. I looked down at my hands lying uselessly in my lap. They were trembling, so I clasped them together tightly.

"Well, sugar, I am a lover to the nth degree. Sometimes I'm like a stud dog after a bitch in heat. Yessir, I'd love to show you how that works, honey, but maybe later. After our big deal is completed. Okay, you go on back to your room now like a good girl and get yourself all rested up for the biggest performance of your life tomorrow!"

I assumed that was my cue to leave, so I stood up. I was somewhat shaky and unsteady so I held onto the chair. Luca came over and took my arm. My face was still stinging.

"I'd better help her out, Boss. We don't want her to fall. If she has any scars or bruises on her, Mancuso might get suspicious. Hopefully, her swollen lip will be totally back to normal by tomorrow. That happened when Inez and Milo put her in the closet."

"Goddamn it! You're right, Luca. I shouldn't have hit her on the face. Probably should have broken a finger. That we could explain. Shit! The face is the first thing he'll see. Why didn't I think of that before? I just got carried away. You're right as always, my man. Help her out. Hell, stay with her tonight and watch her to make sure that she doesn't pull any more dumb stunts."

Luca helped me, and we were halfway out the door when Carlo spoke again.

He had lit another cigar. "Oh, doll, by the way, Mark is doing fine in Sicily."

Something snapped in my brain. What? What did he know about my son, Mark?

"What?"

"I talked with him by phone today, darlin'. He's okay . . . for the time being, I should say."

Luca squeezed my arm. Careful.

"You talked to my son, Mark?" My voice was cracking.

"Yeah. He's in Sicily right now. Just as a little added insurance that you would mind your manners with Mancuso, I'm having Mark detained. I decided to sweeten the pot a little, raise the stakes, up the ante. Well, anyway, tonight good old Mark is spending the night in a Sicilian jail, compliments of my longtime poker buddy, the police chief there, Salvatori

Campisi. He'll be holding your boy in a cell checking into some drug-possession allegations. Hell of a poker player, that Salvatori! Anyway, I imagine Mark will be fine as long as his mama doesn't screw up tomorrow." He smiled malevolently.

He paused to blow large, perfectly shaped smoke rings. Totally enthralled with his finely honed skill, he watched them form and then dissipate into the air.

"If all goes perfectly here, Mark will be out of jail soon, looking for new skirts to conquer. On the other hand, doll face, if you mess up, then Markie boy is in deep shit. He may be looking at life imprisonment in a filthy, rat-infested, disease-ridden prison, full of nasty murderers and drug addicts. But most likely he'll be facing a firing squad. Drugs are not taken to kindly in Sicily. 'Bye now, love!" He waved his cigar-holding hand at me.

Luca guided me out of the office and toward the outer door of the building. Just as Luca turned the knob, Carlo's voice called out again from where he now stood in his office doorway.

"Hey, sweetie!"

I turned my head to look at him.

"Don't forget, doll. I'm expecting an Academy Award–winning performance out of you tomorrow. Sleep well, darlin'!"

Luca nodded to Carlo, and we left.

CHAPTER 22

Luca and I walked back to the main house together in complete silence. We spoke not one word as we passed some gardeners mowing and trimming. Once inside the house, Inez and her crew, minus Elisa, were busy gathering silver pieces to polish.

Luca escorted me straight to my room and sat me gently down on the edge of the bed. He quickly shut the door and locked it.

"We have to keep our voices low," he cautioned. "Do you want some brandy?" he asked.

"No." Still standing, he gently tilted my chin up so that I was looking at him instead of straight ahead like a zombie.

"Catherine, I wouldn't blame you if you never spoke to me again."

I was still in a daze. "What do you mean?"

"I knew the bastard didn't have any bullets in his gun. He never loads it. He never has. But you didn't know that I knew that. Didn't you wonder why I didn't do something to stop him?"

"Not really. I wasn't thinking anything except what it would feel like to die."

"To hell with this damned assignment!" he whispered. "I wouldn't just stand by and let him kill you, Catherine. I would have taken the bullet myself. You have to know that above all else." His face reflected the depth of his anguish.

"I know that, Luca. I never questioned it."

He sighed deeply and sitting down next to me, put his arm around me. He studied my face and the cheek that Carlo had slapped. His eyes were sad and filled with pain.

"Why don't you lie down for a while? I'll go get some ice for your face."

I sat numbly on the side of the bed. I felt paralyzed. All I could do was think about Mark and what he was going through right now. My vivid imagination wasn't doing me any good. The physical pain of Carlo's slap was nothing compared to the mental anguish I was experiencing over Mark's present situation. Carlo had dealt me the ultimate blow. My heart ached for my son. The shock of being wrongfully arrested. The terrible fear of being imprisoned in a strange country. Drug offenses in foreign countries were extremely serious. Of course, this was a bogus arrest, so there was not even the hope of being able to prove his innocence. What had Carlo said to him on the phone, if in fact, he had spoken directly to Mark? What had Carlo told him about me? Good God! What were we going to do? We were helpless, cornered, trapped like . . . like innocent lambs headed to the slaughter.

My tortured mind was churning with trepidation. My thoughts were racing madly down dark corridors studded with an endless multitude of dire possibilities. *Stop it! Pull yourself together!* I had to get a grip on myself, or I would be utterly useless to anyone. I took some deep breaths and exhaled slowly.

Luca returned, bringing the promised ice pack. He closed the door behind him and locked it. Then he sat down next to me and carefully held the ice pack to my face.

"Catherine, are you okay?"

"No, I'm not. I'm mad as hell and . . ."

He interrupted my flow of speech by holding his index finger to my lips. He got up and spent five minutes giving the room a thorough going-over to check for bugging devices. Satisfied at last that there were none present, he went to a corner shelf and picked up a portable cassette-tape player.

Bringing it over to the bedside table, he pressed the "Play" button, turned the volume up, and soon the sounds of Frank Sinatra singing "My Way" filled the room.

He came back and sat next to me on the bed. He looked tired.

Holding the ice pack against my tender cheek, I whispered into his ear, "Why don't you just go ahead and say it?"

"Say what?"

"Say, 'I told you so.' He wouldn't have slapped me if I hadn't questioned him."

"In the mood he's in, I don't think it would have taken much of anything to set him off. I've never seen him this volatile. He's in an extreme state of anxiety over this drug deal. If I didn't know how much he despises taking drugs himself, I would have thought he was on something."

"I'm sorry, Luca. You warned me. I should have answered his questions and never challenged him. It was my tone. I ticked him off, and you know it. Dear God! I hate the bastard and what he's doing to all of us, his victims!"

Luca looked grim. I could see him fight to control the anger that was smoldering beneath the surface. "My God, Catherine! He was acting totally nuts. I've seen him mean and obnoxious, but he's hit a new low. All I wanted to do was shoot the fucking bastard's head off! Instead, I had to sit there and watch while he scared the hell out of both of us and hurt you. Damn him! Nothing is going to make me happier than to nail his sorry butt to a prison cell for the rest of his miserable, shitty life!"

His depth of caring touched my poor, aching heart. I rested my head on his shoulder, and he put his arm around me. Frank Sinatra was singing "Strangers in the Night" as our eyes met in mutual frustration and misery. We stayed that way for several minutes. Then Luca whispered in my ear, "Catherine, I'm going to go back and talk to Carlo. I'll see what I can find out about Mark."

I frowned. "No. Won't it just make things worse?"

"I don't think so. I'll reassure Carlo that you're going to do a great job tomorrow. I can smooth things over. I know how."

"Be careful."

"Always. Try to rest. I won't be gone long. And lock the door when I leave."

He squeezed my hand and left.

I got up, locked the door, and returned to the bed. I lay down and put the ice pack back on my cheek. I had only lain there for a few minutes when there was a slight knock at the door. I wasn't sure that I'd heard anything at first, because Frank Sinatra was still crooning his heart out in a duet with his daughter. I got up and went over to the door. Someone knocked again.

I was immediately suspicious.

"Who is it?" I finally asked through the door.

"It's Elisa," the soft voice answered.

"Just a minute." I shut off the tape. Elisa? What did she want?

I unlocked the door and opened it.

Elisa gave me a nervous smile.

"Can I come in, please?"

"Sure. Come in."

Puzzled, I opened the door wider, and she came in closing the door quietly behind her. She looked very nervous and embarrassed.

"You're probably wondering why I came."

I nodded.

"I, um, I was cleaning in one of the other offices when you came to see Carlo. And, I, well, I know I shouldn't have come, but I think you're a nice lady, and I was worried about you."

"Oh, well, I'm okay, Elisa. Really."

"I waited until Luca left before I came. I didn't want anyone to see me come here."

"I understand." I really didn't, but maybe she was going to tell me why she had come if I made it easy for her.

"Do you want to sit down, Elisa?"

"Oh, no, *gracias*. I have to be going. I just wanted to bring you something." She was wearing a pale pink uniform that consisted of a blouse with a type of pinafore over it. The pinafore had two deep pockets. She pulled a small, black object out of one of them and handed it to me.

"What's this?" I asked, accepting a small black doll.

"This is what my people call a *resguardo*. It is a protector. It keeps bad people away. Maybe it will help you so that nothing else bad happens to you."

"Thank you, Elisa."

She smiled shyly. She looked as though she wanted to say something else but was afraid to.

"Is there something else you want to tell me?"

"Um, yes. I . . . uh . . . Carlo, he has hit me, too. I am sorry for your pain . . . he . . . he has a terrible temper. I think that is all I should say now. Please tell no one I was here. Take care of yourself, señora."

"Thank you, Elisa. Good-bye."

She left. How very odd, I thought.

CHAPTER 23

True to his word, Luca returned in less than an hour. I was still lying on the bed when he came, still holding the ice pack to my face in the hopes that there would be no bruising. Makeup could only camouflage so much.

He knocked, and I unlocked the door and let him in. He was carrying a large tray.

"How're you feeling?" he asked, setting the tray on a corner table.

"Considering that my life and the lives of those I hold dear are hanging by a fine microscopic thread, okay, I suppose. I'm sick with worry, I'm emotionally and physically exhausted, and I can't for the life of me figure out why I'm still sane. Oh, yes, and now I have a skull-crushing headache."

"Have you taken anything for it yet?"

"I didn't have the energy to get up. I'll take something now." I went into the bathroom and rummaged around in my bag of medical supplies and located some Tylenol.

When I returned to the room, he was arranging the plates of food on the table.

"Luca, I'm not hungry. I don't think I can eat anything. No appetite under the circumstances."

"I know you don't feel like eating, but you need to try. It'll make you feel better. Besides, you need to get something in your stomach if you're going to take that Tylenol."

"I guess you're right. I'll attempt a few bites."

"I don't feel like eating either, but let's try. Want to turn on

'Old Blue Eyes' again? We need a little background music for conversation."

"Sure."

I turned on the cassette player again. This time Frank was singing "New York, New York." Frankly, "Old Blue Eyes" was beginning to get on my nerves.

"What's this?" he asked, holding up the little black doll that Elisa had brought me.

I told him about her visit, what she had said about Carlo, and what the significance of the doll was.

He said nothing but "Hmmm," and left it at that.

I looked at the plate in front of me. It consisted of a T-bone steak, a baked potato, a mixed green salad, and a big doughy-looking roll.

"Who is the chef now?" I asked, trying a bite of baked potato.

"Now that's an interesting topic. Carlo hasn't hired anyone permanent yet. Right now, one of the men who had assisted Genesis is filling in. As you can tell, he's not in Genesis's league. Strictly plain fare, meat-and-potatoes stuff. Poor guy. Carlo's already laid him out a couple of times."

"It's not bad, but it's certainly not gourmet."

I picked at the food, somehow managing to eat small portions of the steak and baked potato. Then I took the Tylenol. Luca's appetite wasn't much better than mine. We stacked the dishes, and Luca loaded them onto the tray and set it outside the door. Relocking the door, he beckoned for me to come over to the bed. He stretched out on the side of the bed closest to the door and fluffed up a pillow for me to lie on next to him.

"Close your eyes, and let the Tylenol take hold."

"Luca, I'll close my eyes, but we need to talk. What did you find out from Carlo?"

"He said that he's really worried about this drug deal and that he wants to make sure that you'll give one hundred percent to your impersonation of Nikki tomorrow with Mancuso."

"Did he actually talk to Mark?"

"Yeah. He said Mark handled himself well over the phone even though he had to be scared to death. He said Mark seemed to be more concerned about you than himself."

A sob escaped from my lips, and soon warm tears were running down my cheeks.

Luca pulled me close to him and held me tight as I continued to cry.

"Hang on, my love. We'll beat Carlo at his own game. From what you've told me about Mark, he's a fighter like his mother. He'll make it, and we'll get him out of there. Trust me. Soon this will all be over." He kissed my forehead and then my cheeks, and then ever so tenderly my lips.

Suddenly a strange calm came over me. It was something I had never experienced before. I knew what I had to do. I felt like a robot with a mission. Emotionless but well equipped to do the job that had been programmed into me. I needed sleep now to regenerate mind and body and prepare me for the following day.

Hurriedly I brushed my teeth and put on my nightgown. Luca pulled back the covers for me, and I climbed into bed. He turned off the bedside lamp. He lay on top of the bedspread beside me, on his side and facing the door. Fully dressed and poised for action if necessary. At least for tonight, he stood between me and whatever dangers lay outside the bedroom door.

CHAPTER 24

The day of reckoning had arrived. I awoke early, at six A.M., on my own. According to my calculations, I had slept a full eight hours. Strangely enough, I felt totally rested and unbelievably calm. I knew the butterflies were bound to return, but for the time being they were AWOL. Luca had already shaved, showered, and dressed and was watching me from across the room when I awoke. He came over to the bed and leaned down to kiss me. As usual, his kiss left me breathless.

"I hope you don't mind, but you're definitely habit forming," he said, smiling.

I smiled back. "How long have you been watching me sleep?"

"Oh, ten or fifteen minutes. You appear to be very angelic in your sleep, which just goes to prove that looks can be deceiving." I tossed a pillow at his head, which he expertly dodged.

"Well, *you* sleep like a bear!" I laughed.

"Meaning?"

"Meaning you pawed me all night!"

"Sorry, my love. It's virtually impossible to sleep next to you without touching you. I think I deserve a medal for being the gentleman that I was."

"Very true. Now forget all that gentleman stuff, and give me one more of those passionate kisses you should have a patent for."

He did.

We looked straight into each other's eyes. Neither one of us said a word, but a great deal passed between us in that look.

"Let's get on with this charade and get it over with. I'm ready to do what I have to do, Luca."

He nodded in agreement.

With that said, I quickly showered, dressed, and put on my makeup. My cheek was tender, and my hand still hurt, too. I took extra time in camouflaging my cheek. I was still one of the walking wounded. Together we went to the kitchen and breakfasted on coffee cake, juice, and coffee. The kitchen was already crowded with staff preparing for the all-important dinner at which Mancuso would be present. The new chef was there giving orders and checking a stack of lists. He tried to appear unharried and in control, but at seven A.M., he was already sweating profusely. He was definitely in over his head.

After breakfast, it was time to go to Nikki's room. I needed to select something appropriate to wear to greet Mancuso. He was due for cocktails around six that evening. On the way to Nikki's room, we passed by Inez and her crew working diligently to make everything look perfect for Mancuso's arrival. As we walked through the dining room, we saw five male servants washing windows. From experience, I knew that the early morning was usually quiet. But today the drones were working against their four P.M. deadline. There were no smiles or courteous nods this morning. Their faces looked grim, determined, and afraid. The air was thick with tension. Apparently the lord of the manor had issued threatening ultimatums to everyone. Obviously, they had all been frequent witnesses or recipients of his unfounded cruelty. They were not anxious to be on the receiving end of his tyrannical disapproval. I was certain that each one had his or her own personal tale of Carlo's brutal behavior. My heart went out to each one of them. As his victims, we all shared a common bond.

Once inside Nikki's room, I shivered. Luca noticed. "Catherine, are you cold?"

"No, just a fleeting moment of déjà vu. I'm all right now."

"Okay, then, let's take a look in her closet."

Nikki's closet was huge and well organized. In spite of the situation, I laughed.

"What's funny?" Luca asked, looking puzzled.

"This closet. It's so neat and organized. Obviously the work of Inez. In college, Nikki could have won a prize for untidiness. We used to kid her all the time about it. The funny thing was she knew where everything was amid the clutter. She could find whatever she needed almost instantly. Once, in a matter of minutes, she retrieved a delicate gold bracelet from underneath a pile of dirty laundry several feet deep. Talk about the proverbial needle in a haystack! She had a real talent for finding things that were lost or misplaced. She even helped other girls find lost things. Nikki had a tenacious quality that never allowed her to give up. I hope to God she still has it now." I sighed.

I looked through the evening clothes that were hanging neatly together in a special section all their own.

"What do you think, Catherine?"

"How did Nikki dress around Mancuso? Girl next door, genteel, sexy, sophisticated?"

Luca closed his eyes and thought for a moment. I knew he had an excellent eye for detail because of all the minutiae he had had to commit to memory about Nikki in preparation for this magnificent deception.

"Sophisticated elegance. Feminine and alluring, but not provocatively sexy."

"Good, because sexy is not something I particularly care to express in front of Carlo. Okay, let me look a minute."

With Luca's approval, I selected a gorgeous, white silk cocktail dress. It was sleeveless with a straight skirt, not tight but fitted, and a respectable, square-cut neckline. All in all, it made a statement of refinement, gentility, and classic beauty. We agreed it was perfect. Her jewelry box sat atop the dressing table I had invaded recently looking for clues about Nikki's disappearance. We opened it and found lovely pearl-drop earrings with necklace and bracelet to match. Her feet were a size larger than mine. Fortunately, I had some pretty high-heeled crystalline sandals that would be stunning with the rest of the outfit. That task was completed. Pity the rest of the day could not be as easy.

"I need to go check in with Carlo and try to keep him in as mellow a mood as possible."

An awful thought popped into my head. "Luca, Nikki's room adjoins Carlo's, doesn't it?"

"Yes, but he's not there now. He spent the night with Laura."

"What a loving gesture on the part of the new father-to-be. He is the father of Laura's child, isn't he?"

"Yes."

"Luca, you know he's been having an affair with Elisa, don't you?"

"Yeah," he said in a flat tone. "And there's a lot more that you don't know, Catherine."

"What do you mean?" He seemed reluctant to answer.

He shook his head. His voice sounded strained and distant when he spoke. "I might as well tell you. Carlo has sunk as low as a man can in this world. He raped Genesis's daughter."

"What?" I gasped. I was so repulsed and stunned that I couldn't speak for a few minutes. "What . . . what happened?"

"Last week before you arrived, Carlo, Milo, and I went to San Juan. On trips to San Juan, I always told Carlo I was out on the town with one woman or another, so I never stayed with Carlo at his posh house there. I was really making contact with another FBI agent, a woman, in fact. Strictly business. Setting up this drug bust has taken a lot of advance planning, and that was our last chance to finalize all the details.

"As usual, Milo stayed at Carlo's, since he's Carlo's real bodyguard, and he does all of Carlo's dirty work. Milo's a bona fide henchman. Very deadly.

"We did all return by plane together. Unfortunately, Carlo had a few drinks and told me what he'd done to Sally. It was all I could do to keep from shooting the SOB on the spot. He also said he'd warned Sally that he would kill her and Genesis if she told Genesis or anyone else about what he'd done. Poor Sally, she's been to hell and back."

"The bastard! So that's why Genesis's daughter was so upset! My God! Did Genesis know what . . . what Carlo had done?" My voice broke. I couldn't bring myself to say the word "rape." I was filled with loathing and utter outrage.

"No. Milo told me today that Carlo couldn't take the chance of Genesis finding out about the rape, so he had Milo kill him before Genesis had a chance to talk to Sally in person. Remember, Genesis's phone was bugged, so Carlo knew about his conversation with the nun. He knew that Sally was close to cracking.

"Carlo is a filthy, nefarious, amoral monster, Catherine." He spat the words out as if speaking them was physiologically acrid to his mouth.

I nodded in the chilling realization of what Carlo actually was. I shook with anger and revulsion. I wanted to claw Carlo's eyes out. I wanted to shout his heinous acts to the heavens and see him rot in prison.

"Dear God in heaven!" I cried. "There is no end to his malignant depravity."

In the womb of the closet, Luca took me in his arms and held me close as once again I sobbed. We held each other for a long time. I was still shaking with rage. The wracking sobs eventually abated and stopped.

At last Luca spoke. "Catherine, we've got to move on. For all our sakes, we've got to finish this thing, and in so doing, finish him off."

"I know. Give me your handkerchief, please."

He did. I wiped my eyes and blew my nose. I took some deep breaths. Just like my sister had taught me to do so many years ago.

I squared my shoulders. "Luca, I'm ready. Let's finish this snake off so he can never, ever harm anyone again!" I was frightened at the degree of hate that burned like a raging fire in my gut. It was the hate that would empower me. The hate that would sustain me. The hate that would allow me to stop Carlo from hurting anyone else once this was completed.

"Let's do it, slugger!" he said quietly but firmly.

As we left the closet, I mumbled something to myself.

"What did you say, Catherine?"

"I said we must do it for the lambs, Luca. The ones who cannot save themselves. The helpless victims whose only mistake was to cross paths with Carlo Cappelli, the devil incarnate."

CHAPTER 25

The rest of the day passed quickly. Luca left after one last hug for luck. A part of me left with him. My anger for Carlo remained within, smoldering deep inside. I knew my self-control would be severely tested when Carlo, the object of my rage, was actually in my presence once again. I spent the rest of the afternoon preparing myself physically and mentally for Mancuso's arrival. I ate a light lunch of soup and salad in my room. Next I took a long shower, washed my hair, and spent an inordinate amount of time on my hair and makeup. I took special care in applying my foundation. Surprisingly my bruised cheek was fairly easy to conceal. It still hurt, though. Then I gave myself a manicure and pedicure. Everything had to look perfect. The main problem was that none of these beauty preparations totally occupied my mind. I was constantly trying to divert my thoughts from Nikki, Mark, and Luca. By four-thirty, I was completely ready. I reminded myself to keep my anger in check and use it for my best interests, not Carlo's. I stood waiting by the French doors, looking at the beauty outside. The natural world seemed light-years away from the man-made evil within the house. I took a few slow, deep, empowering breaths, and declared myself ready, or as ready as I would ever be.

There was a tapping at the door. It was the irrepressible Inez.

"Mr. Cappelli would like for you to join him on the terrace now, *Mrs. Cappelli.*"

I didn't blink an eye. Nothing was going to fluster me. I was not playing a character. I was the character. I was Nikki Cappelli.

"Thank you, Inez." She raised her heavy black eyebrows and scurried off in front of me.

I had to admit that the staff had really outdone themselves. They had spent a great deal of time and effort making the beautiful mansion appear even more splendid than usual from floor to ceiling. The huge front entryway was bedecked with several dozen large baskets brimming with luscious, exotic flowers. The large lead-crystal vase in the center of the entryway was overflowing with glamorous, fragrant flowers in varieties that I had not seen before. The overall effect was breathtaking, and the air was heady with the combination of their natural perfumes.

I walked at a slow, stately pace, practicing the look of elegance and femininity that I wanted to achieve.

Carlo was standing at the far edge of the terrace, his back to me, looking out to the ocean. With a drink in one hand and a Cuban cigar in the other, he must have been plotting some new evil contrivance as he stood there. He was truly an enigma to me. What made men, or women for that matter, turn into pompous, cold-blooded, money-grubbing, amoral swine? Some major flaw in personality probably. My guess is that Carlo could have had more than his share of wealth, power, and happiness if he had lived within the rules. Although he was certainly not my type, I was forced to admit that many women would find him physically attractive. He was smart, and according to Luca, very talented in matters pertaining to business. Unfortunately, he was all twisted inside. So twisted that he had to dominate everyone and everything he came in contact with. And if he couldn't dominate them, then he would destroy them. I was willing to bet that he had not the slightest clue as to what real happiness felt like.

Enough of Psychology 101. *Get on with it, Catherine.*

I walked across the terrace toward him. Hearing the clicking of my heels, he turned and gave me a full-toothed smile.

"Ah, my darling! You are a vision tonight! Absolutely beautiful!"

"Good evening, Carlo," I replied stiffly but politely.

He walked to meet me. I knew it was coming, but I had to steel myself for his touch. It made me sick all over for him to put his arm around me, so I pretended that it was somebody else's skin and not mine that he was touching.

"Nikki, you look stunning, my dear."

"Thank you." It was difficult for me to feign civility, but I knew I had to be convincing. I looked him over. He was very polished in his expensive, light summer suit. At least he had a knack for selecting stylish and attractive clothes. As far as I was concerned, it was the only redeeming quality he possessed. His cologne was overpowering.

He lowered his voice and spoke almost in a whisper.

"Are you ready, doll? This is it."

I answered in a whisper. "Yes, I'm ready, Carlo. He'll be totally convinced that I'm Nikki."

He resumed his normal speaking volume. "Excellent! Excellent! You really do look fabulous, darling. That's one of my favorite dresses. You're an absolute knockout!"

Finding his compliments loathsome, I changed the subject. "Has Mancuso arrived yet?"

"Yes, he arrived exactly according to schedule. I greeted him and left him to shower and dress for dinner. He should be here any minute."

"Good," I remarked.

I had barely said "good" when Mancuso arrived. I was quite surprised at his appearance. I hadn't expected him to be so handsome. He was not a large man in height or build. He was of average height with a slender build. Sixtyish, full head of thick salt-and-pepper hair, evenly tanned, and a firm-looking body. His looks and demeanor exuded elegance and suavity. Impeccably dressed in a perfectly tailored expensive Armani suit, he reminded me very much of the distinguished and attractive actor Efrem Zimbalist, Jr. He carried himself like a king. I was certain he rated a cover photograph on *GQ*. Without a doubt, he had presence, charisma, and a rare quality that exceptional movie stars are born with and that savvy directors recognize instantly.

Fortunately, Luca had filled me in on Mancuso's background. His real name was Massiliano Mancuso. But his friends, family, and close business associates knew him by his nickname, "Gentleman Johnny," Johnny for short. He had earned this nickname at a very young age because of his charming personality, his good looks, and his genuine affection for people. Johnny, because it sounded American. The "gentleman" part alluded to the fact that, even as a young boy, and especially later in the Mafia world, he was known as being fair and honest, whatever that meant in their terms. He was a staunch ally, if people were honest with him, and a man of his word. As head of the Mancuso family for many years, he had retained the reputation because of certain values that he lived by. He refused to have anything to do with drugs, and in reality, most of his family businesses were totally legitimate. A shrewd, intelligent businessman, he was tough but well liked by other Mafia families, and loved and revered by his own. Women were mesmerized by him. Other families sought his advice. He was immensely powerful. And the Mancuso family remained highly successful because of the high degree of respect they had for their leader, Gentleman Johnny.

As soon as he caught sight of me, his handsome face lit up.

"Nikki!" he called out exuberantly in his full, rich, commanding voice as he made his way across the terrace to see me.

"Johnny!" I called out in response. I started walking to greet him.

We met halfway. We hugged each other warmly, and I kissed him on the cheek, apologizing for getting lipstick on him.

"Oh, Nikki! I'm so glad to see you! It's been much too long, much too long."

"Yes, it has been too long, Johnny. It's wonderful to see you. I'm so glad you're here. I've really been looking forward to your coming!"

"Let me look at you for a while, Nikki. You're glowing! Carlo, I don't know what it is, but Nikki is even more lovely than the last time I was here. All that inner beauty is overflowing." He stepped back and scrutinized me carefully in an admiring way.

"It must be love, Nikki. Only love brings out that inner glow. I'm surprised, I must admit, that you would find this type of love with Carlo, but I'm happy for you. I'm quite relieved to find that he has been obeying my orders concerning you." He seemed to be very serious.

He directed his gaze to Carlo who was beaming.

"Carlo, I admit I'm surprised and overwhelmed. Is it true? Do you actually realize the rare treasure that you have in Nikki? Have you truly changed?"

"I have, Johnny. She's all the world to me. What else could I ask for with Nikki at my side? She's brought out the best in me. She's turned me around for the good. She is the love of my life. She *is* my life!" He sounded completely sincere. Bravo! What a performance. I wanted to puke all over his fancy designer suit. I looked at Johnny to see if he was buying all of this. I don't think he was quite certain yet. Smart man. Uh, oh. I was forgetting. Not only did I have to convince Mancuso that I was Nikki, but also that Carlo was a devoted, loving, faithful husband.

All this time, Carlo had had his arm wrapped affectionately around my shoulders. Now he gave me a modest kiss on the lips. Outwardly I appeared to be the adoring wife, totally enthralled with her equally adoring husband. Inside I felt as though I had just kissed a disgusting, warty toad.

At that moment, a tuxedoed servant appeared with fluted, crystal glasses of sparkling champagne.

"Ah, champagne! This is our finest, Johnny. We've been saving it just for you, haven't we, darling?"

"We certainly have, Carlo," I said, positively beaming at him.

Carlo handed a glass of ice water to me and champagne to Johnny. Then he took his glass and raised it.

"A toast to our wonderful, generous friend, Johnny!"

Johnny paused, and then, raising his glass, looked me straight in the eye. "To the incomparable Nikki! There is no other like her in this whole wide world! To our stunning hostess!"

I smiled warmly at Johnny. Then we all clinked glasses. We were making progress, slowly but surely.

So far, so good. Johnny seemed to accept me as Nikki. Again, thanks to Luca's expert tutoring, I knew that Johnny was very taken with Nikki, in a fatherly sense, because Nikki's personality reminded him so much of his own cherished daughter, who was a dedicated doctor working somewhere in a remote jungle in Africa. They seldom saw each other because she was so intensely committed to her work that she rarely left the area. Nikki was like a surrogate daughter to Mancuso. I hoped with all my heart that I could continue with this magnificent deception.

CHAPTER 26

The three of us continued to chat amicably. I could tell that Carlo was extremely pleased with my performance. He was attentive, pleasant, and very warm toward Mancuso and me. I, too, was feeling confident that I was doing an outstanding job and would without a doubt convince Mancuso that I was Nikki. Soon, the excellent little combo that had performed the first day I had arrived came and began playing their music. Shortly after that, the rest of the dinner guests arrived. Laura came in with Alberto, and then Luca, followed by two large, swarthy-looking men who had to be Mancuso's bodyguards. They were massive, hulking creatures who seemed vastly uncomfortable in their evening wear. They stood away from the rest of us on the perimeter of the terrace where they could monitor the activity.

Laura, Alberto, and Luca joined our group, and soon we were all talking and laughing. Laura looked quite lovely in a sunshine yellow swing dress that was enhanced by her beautiful, sun-tanned skin. She had a certain radiance now, most likely nature's gift to pregnant women. The contrast between her beauty and Alberto's ugliness made her stand out even more. Apparently Mancuso was well acquainted with her from past visits, because he spent a great deal of time talking with her. Of course, Luca looked very handsome in his evening wear. It accentuated his natural good looks.

It wasn't long before a favorite song of Mancuso's was played by the combo, and he asked me to dance. Naturally I agreed, and I hoped that I was as accomplished a dancer as Nikki. I had always considered myself an adequate dancer, but Nikki was the more dramatic one, more flamboyant in all of her actions, especially on the dance floor. The atmosphere had relaxed me a bit, so I felt confident that I could carry it off. Mancuso turned out to be a fantastic dancer, and thankfully, I was able to follow him in all of the complicated dips, turns, and twirls he executed. When the combo began to play a tango, I was a bit concerned, but Mancuso was such an excellent dancer that I needn't have worried for a moment. I think we would have made even Ginger Rogers and Fred Astaire take notice. At the end of the tango, I realized that everyone else had been watching us in admiration. They applauded with great enthusiasm, and as Mancuso and I took our mock bows, I felt a blush coming on. Oh, God! I didn't think Nikki had ever blushed in her life! All I could do was hope that everyone would believe my high color was due to the flush of excitement and overheating caused by the dancing. Mancuso smiled brilliantly and hugged me.

"Nikki, my dear, you were wonderful! Now let's sit down and have a cool drink and a rest." I agreed, and he led me over to our chairs at the table.

"What'll it be, Nikki?" Mancus asked.

"A glass of ice water would be perfect, thank you." Mancuso motioned for Eduardo to come over, and he gave him our drink order.

"Excuse me for a moment, my dear," Mancuso said, and walked toward the house.

Carlo came and sat down next to me. He took my hand and kissed it. Nausea threatened to envelop me.

"You never cease to amaze me, darling. Your talents are endless. I would sincerely like to reacquaint myself with some of them later this evening, in private. A woman who can express herself that sensually on the dance floor definitely has a wealth of hidden passions waiting to be explored." He raised his dark, heavy eyebrows and licked his lips lasciviously.

Repulsed, I turned away, hoping to keep up my charade and regain my composure. Eduardo arrived with our drinks, just as Mancuso returned.

I was really thirsty, but I refrained from gulping it down. I smiled at Johnny, and he smiled back.

Out of the corner of my eye, I noticed Laura asking Luca to dance. They walked out to the dance floor, and I was surprised that I felt truly jealous. *Get your mind back on track, Catherine.* I turned my attention to Johnny, who was busy talking to Alberto about the hotel Carlo was building on the island.

"We'll take you to see it early tomorrow morning, Johnny. You're going to be very impressed with the progress that's been made. And, with the extra money you've so generously offered to loan Carlo, the hotel can be finished with all the grandeur that will make it a world-class facility, and of course, a great financial success."

Johnny smiled pleasantly and changed the subject to the beauty of the island. He was impressed with the landscaping and expressed admiration for the crew needed to produce such outstanding results. This pleased Carlo immensely, and he went on at length about how he had hired a professional gardening staff away from a large hotel in San Juan. Nervously I watched him go into his bragging mode, a characteristic I was certain would not be appreciated by Mancuso. I needed to rescue him by changing the topic of conversation before he started undoing all the points I had earned.

The combo began playing a beautiful rumba. Its melody was hauntingly familiar and its rhythm hypnotic. Laura and Luca continued to dance. I swallowed hard. *It's just a dance, Catherine. You've got more pressing things to worry about now, like saving your life, stupid. For heaven's sake, stop acting like a jealous teenager.* I sighed.

Carlo stirred next to me and taking my hand, led me to the dance floor. His touch was repellent to me, but I pasted a loving smile on my face and kept reminding myself that after tomorrow, I would never ever have to look at his disgusting, egotistical face again, much less touch him.

Carlo was a fairly decent dancer, but he was certainly not in either Mancuso's or Luca's league. The combo slid neatly into a samba next, which we also danced. And so, to my heart's dismay, did Laura and Luca. After that dance, the combo played a bossa nova, and thankfully Laura and Luca sat down. There was no doubt they made a handsome couple.

Mancuso claimed me for the next three dances, and even under the adverse circumstances, I enjoyed them immensely. After that, Mancuso politely delivered me back to Carlo, and Johnny asked Laura to dance. Each time Carlo touched me, a wave of nausea washed over me, so I was grateful when, out of the corner of my eye, I spotted our salads being served, and we could sit down.

We all returned to our seats. Eduardo, the friendly servant with no tongue, was in charge of the serving. Usually very confident in his duties, he revealed a nervousness tonight that I hadn't seen in him before. Perhaps he was worried about the new chef's cooking. Standing to the left of Carlo's chair, he monitored Carlo's facial expressions carefully.

"Darling?" questioned Carlo, raising his salad fork.

"Oh, yes. Please, everyone, begin," I said, lifting my fork. It was supposed to be a Caesar salad. With the first bite, I felt my spirits drop, because I realized that there was no dressing on the salad greens.

Carlo took a bite. Eduardo stood by quietly patient, ever the perfect servant, awaiting his master's approval. Carlo choked, and picking up his water glass, tried to wash the dry bite of lettuce down.

Immediately after swallowing the water, he turned beet red with anger.

"Eduardo! There is no salad dressing on this salad! How can you have a Caesar salad without dressing? Collect our salad plates immediately and tell that cockeyed chef, Jorge, or whatever his name is, to take care of this! Do I make myself perfectly clear?"

Deeply humiliated, Eduardo cast his eyes downward and nodded his head dutifully in agreement. Picking up our salad plates, he practically raced to the kitchen.

Carlo looked around the table trying to contain his obvious anger. He was ready to explode.

"My apologies to everyone. Darling, Johnny, Laura, Alberto, and Luca. This is inexcusable. I'm very embarrassed and ashamed. We have a new chef and from his performance so far this evening, he'll be looking for a new job after tonight. I'm very sorry. Please, have some more champagne. I promise you that this mistake will be rectified immediately." He snapped his fingers, and instantly one of the tuxedoed waiters standing close by moved to efficiently refill the glasses.

Mancuso spoke to Carlo in a quiet, comforting voice. "Carlo, please relax. This kind of thing just happens sometimes. We all know what a fine host you are. By the way, what happened to that excellent chef you had the last time I was here? He was one in a million."

"You mean Genesis? Yes, yes. He was a magnificent chef. Good man, Genesis. He, uh, committed suicide very recently. Apparently suffered from a deep-seated depression. Terrible thing, Johnny. It was a very sad occurrence here on the island. Genesis was a truly brilliant chef, as you said. We certainly miss him and his culinary skills, uh, but not just for that, of course. He was a good, hard-working fellow. This brainless wonder, Jorge, is simply filling in until I can locate a suitable replacement for Genesis."

Mancuso's eyes had a knowing look about them.

Within minutes, Eduardo returned and served everyone a fresh plate of salad—I hoped with dressing this time. Carlo narrowed his eyes at Eduardo and said in a low, threatening voice, "This had better be right, Eduardo, or there'll be some heads spinning soon."

Eduardo nodded meekly. Carlo took a bite, chewed it carefully, and swallowed. "It's okay, Eduardo. Tell Jorge not to screw anything else up on this dinner."

The rest of us began to eat and talk. Soon the main course arrived. It was some kind of exotic chicken dish with rice and vegetables.

Taking a bite of the chicken, I determined that it was quite good, but very spicy. I noted that it contained a lot of cilantro. I could detect cilantro a mile away ever since my college days when, as an immature act of revenge, Nikki and I had secretly mixed copious amounts of it—every night for a week—into the dinner of a fellow sorority sister who had underhandedly stolen one of Nikki's boyfriends. Her loud sneezing attacks had left her red-nosed and virtually unattractive.

Laura was sitting directly across from me. Hungrily she had taken a big bite, and after swallowing, she tossed down her fork. She froze for a few minutes, as some kind of shocking realization set in.

Suddenly her lovely face became distorted with rage.

"Carlo, is there cilantro in this chicken?"

Carlo glanced down at his plate. "I don't know, Laura. Well, I . . . I guess so. Damn it! I told that chef specifically to never use cilantro. Christ! I know you're allergic to it."

Laura looked down at her plate. She was ready to explode.

"Are you certain this was a mistake?" she shouted at Carlo.

"Well, of course, it was a mistake! You don't think that I would deliberately poison you with this stuff, do you? What kind of person do you think I am?" he demanded.

The question floated in the air and lingered there as if it were a tangible object. Laura, who was still fuming with anger, looked as though she might kill Carlo with her bare hands right in front of all of us.

"Laura, now really, stop behaving this way!" Carlo jumped to his feet.

"Laura, will you have an extreme allergic reaction to the cilantro? Perhaps we should call the doctor," I said in a calm voice.

"In just minutes, I'll be covered with ugly red blotches!" she responded furiously.

"Do you have a medication to counteract the allergic reaction?" asked Mancuso.

"Yes, of course. It's . . . it's in my room. I'll have to go to my room and give myself a shot immediately. Even then, it might be tomorrow before the blotches go away!"

"Laura, do you want me to call Dr. Laurenza?" asked Alberto meekly.

"Dr. Laurenza? That quack? You've got to be kidding, Alberto! I can deal with these damned blotches myself. He couldn't treat a hangnail! I have a prescription for this from a *real* doctor." She got up and threw her napkin down. She was trembling with rage.

Carlo arose from his chair and rushed over to her.

"Laura, I'm very sorry. Let me help you! Your getting upset will only make things worse." He reached out to take her arm.

Pulling away from him as if he had the plague, she proceeded to scream at him at the top of her lungs, "Don't you touch me, you asshole, and don't you ever tell me what to do! I'll get upset wherever and whenever I damn well please! You deliberately tried to poison me, you bastard, and you know it!"

Carlo stepped back surprised, humiliated, and angry with her for her hysterical outburst and her appalling accusation.

"Eduardo, get Inez immediately to assist Laura," Carlo said.

"Don't send that goddamn spic to help me do anything! I can take care of myself, you lousy son of a bitch!" Having made her vitriolic remarks, she stalked off with Alberto dutifully trailing two steps behind.

An embarrassing silence hung over the table as thickly as the cloud after the explosion of an atomic bomb. Even the combo had stopped playing as soon as Laura had begun her tirade.

Carlo was still reeling from Laura's tongue-lashing. He just stood there looking dumbfounded, staring in the direction she had gone. Still dazed, he sat down. Turning around in his chair, he looked at the leader of the combo, pointed his index finger, and said, "Play."

He sat very still for a few minutes staring at his plate. At last, he spoke in a controlled voice. "Luca, go check on Laura and make sure she's all right. She may need a doctor. After all, she is pregnant. I'll go to the kitchen and get this dinner business straightened out."

I looked at my plate. The dinner was, of course, cold and completely ruined by now. Not that I felt like eating it anyway.

"Wait, Carlo. Let me handle this," I said, rising and heading toward the kitchen. Once in the kitchen, I encountered the trembling chef, who was so frightened, I thought he might drop dead of a heart attack. The rest of the kitchen help were equally afraid. Calmly I gave the chef instructions and told him to follow them to the letter. Within minutes the table had been cleared by the servants, and I remained in the kitchen standing next to the shaking chef as he and his helpers prepared a quick meal. He thanked me profusely, and I returned to the table.

Carlo looked worried. "Darling, what did you tell them?"

"You'll see. It's nothing fancy, but we're all starving, and we need to eat."

Luca returned, reporting that everything was under control. Laura had taken her injection, had calmed down, and was feeling somewhat better. She was resting comfortably, and Alberto was going to stay with her to make sure she was all right.

Carlo was still unhinged over Laura's verbal attack.

"Johnny, I must apologize for Laura's outburst. As you know, she's usually a levelheaded individual. I understand her getting upset, but losing control like that and accusing me of poisoning her! A type of temporary insanity, I suppose. The only thing I can figure is that, due to her pregnancy, her hormones are all in an uproar, causing her to behave in a completely irrational manner."

Mancuso took a sip of wine. "Odd thing for her to say, that

you had poisoned her. Strange choice of words. Where would she get such an idea, Carlo?"

Carlo shook his head. "I don't know, Johnny. I'm sure she's sorry she said those things. In all the years we've worked together, I've never seen her behave that way. As I said, it must be the hormones talking."

Very soon, piping hot plates of perfectly scrambled eggs, crisp bacon, spicy sausage, three kinds of toasted breads, hash brown potatoes, and fresh fruit cups were served to us.

Mancuso seemed delighted and smiled broadly. "Breakfast is my favorite meal, whenever it's served. You remembered, didn't you, Nikki?"

"Of course I did, Johnny." Once again, I was grateful for the background information that Luca was privy to and had drummed into my head.

Carlo seemed greatly relieved and beamed proudly at me.

"Isn't she wonderful, Johnny?"

"I've always known that, Carlo."

After the satisfying meal, it appeared that the evening had been salvaged. Coffee was served, and of course, Carlo passed around his prized Cuban cigars. Neither Mancuso nor Luca smoked, so only Carlo lit up. We moved from the table to the wall of the terrace to look at the moonlight on the ocean. For a half hour, the four of us conversed about the weather, baseball, and even politics.

It was getting late, and I didn't think I could handle much more. Being tired might cause me to make mistakes, something I couldn't afford.

"Johnny, I hope you'll excuse me. I'm very tired. Would you mind terribly if I called it a night?"

Johnny smiled. "Of course I'll mind terribly, my dear. But I do understand, Nikki. It's been an interesting evening, hasn't it? Spending time with you is always a memorable event. You're right though. It is late, and I'm going to call it a night, too. But only if you promise to meet me in the morning for our private chat. I have to leave around noon, but you promised that you and I could spend some time together."

"Of course. What time is good for you, Johnny?"

"Well, Carlo, Alberto, and I are meeting at the hotel at six-thirty. That shouldn't take long. How about seven-thirty? Is that agreeable to you?"

"Perfect. I'll meet you in the dining room. Good night, everyone."

"Good night, Nikki. It was, for the most part, a lovely evening." Mancuso kissed me on the cheek.

I turned to go, but Carlo caught me by the arm.

"Wait, darling. I'll go with you," he said.

"Oh, no, Carlo. That's okay. Take your time. You haven't even had a chance to finish your cigar."

"No. I want to come with you, Nikki." He took one arm and Mancuso took the other. As we left, I managed to look over my shoulder and cast an anxious, fleeting glance at Luca.

He nodded solemnly.

CHAPTER 27

Fear, my familiar nemesis, began to well up inside me once again. I knew what Carlo was capable of, and the last thing in the world I wanted was to be alone with him. I was counting on Luca to somehow rescue me.

Carlo and Johnny were talking about the beautiful weather here on the island, and how hot New York always is in the summer, etc., etc. I realized we were not headed in the direction of the regular guest rooms.

Carlo spoke.

"Oh, you know what, darling? I had Inez put Johnny in a suite across from ours. I didn't think the regular guest rooms were comfortable enough for our special guest."

"This room is definitely comfortable," commented Johnny.

We reached the door of his suite.

Johnny kissed my cheek affectionately once again, and we said good night.

Carlo steered me to his bedroom door. We went inside, and my heart began to pound fiercely. The adrenaline rush was back. It was not a pleasant feeling.

Carlo closed the door and began taking off his jacket, tie, shirt, and shoes. He was smiling.

"Well, well, here we are, my lovely bride. Alone at last! I didn't think I could stand another moment in the company of that fucking, egotistical Johnny! He thinks he's so damned smart. He may have money, but that's all. He's an old geezer, over the hill, a has-been." He tossed his things carelessly onto the floor and began taking off his slacks.

"Look, Carlo, I'm really tired. I'm going back to my room and get some sleep. I have to be rested for tomorrow's performance. I can sneak back there very quietly. Johnny will never know."

Carlo stood across the room wearing nothing but bright red bikini underwear. He had a stupid grin on his face, as he came over to me and reached around me to get at the back zipper of my dress. I moved his hand away firmly.

"Stop it, Carlo. This isn't part of the deal."

"Doll face, you are one hell of a sexy lady. Those moves out there on the dance floor really turned me on." I was almost backed up against the wall, but I managed to somehow scoot out of his reach. He followed me.

"No, Carlo, don't do this," I warned, deliberately keeping my voice down. He reached out and pinched my breast.

"What's wrong, baby? Am I coming on a little too fast for you?"

"Stop, Carlo," I insisted, moving away as he turned to follow me.

"Okay, so you're playing hard to get. This'll be fun."

I retreated across the room with no good ideas as to how to actually prevent him from getting what he wanted. He was faster on his feet than I thought, because now he had me trapped in a corner.

"No, Carlo. Please. I don't want to scream. Johnny might hear me and get suspicious. Stop it, now!"

"Then don't scream now, baby. Save that for when we're one on one, in the heat of passion." I tried to push past him, but obviously he was much bigger than I, and he was blocking my escape. I was petrified. I knew what he was capable of doing.

"Gotcha, doll!" he said, reaching out with his right hand to rip my dress right down the middle. The sound of the material tearing sent strong shock waves throughout my system. I gasped, and in a flash he grabbed me tightly. I realized the magnitude of his strength as he held me in his viselike grip. I couldn't move at all, as I struggled to get free.

He was in complete control and aware of his overpowering strength. He threw me down onto the bed like I was a rag doll and fell on top of me. My God! I had to stop him!

I could hardly breathe beneath his weight. Frantically I tried to claw at him with my hands, but laughing, he pinned my arms down and tried to kiss me. Suddenly the door flew open. The sound surprised us both. He stopped mauling me and stood up. Tears were rolling down my face as I jumped up and tried frantically to pull the remains of my dress together in the front.

It was Laura. She was wearing a black, lacy peignoir, and she had small red blotches all over her face, on what I could see of her chest, and down her arms. She closed the door and came over to Carlo.

In a rare moment, Carlo was at a loss for words.

Immediately Laura garnered control over her emotions. There was pain, anger, and contempt on her face.

"You swine! I finally caught you at your little game. I've suspected this for a long time. You're after anything and everything that has ovaries in this household! You scumbag!" She spat in his face. Carlo reached out to grab her wrists, but she stepped back. Carlo actually looked repentant. Then he looked down and, realizing he had on nothing but underwear, hurriedly grabbed his pants off the floor and pulled them on.

"Laura, this isn't what it looks like. She came to my room, begging me to have sex with her. I was changing my clothes, and she came in and tore the front of her dress. Imagine that—she was throwing herself at me! I've never seen anyone so brazen. . . . Why, she . . ."

Laura remained amazingly in control as she spoke in an even, low voice. "I can't believe I was so stupid about you. I believed you really loved me, and that we were going to get rid of Nikki and live happily ever after, with me as the new Mrs. Carlo Cappelli. We could have had it all, Carlo. The plan was so perfect. I was going to give you a son, and we were going to be rich and live in luxury and have it all! If you had only thought with your brain instead of your dick!"

"Laura, listen to me . . ."

"No, Carlo, I'm not going to listen to you anymore. When Johnny gives you all those millions of dollars in cash tomorrow, I want you to give me two million dollars. I won't mess up this deal with Johnny, because I've worked as hard as you have to make this plan a success. Don't try to bully me, and don't try to sweet-talk me either. I'm through listening to your bullshit. There's no future for us, Carlo. I won't share you with a cast of thousands. Find another filly for your stable. This one got fucked, but she also got smart!"

"No, no, Laura! Sugar, you don't know what you're talking about. You're still sick; you're not thinking straight. Tomorrow you'll feel totally different about me." Nervously he ran his hands through his hair and drew in a deep breath. "Laura, why did you come here tonight?"

"What does it matter? I'm here now, and I know that you've been lying to me all along."

"But why did you come?"

"I came because someone stuck this damn note underneath my door."

"Let me see that." As Carlo read the note, Laura went to the closet and came back with a red velour robe that she tossed to me. I put it on. I was shivering with fear and shame and disgust.

Carlo looked puzzled. "This note says to come to my room at midnight. It's typed. Didn't you think that was odd?"

"Who cares, Carlo? There's a hell of a lot more at stake here than a stupid note and whether it's typed or handwritten. My God! Don't be such an asshole!"

"Now look, baby, you're wrong about this whole thing. Let's not say another word about this tonight, because tomorrow you're going to feel differently about the whole thing. You know I'm crazy about you, and you've gotta have me, Laura. You know you can't get me out of your system. We're just alike." He moved closer to her and reached out to pull her close to him.

Laura stepped back. "No, Carlo. I'm not buying any more of your crap. I told you how it's going to be. Now, I'm going to bed. I'm so tired . . . so very tired." She turned to leave.

"Wait, baby . . ." Carlo followed her to the door.

Right before she opened the door, Laura spun around and said in a voice filled with contempt, "And for Christ's sake, Carlo, leave Catherine alone. She's not one of your mindless whores!"

And then she left.

Carlo appeared to be uncharacteristically subdued, as he sat down on the bed, a defeated man, and put his shoes on. Oddly enough, it occurred to me that his demeanor toward Laura was psychologically revealing. He treated all other women like doormats, but he had demonstrated a kind of demented affection for her. Sexually he had cheated on her innumerable times, but he still maintained a type of twisted respect for Laura that he reserved for her and no other woman.

"Go on, Catherine, get out of here. Use the adjoining door to Nikki's room and sleep there tonight. I don't want Mancuso to suspect anything. Tomorrow is an important day. Get some rest. Do as well as you did with Mancuso tonight, and we're in. Don't forget what's at stake here. Make no mistake. I won't hesitate to strike back if you try anything stupid. It only takes two phone calls. One for Mark and one for Nikki." His threat chilled me to the core. I shivered.

Wrapped in his robe, I made my way on rubbery legs to the adjoining door and went into Nikki's room. Feeling like a wounded animal, I slunk off to my lair to lick my wounds. Once inside, I closed the door, locked it from the inside, and switched on the light. I was obsessed with protecting myself. I glanced around for something heavy to put in front of the door. I saw a chest of drawers that looked substantial enough to make entry through the door difficult. It was heavy as I pushed it across the wood floor. At least I would have warning if he tried to get in that way. Next I went into the closet, dropped Carlo's robe on the floor, and slipped into a robe of Nikki's. I wanted nothing next to my skin that had touched his.

Suddenly the tension of the evening settled heavily upon me. I sought refuge in a comfortable armchair over by the bed. Utterly drained, I tried to relax and go limp, leaning my head back and letting my arms fall loosely over the sides of the chair. I felt completely exhausted. I sat there motionless for about five minutes, unable to move, unable to think. There was a slight knock at the door. Cautiously, I opened it only a couple of inches to see who it was.

It was Luca. He looked worried.

I opened the door wider, and he slipped in.

"Catherine, are you okay?" he whispered.

"Yes, thanks to you. You wrote the note and slid it under Laura's door, didn't you?" I whispered back.

"Yes. Thank God you're okay! It was a close call though."

"Very close. Almost too close. Luca, you'd better go now. We don't want anyone to see you and get suspicious."

He looked over and saw the chest in front of the adjoining door.

"Good thinking. Will you be all right?"

"I'll survive. I don't think he'll try anything else tonight. Now go. Hurry, before someone catches you here."

"Be careful, Catherine."

He looked at me with compassion in his eyes and squeezed my hand. Opening the door, he peered out carefully and then left as noiselessly as he had arrived.

Quietly I closed the door to the hall and looked for a piece of furniture to slide in front of it. A heavy keepsake chest would do. I moved it and then sat down on the edge of the bed. I was emotionally and physically drained. I felt as though someone had given me a megashot of Novocain that affected my entire body. Sadly, the complete numbness of body and mind was welcome. Emotionally and physically, I was bankrupt.

I sat statuelike for the next half hour. I looked at my watch. It was one A.M. Time to get some sleep. I left on two bedside lamps and went into the bathroom. Checking the vanity counter, I found exactly what I was looking for. A can of aerosol hairspray. A makeshift deterrent of sorts. If Carlo did manage to get through my barriers, I would simply give him a big shot of hairspray right in the eyes. It would certainly discourage him from any further activity. I doubted that he would try anything, but I wanted to be prepared.

I purposely avoided looking at my image in the mirror. It would tell me what I already knew: I had had more on my plate than was humanly possible to deal with.

I went back to the bed, turned back the spread, and took out a fluffy pillow. Lying on top of the spread, I curled up in the fetal position. With any luck, I would be able to sleep. Sleep. Escape from reality. They seemed one and the same to me, and I needed them both desperately.

CHAPTER 28

I was still asleep the next morning when the telephone rang. It sounded muted, as if it were ringing from someplace far away. Startled, I opened my eyes, but I was confused as to exactly where I was. I must have been in a deep sleep. While I was still getting my bearings, the phone jingled softly two more times. I picked up the receiver.

"Hello?" I said.

"Hello. Señora Cappelli?" said a familiar voice.

"Uh, yes."

"This is Inez. Señor Cappelli asked me to call you at six-thirty to remind you of your seven-thirty meeting with Mr. Mancuso."

"Oh, yes. Thanks." I scolded myself for saying thanks to a woman who had had me chloroformed and held prisoner for hours in a closet.

I hauled myself out of the bed and headed straight for the shower. The warm water felt almost healing. It wasn't long before I felt better. After the shower, I put on Nikki's robe again and blew my hair dry. Then I sat down at Nikki's dressing table and took out the makeup that I needed.

Today of all days it was important that I look my best. My cheek still needed extra coverage. As I worked, I realized how amazing it is that makeup can camouflage a great deal: the lingering physical effects of too little sleep and too much worry, frustration, and sadness. Makeup could conceal and mask the truth. In this case, it was an important tool in a deadly game of deception.

Next I dug around in Nikki's chest of drawers to find a bra and some panties. With that accomplished, I perused the contents of Nikki's closet hoping to find something suitable as outerwear. At last, I found a pretty, yellow, cotton-gauze outfit consisting of a sleeveless blouse and a long, flowing, matching skirt. It gave the illusion of softness and femininity. Shoes were the next problem. But after looking for a while, I discovered some white sandals with adjustable straps that would work fine. The finishing touches were dangly white shell earrings and a matching bracelet from Nikki's jewelry box, and two healthy sprays of a powdery, subdued perfume.

I checked the full-length mirror in the bedroom to make sure that the picture was complete. The person looking back at me bore no resemblance whatsoever to the face that I had seen in the mirror thirty minutes ago. Mission accomplished.

I looked at my watch. Seven-twenty-three A.M. Time to go to the dining room. No time to worry, just time to be what I had to be and do what I had to do.

When I reached the dining room, Inez left her plant-watering duties momentarily to tell me that Mancuso was already seated at a table down by the ocean. She had set things up as he had requested with coffee and breakfast. He was waiting for me now.

I passed through the dining room, out onto the terrace, and down the steps to the beach. I could see Mancuso through the trees. He was impeccably and fashionably dressed in white cotton casual pants, burgundy knit shirt, and white canvas loafers. Seated at a small glass-topped table for two, complete with red-and-white striped umbrella, he was sipping a cup of coffee.

"Johnny!" I called out, waving.

He stood up, smiled, and waved back.

"Good morning, Nikki! You look as fresh and lovely as this beautiful day!"

"Good morning, yourself. You really should be on the cover of *GQ*, you know."

He seemed pleased.

"What a perfect way to start my day. A beautiful young woman and a beautiful morning! Now that's what I call an unbeatable combination."

"Johnny, you always know the right things to say."

"That's because they're from the heart, Nikki."

Mancuso helped me with my chair, and we set about the business of pouring coffee and serving ourselves from the large picnic basket Inez had sent down. We had fresh cantaloupe, honeydew, and watermelon balls. There was also freshly squeezed orange juice and plump, fresh-from-the-oven cinnamon rolls. We helped ourselves to the food and chatted about nothing in particular as we ate.

On our second cup of coffee, I felt the conversation shifting into a higher gear.

"Nikki, we've always been able to talk freely. Do you still feel comfortable in confiding in me?"

"Of course, Johnny."

"I wanted to talk to you alone because I want to make sure that Carlo is truly treating you well. Has he really changed, Nikki? Has he truly committed himself to loving you and you only?"

"Yes, yes, he has, Johnny. Carlo has changed tremendously in the last few months. I know he loves me very much. He's cut back on his travel so that he can be with me. We spend more time together now, and it's made a big difference in our relationship. He's thoughtful and attentive, all the things that a loving husband should be."

"Hmmm. So he treats you with respect?"

"Yes, he does. I know he still sounds egotistical at times, but that's just Carlo. As far as I'm concerned, Johnny, he couldn't be more caring. Our marriage is the strongest it's ever been."

"Then he hasn't hit you or abused you, verbally or physically?"

"Absolutely not. I couldn't and wouldn't put up with that."

"I'm glad to hear that, Nikki. You know how much I care about you. You're so much like my own daughter. I hope that never changes."

"We won't let it, Johnny. I care a great deal about you, too. Your friendship is invaluable to me." I reached across the table and placed my hand on his. I liked him a lot. At least, Nikki had had this man as her friend. Regardless of his profession, he seemed to be a sincere person who held my friend in high regard and had treated her with kindness. For that I was grateful.

"Nikki, you know that today I'm prepared to loan your husband a great deal of money. This money is to be used to complete your grand hotel in all its splendor."

"Yes, Johnny. And you can't imagine how grateful I am to you for doing this. This hotel is part of Carlo's dream, and you are the one responsible for fulfilling it. I don't know how to thank you enough for this act of faith. It means a great deal to me. You're a very generous man."

"It's my pleasure and privilege to be generous as long as the money is spent in a positive, potentially lucrative venture. Besides, it allows me to continue to hold Carlo responsible for treating you as he should."

Our eyes met in a straightforward way, and I didn't blink once, hopefully assuring him of my sincerity.

"Our friendship is important to me, Nikki. From the very beginning, there was a meeting of the minds, and more importantly, of the souls. Remember our first meeting when we discovered a shared admiration for *The Prophet* by Kahlil Gibran?" He recited:

> "When your friend speaks his mind you fear not the
> 'nay' in your own mind, nor do you withhold the
> 'ay.'

> And when he is silent your heart ceases not to listen to his heart;
> For without words, in friendship, all thoughts, all desires, all expectations are born and shared, with joy that is unacclaimed.
> When you part from your friend, you grieve not;
> For that which you love most in him may be clearer in his absence, as the mountain to the climber is clearer from the plain.
> And let there be no purpose in friendship save the deepening of the spirit.
> For love that seeks aught but the disclosure of its own mystery is not love but a net cast forth: and only the unprofitable is caught."

"Go ahead, Nikki, finish the rest."

I was trapped. I loved literature, too, but I had not committed this piece to memory. Oh, God, what could I say?

I remained silent for several minutes trying hopelessly to explain my way out of this. "I . . . I'm sorry, Johnny. I can't seem to . . ."

He interrupted me. "Can't remember it? Not even part of it?" He looked sad and gravely disappointed.

"I . . . my mind is . . . I . . ."

"I'll finish it for you:

> "And let your best be for your friend.
> If he must know the ebb of your tide, let him know its flood also.
> For what is your friend that you should seek him with hours to kill?
> Seek him always with hours to live.
> For it is his to fill your need, but not your emptiness.
> And in the sweetness of friendship let there be laughter, and sharing of pleasures.

> For in the dew of little things the heart finds its
> morning and is refreshed."

He sighed deeply and looked out across the deep blue Caribbean. I was inwardly panicked, but I could only sit and wait.

When at last he spoke again, it was with a new perspective. It was as though he saw me totally naked, stripped of all pretense. He knew.

Inside I was dying a thousand deaths.

He kept staring at me, a piercing stare that frightened me.

"Who are you?" he asked.

"Why, I . . . I'm Nikki, of course."

"No, you are not Nikki! Who are you and why are you putting on this devious charade?"

"You don't believe that I'm Nikki? Who else would I be?"

"Look, I don't know who you are, but you're not Nikki. You're incredibly like her in almost every way imaginable, but you're not Nikki. You had me ninety-nine percent convinced, until today, when I gave you the ultimate test."

"Why would you say ninety-nine percent convinced?"

"You weren't wearing the ring that I gave Nikki. It was a ruby. A beautiful, exquisite ring that Nikki always wore. I started to ask about it, but I thought perhaps you had just forgotten to wear it. All the other times that I visited, Nikki was wearing it. Without exception."

"Oh." I looked down at my hands. Carlo had remembered to get Nikki's wedding ring for me, but not the ring that Mancuso had given her.

"I demand that you tell me where Nikki is. Now!"

I nodded. "I . . . I guess you deserve to know. Even though my telling you is a virtual death sentence for my son, Nikki, myself, and Luca."

His eyes grew wide. "Tell me."

"I . . . I can't, Johnny."

"You must. You have no choice."

I knew he was right, but I was terrified of the dire consequences. He continued to glare at me. "Okay, I know I have to tell you. But first, can anyone overhear us here?"

Mancuso scanned the area. "My men are close by. Let's walk up the beach to make certain that no one else is listening." He signaled to his men, and they followed behind us keeping a reasonable distance between us.

I told him everything. About Nikki. About Carlo. About me. About Mark. Reluctantly I told him about Luca and the big drug deal. I was really afraid to tell him about that, because of how he might react to Luca's connection with the FBI.

Although I gave it to him in an abbreviated form, it took me a good thirty minutes to include all the relevant information. When I finished, I felt a peculiar sense of relief. I didn't understand that, because telling Mancuso meant the actualization of my greatest fears.

We had walked a long way on the beach. With the conclusion of my story, we stopped and faced each other.

"Johnny, I'm sorry about deceiving you. But you can see why I had to do it. What'll happen to all of us now? If Carlo doesn't get this money for the drug deal, he'll kill us all. Nothing can save us now!" Tears began rolling down my cheeks. When I looked at Mancuso again, his expression had changed dramatically. He was no longer angry with me. He reflected warmth and caring and strength. Gently he took me into his arms as a father would a distraught daughter and held me in a loving gesture of comfort. I continued to sob. Finally my tears subsided. He handed me a monogrammed handkerchief.

"There, there, Catherine. I'll take care of things with Carlo. I have a score to settle with him. Trust me, my dear, because now I'm your friend, too. You're Nikki's best friend, and she's like a daughter to me. I want to help you. As a friend, I share your pain. Poor Nikki! And your son, too. And what about all that you've had to endure? My heart aches for you all. The man is despicable! There are not enough words in any language to describe the depths of his depravity. He's the devil incarnate! Be assured that today justice will prevail."

A tiny ray of hope glimmered in my brain.

"Then you'll help us?"

"I'll take care of Carlo, Catherine."

"But what will you do, Johnny?"

"Let me worry about that. For the time being, I want you to return to the house and tell Carlo that your performance was perfect, and that I've agreed to loan him the money. Stick with that story. Leave everything to me. Above all, we've got to rescue Nikki and your son. That comes first."

I wanted to believe him. I had no choice.

Something was nagging at the back of my mind.

"What about Luca? What should I tell him?"

"Nothing. Leave everything to me."

"You're not going to hurt him, are you? After all, he's here to nail Carlo on drug trafficking charges and arrest the people who're delivering the illegal drugs."

"I have no reason to dislike or distrust Luca. He appears to be an honorable man. And the drugs. The drugs! What a filthy business! Luca's cause is to put these peddlers of death away. That's a noble venture." He paused a moment and then asked, "What do you think of Luca, Catherine?"

I was flustered by the question. "He's only meant to do good, Johnny. He's guided me through this mess. Without him I wouldn't have survived for long. I know that he tried to help Nikki, too. He told me he knew nothing of Carlo and Laura's plan to poison Nikki. Carlo had told Luca that Nikki wouldn't be harmed at all, just sedated temporarily in order to take her unharmed to San Juan, so he could coerce me into masquerading as Nikki and fool you. Luca's only intent has been to catch Carlo, present an airtight case against him, and put him away for life."

Johnny chuckled. "I'd say you have a very high opinion of Luca, my dear."

"Well, yes . . . I guess I do."

He grinned. "Ah, hah! I was right about the glow I detected in you. I said it was the result of love. Am I right?"

I blushed. "Well, I . . . I . . ."

"Catherine, we'd better head back now. Carlo will get suspicious if we stay any longer."

With that said, he put his arm around my waist, and we began the walk back. All kinds of thoughts were spinning about in my head. Fears, questions, possible scenarios. With all my heart, I hoped everything would turn out okay. I could only hope.

"What other score do you have to settle with Carlo?" I asked.

"It's a question of honor."

"Honor?"

"Yes, without honor, a man is nothing but an empty shell."

"Then I would say that that accurately describes Carlo."

"My point exactly."

CHAPTER 29

Coming up the steps of the terrace, we ran into Carlo.

He was dressed in an off-white summer suit, imported blue silk shirt, and a coordinated designer tie.

"I was just coming to look for you two. I trust that your breakfast was fine and you enjoyed your talk. Did everything go well, Nikki?"

"Yes, everything is perfect, Carlo," I said, stressing the word *perfect*. "And by the way, Johnny has generously agreed to loan us the money we need. Isn't that wonderful?" I gave him a brilliant smile.

He looked relieved. "Excellent! Johnny, why don't we step into my office and take care of a little business?"

Mancuso checked his watch.

"Carlo, it's eight-thirty now. I need to make a few phone calls, tie up a few loose ends. Why don't we meet in the library at eleven? Is that all right with you?"

Carlo shrugged. He was so happy about getting the money that he didn't mind being agreeable. "Okay, sure. The library at eleven. As a matter of fact, I've got a few loose ends to attend to myself over at the hotel. See you at eleven."

Johnny went into the house closely followed by his two bodyguards. Carlo set off in the direction of the hotel, looking back over his shoulder to flash me a cocky grin and a wink.

I swallowed hard. A bad case of nerves was setting in. Having stood indecisively in the same spot for several minutes, I decided the best place for me was my room.

Once I reached my room, I sat down on the edge of the bed. A million questions were whirling around in my mind, but I had no answers to any of them. I was too uneasy to do anything remotely productive. Besides, what could I do that wouldn't endanger me or someone else? I wanted to find Luca and tell him about my meeting with Mancuso, but I didn't know where he was, and it was much too risky under the circumstances. Frustrated, I moved over to the wing chair in front of the French doors. It was going to be a long morning. What was I going to do to keep from going mad? Searching for any available distraction, I gazed out at the magnificent scene outside the French doors. The flowers, the trees, the profusion of brilliant colors, the deep green carpet of grass. Out of the blue, something clicked in my brain, reminding me of the old crone on the airplane and the frightening premonition she had had about me that had caused her to have a heart attack. Those kinds of thoughts were not going to do me any good at all. I had to do something to occupy my mind for the rest of the morning, or I really was going to go crazy. I didn't feel like reading, but it was something to busy my mind, so resignedly, I picked up the Lawrence Sanders novel.

I had been reading for well over two hours, when I heard a knock at my door. My mouth went dry. As I reluctantly went to answer the door, I couldn't help wondering if there would ever be a time in my future—if I managed to survive this nightmare—when I could answer a knock at the door without breaking into a cold sweat and feeling a terrible sense of dread. I opened the door. Surprisingly it was Mancuso's goons. Their size alone was intimidating, and let's face it, they were not exactly hired for their friendly facial expressions.

"Oh, hello," I said meekly.

The larger one spoke. "Mr. Mancuso wants you to come with us." His voice was deep and guttural.

"Come with you?"

"Yeah, come with us, ma'am," added the slightly smaller one.

"Well, I . . . okay," I agreed. What choice did I have?

They split up so that one stood on either side of me. This definitely bothered me. And why did Johnny want me in on all of this? I went with them, feeling like a dwarf sandwiched between two giants. We walked briskly toward the library. The slightly smaller one opened the library door and gestured for me to enter.

Inside, Carlo was seated behind a massive desk located in a corner of the large room. His feet were propped up on the desk in a typical Carloesque pose. Mancuso sat in a leather chair facing the desk.

Carlo seemed very surprised to see me. Enough so, that he took his feet off the desk and sat upright, all the while puffing on a big, smelly cigar.

"What . . . what's all this about? Darling, why don't you go for a swim or something? Johnny and I have to finish our business first. We'll be done soon, and then we can all have a nice lunch together. Run along, now."

Mancuso turned around to face me. "No, stay where you are."

About that time, Luca, Alberto, and Milo appeared at the open door.

Carlo looked somewhat relieved. His own forces had arrived.

"Come in, guys," he said.

Luca, Alberto, and Milo came in and stood next to the two goons. Luca looked wary. He reached inside his jacket, but the larger of the goons had already drawn his own gun and caught Luca's wrist in motion, stopping Luca from arming himself.

In a flash, the other goon drew his revolver and pointed it at Milo and Alberto. They were ordered to put their hands up in the air. Stunned by the unexpected show of force, they obeyed the order without any argument. Next Mancuso's men frisked the three thoroughly, relieving them of their respective weapons.

Carlo looked angry.

"Hey, Mancuso, what is this crap?"

He reached out to open the middle desk drawer, but Mancuso was faster than he was. He had his revolver already out, and it was pointed directly at Carlo.

"Step back from the desk now, Carlo." In a foolhardy attempt, Carlo yanked the drawer open at the same time that Mancuso shot him in the upper arm.

I gasped. I had never seen anyone shot before.

Carlo moaned and looked at his arm.

"You don't follow instructions very well, do you, Carlo?" said Mancuso. I was frozen to the spot. "Boys, tie them all up and gag them, too." The bigger goon held his gun on me, Luca, Alberto, and Milo, as the smaller one proceeded to take rope out of a briefcase and tie our hands securely behind our backs.

The smaller thug stuck his gun in Luca's back and told him to start walking. He marched Luca out to the hall, and I could hear their footsteps passing down the marble floor to God knows where. Now I was really panicked. Why would he single Luca out? Where could he be taking him? All kinds of horrible possibilities flitted through my mind. The larger thug, who was called Rocko, told us to sit down, and he tied our ankles. Next he gagged us. I was in a living nightmare. Everything was happening so fast. Nothing seemed real.

After a few minutes, the smaller thug, called Dom, returned to the room. Alone. Oh, God! Where was Luca?

Never taking his eyes off Carlo, Mancuso spoke to me in a calm, even voice. "Don't be afraid, Catherine. You won't be hurt. Tying you up is a sort of . . . protection to keep you out of harm's way."

Fear had me in a death grip now. I was worried about Mancuso. Why should I believe him anyway? What had he done with Luca?

All this time, Carlo had been standing, holding his wounded arm next to his body, breathing hard, and sweating profusely.

Mancuso finally spoke. "Sit down, Carlo. We don't want

you to pass out. You're an important character in this little scenario." Reluctantly Carlo sat down in the desk chair.

"For Christ's sake, Johnny! What are you doing? What's going on around here? Shit! My arm hurts like hell! You've got a lot of explaining to do."

Mancuso laughed. "Me? Explain? No, pal, it's you who has to do the explaining." As he was talking, he had crossed around to the other side of the desk. Still holding the gun on Carlo, he pulled open the middle drawer. Reaching in, he removed a big handgun, bigger than the others that were presently drawn in the room. He opened the other drawers and checked them quickly.

"I guess you were looking for this, Carlo. But you won't be needing it, my friend." He handed it to one of his thugs. Then he picked up the phone and pressed a number. "We need a little first aid in here, please."

Only a few minutes passed before Inez entered the room. I guess Carlo expected her to do something to rescue him, but it didn't happen. Inez seemed smugly at ease as she carried a small, metal case over to the desk and set it down.

"Take off your coat and shirt," she ordered brusquely.

Carlo looked annoyed. "Since when do you give *me* orders?"

Inez slapped him hard across the face. "Since now, you sorry son of a bitch!"

Though wounded, he jumped up to attack Inez, but Mancuso shoved him down hard into the chair.

Carlo was stunned and confused. Roughly Inez helped him take off his jacket, his tie, and his shirt. He winced.

Inez examined the wound carefully. "It's only a flesh wound, Mr. Mancuso. I've seen worse," she reported. She rummaged around in the case and took out some antiseptic and gauze. After cleaning the wound thoroughly, she covered it carefully with gauze. "That'll do for a while," she said, putting the things back in the box.

"Dom, come over here and tie his good arm to the back of

the chair. And tie his ankles together, too. I don't trust him." Dom did as he was told.

"Thank you, Inez. You can stay if you like," said Mancuso.

Stay? Stay for what? My heart was pounding fiercely. Inez sat down in a chair across the room. What exactly was going on here?

"Carlo, I want you to pick up the phone and call the person in charge of holding Nikki captive," ordered Mancuso.

"What? What are you talking about? Nikki is being cared for in a private facility by a very competent nurse."

"Carlo, you seem to be missing the point here. You are no longer in charge. Your soldiers are all tied up. You have no choice but to do as I say. You were lucky the first time I shot you. I grazed you on purpose. Don't push your luck, buddy, because it's run out. Let's see, I believe I'll start with your left ear. With one less ear, you'll have something in common with van Gogh," he said, holding the gun right up against Carlo's ear.

"Punch the number, asshole!" commanded Mancuso.

Carlo groaned. "Okay, okay. Bring the phone a little closer."

Johnny did. Using his injured right arm, Carlo gritted his teeth and punched in some numbers. Then he whined, "Johnny, could I at least have some Scotch? Goddamn! This hurts!"

"In a minute. Go on with the phone call. When they answer, tell them to call the police and the paramedics immediately to come and take care of Nikki. Or else you're minus one ear."

"Hello, Juanita? This is Carlo. I . . . uh . . ." Carlo was stalling.

Johnny spoke through clenched teeth. "Say it, you bastard!" he said, cramming the gun hard up against Carlo's ear.

"I want you to call the police and the paramedics to come and get Nikki," said Carlo.

He listened to Juanita.

"Hell, I don't care what you do afterwards! Look, let me

speak to Nina. Hurry up!" A few moments passed. "Nina, this is Papa. Listen carefully. I want you to call the police and the paramedics to come and get Nikki. Right now!"

He listened to Nina.

"Yeah, yeah, I know. There's been a change in plans. Just make the call, and then you and Juanita can leave. I'll talk to you later. I'm kind of tied up right now." He just couldn't resist the wisecrack. "Yeah, yeah, you'll get paid. Nina, quit being a smart ass and do what I fucking tell you to do!"

The conversation was over. Johnny hung up the phone. Carlo looked at Johnny. "Okay, I did what you told me to do, Johnny. Now, how about that drink?" Sweat was dripping from his forehead.

"You've got one more phone call to make. Call Sicily. Your police chief friend there. Tell him to release Mark Hanson immediately and drop all charges. Is that clear, or do you need any more convincing?"

"No." Frowning, Carlo punched in some numbers. He spoke in Italian. He had to wait a few minutes before they located his "friend." The conversation was brief. I was glad that Mancuso spoke Italian and could be certain that Carlo was saying exactly what he was supposed to say. Carlo was ready to hang up, but Mancuso took the receiver. He chatted briefly in fluent Italian with the Sicilian policeman. He even laughed over something that was said. Then he hung up. Mancuso turned and looked at me. "It's done, Catherine. Within minutes, they'll both be free."

At that moment, I felt a tremendous release. I imagined Mark and Nikki and their surprise and relief over being set free. My eyes filled with tears as I pictured their faces.

"Inez, would you please fix this jerk a Scotch? A double, I think. He'll need it," said Johnny.

Inez did as she was asked and handed the Scotch-filled glass to Carlo. Carlo leaned his head back and took a big swallow and then another, and then another, draining the glass.

"Dom, come over here and cover this loser. I'm tired of

holding this gun on him." Dom moved into place, and Mancuso sat on a corner of the desk, facing Carlo.

"Johnny, you owe me an explanation for all of this. What the fuck's going on?" Carlo asked angrily. Apparently the liquor had given him a false sense of machismo.

"I don't owe you anything, Carlo. You're the one who owes just about everybody you've ever come in contact with an explanation. So we'll just start with what we have and see where it takes us. This is going to be a little like the old television program, *This Is Your Life*. Remember it, Carlo?"

Carlo mumbled something.

"What did you say, Carlo? You're going to have to speak louder. You've got a captive audience here, and everyone wants to hear exactly what you have to say."

"Yeah, yeah, I remember it."

"Okay, then, Inez, would you bring our first guest in, please? Carlo! Notice the way I say 'please' and 'thank you'? You should have been a little nicer to people. If you had, you might not have found yourself in the spot you're in today. Inez?"

Johnny looked at Inez. She walked over to the desk with a puzzled look on her face.

"Oh, I'm sorry, Inez. Of course. Excuse my forgetfulness. You asked to have first crack at him, didn't you?"

Inez walked around the desk and stood facing Carlo. Her expression was frightening. It was hate in its purest form. When she opened her mouth to speak, I almost expected fire to come billowing out.

"You . . . you . . . are the vilest person I've ever known. You lied to me, and you threatened me, forcing me to do what you wanted. What you've done to my husband is unforgivable. That was bad enough, but when you started using and abusing my daughter, Elisa, you sank to the depths of hell. Yesterday she came crying to me. She undressed and showed me the bruises and burns on her body that you are responsible for. Then she told me she was pregnant by you, you lousy bastard! She asked me for money to get an abortion. I gave her the money, and this morning she left for San Juan. I asked Mr. Mancuso if I could have the pleasure of chopping off your genitals, but he said no because it was important that you remain conscious. You're lucky he said that, because I would have thoroughly enjoyed watching you scream out for mercy in the middle of your agony. I hope you rot in hell, you miserable wretch!" She spat in his face. It shocked Carlo, and he recoiled.

Walking away, she turned to look at Mancuso and said, "I'll get Eduardo now."

Carlo looked miserable.

Eduardo entered and closed the door behind him. He was dressed immaculately as always. Although he was a small man, he carried himself with dignity and pride. Of course, he couldn't speak, but if looks could kill, Carlo would have been dead on the spot. I noticed that Eduardo was carrying something in one hand behind his back. It was the largest hammer I had ever seen. A lump rose in my throat. He walked over to Carlo and spat in his face. Then Inez came and stood beside Eduardo. I was afraid of what was coming.

"Rocko, you'll need to help them out," said Mancuso as he got up from the desk and moved out of the way. The massive Rocko walked around and grabbed Carlo's free hand, holding it down flat on the desk, mashing down hard so that the fingers were separated. Inez took the hammer in her hand. I couldn't bear to watch so I closed my eyes. I could hear Carlo's loud sobs and his voice pleading with Mancuso to stop.

I heard the sound of the hammer smashing down on the desk, not once, but twice. Carlo let out a bloodcurdling scream. I kept my eyes shut tight. I hoped it was safe to open them.

Inez left the room once again. This time she brought the new chef, Jorge, with her. He walked around the desk and stood in front of Carlo who was making an odd mewling sound.

Jorge's dark eyes were filled with rage as he screamed in Carlo's face. "You bastard!" Carlo's face lost all its color. "You murdered my friend Genesis and you raped his daughter! I'm doing this for both of them!" Rocko grabbed Carlo's mutilated hand and mashed it flat on the desk again. Eduardo handed Jorge the hammer.

Carlo moaned. "Please stop, I'm begging you to stop!"

Jorge spoke again. "Finally you will know what it's like to be treated like an animal!" He raised the hammer, and I quickly closed my eyes. I heard two loud crashes on the desk. Carlo was whimpering now. He sounded like a dying animal. I felt sick to my stomach.

Inez, Eduardo, and Jorge took the bloody hammer to the other side of the room where Jorge dropped it into a box, and they sat down together on a large burgundy-leather couch. Mancuso returned to his position on the corner of the desk.

"Stop sniveling, Carlo. Take it like a man, you coward. So far so good. Now we move to a new stage of our little game."

Carlo was slumped down in the chair looking in horror at the bloody mass that once was his hand. He was clinging to consciousness by a single thread. It was a pitiful sight.

"Johnny, please! Give me a chance to explain. You're wrong about this. I . . ." He barely got the last word out before he began to cry.

"You know, Carlo, you really make me sick. You haven't suffered a fraction of the amount that you've made other people suffer. When I think about Nikki and how horribly you've treated her, I want to rip your disgusting face off with my bare hands and cut your lousy no-good heart out, too! You took a beautiful woman and practically destroyed her mind and body. And then you brought her best friend here and put her through a living hell. You had her son arrested on false drug charges and thrown into a dangerous, filthy prison thousands of miles away from home. You murdered an innocent man, Genesis, and you raped his daughter. And the list of your crimes goes on and on. Who knows how many thousands of lives you have destroyed with your drug trafficking! Yes, I know all about what you've done, Carlo. My God, man, there is no end to your depravity! No end!" The air was thick with tension. Mancuso had reached his boiling point. He was a virtual time bomb of controlled indignation waiting to explode at any moment.

Mancuso looked away for a few minutes. He was fighting hard to contain his rage. Finally he spoke.

"Carlo, as part of *This Is Your Life*, I want you to think back about twenty-two years ago. Can you do that?"

Carlo's voice was weak and raspy. "Yes."

"You had graduated from college, and you were running some restaurants, correct?"

"Yes."

"And these restaurants were bought for you by whom?"

"Luigi."

"Inez, please give him a drink of water. I can't hear him. His voice is giving out." Inez brought a glass of water and held it up to Carlo's quivering lips. He managed to drink several mouthfuls and then whispered quietly to her, "For God's sake, help me." Inez's black eyes flashed, but she spoke not a word as she took the glass away with her and returned to her seat.

"I'll help you out, Carlo. Three restaurants were bought for you by your adoptive father, Luigi Cappelli. Luigi Cappelli, the man who took you in when you were a runaway child with no place to go. He and his wife, Anna, took you into their home and raised you as if you were one of their own children. Remember?"

Carlo nodded.

"My good and honorable friend Luigi took you in, fed and clothed you, educated you, loved you, taught you, did everything for you because you had *nothing* and *nobody* in the world! Luigi and Anna treated you like their own flesh and blood. And then, then, what did you do at the age of twenty-three?"

Carlo stared blankly at Johnny.

Mancuso's voice thundered across the room. "I'll tell you what you did, you fucking scum of the earth! You set fire to their house one weekend when they were all at home. Luigi, Anna, and their four daughters, sound asleep. You burned them all alive! Incinerated them like insignificant slabs of meat! Oh, you were a smart bastard then, and even after a detailed police investigation, no one could directly link you to the fire. But you did it all right. For years I suspected you, but there was no proof. I kept hoping that I was wrong about you, that you hadn't committed the most heinous of all crimes. A crime against your own family, for God's sake!"

His agitation was so great that he stood up, unable to contain his wrath any longer. His face was red with rage. He was losing control fast. He paused a few minutes to regain his composure before continuing.

"One week ago, I received something in the mail that confirmed my belief that you had, in fact, murdered them in cold blood!" He reached into his pocket and pulled out a cassette tape and held it up for Carlo to see.

Apparently Carlo recognized it and winced.

"This is the evidence I have waited for for over twenty years! This was sent to me by your ex-chef, Genesis. He had secretly taped a conversation that you had with Alberto. In the taped conversation, you bragged to Alberto about the fact that you had executed the entire family. You were proud of the fact that you hadn't been caught. You did it so that you could inherit all the family money. Your greed consumed you because you were nothing but a little worm, always unworthy to bear the family name. The only problem was that you didn't know about Luigi's two older brothers who lived in Rome. For all of your devious scheming and plotting, you had missed a vital piece of information. The two older brothers inherited the bulk of the estate, and you received a handsome amount, but not nearly what you had expected."

I looked around the room. All eyes were riveted to Johnny and Carlo.

"Today I am here to avenge their deaths, Carlo. Luigi was one of the best friends I've ever had. I must honor my friendship. It is my duty to see that you are punished because of the great dishonor that you have brought on the Cappelli name and the heinous massacre of a family who loved you. You are a disgrace to Italians everywhere. I cannot undo all the terrible wrongs you have committed against the Cappellis and against Nikki, Catherine, Mark, Inez, Elisa, Eduardo, Genesis, his daughter, Jorge, and countless others, but I can make sure that you never defile this world of ours again by being allowed to live in it. Unfortunately, I cannot trust our justice system to lock you away for life. Without a doubt, some hotshot lawyer would come along and get you off. There would be some angle, some mistake, some do-gooder liberal group that would make you a television heartthrob and the symbol of a psychologically screwed-up child who was abused by his first set of adoptive parents and abandoned by his real father. Oh, no, I won't trust this important duty to anyone else! It is up to me to mete out justice and retribution of some kind! The act of vengeance is my responsibility!"

Carlo's eyes were wide with terror.

"What . . . what are you going to do to me?"

"I'm going to let you burn alive, Carlo. It's only fitting, don't you think?"

Upon hearing his death sentence, Carlo began to cry. He was begging, pleading, but Johnny ignored him.

He turned and faced all of us. "I apologize for the violence that you've witnessed here today. Unfortunately, it was necessary. Now, Dom and Rocko will untie you and remove the gags so that you can be driven to the ferry that is waiting to take you to San Juan. Inez, have you followed my instructions so that all of the remaining household help are waiting at the dock?"

"Yes, Mr. Mancuso, I followed all your instructions. No one is left in the house but the people in this room."

What about Luca? Had they murdered him? I was sick with dread.

"Very good, Inez. Thank you. Boys, handcuff Milo and Alberto. Soon Dom and Rocko will direct you in an orderly fashion out to the driveway, where we will use the two available cars to drive you to the ferry launch. As soon as you have all boarded the ferry, the captain will take you to San Juan without delay. Alberto and Milo will be held in separate quarters under armed guard on the ferry, as upon arrival, they will be arrested and taken by boat to a Sicilian prison where they will be incarcerated for life to pay for their misdeeds."

Then he turned to Rocko and said, "Make sure the bastard is tied securely to the chair. I'm not taking any chances."

Mancuso looked down at Carlo. He spoke to him in a low, derisive voice. "You know you'll be in hell very shortly. Or, who knows, maybe even the devil himself will reject you!" He shook his head and walked over to me. Carlo began wailing. Mancuso turned and said, "Put a gag in his mouth, Dom. I'm tired of listening to his pathetic blubbering. Oh and by the way, Carlo, Laura was given the opportunity to be here, too, but she declined. She said the sight of you makes her nauseous, and she has the baby to think of. I know that she helped you to poison Nikki, so she's certainly not blameless. However, I hold you responsible for lying to her and brainwashing her. Early on, you told her that Nikki had actually threatened to have *you* killed in order to inherit your money. She bought it because she was dumb enough to fall for you. At any rate, her cross to bear is giving birth to a child that carries your wretched genes. We can only hope and pray that the child bears no resemblance physically or morally to you. Pitying her, I gave her a nice sum of money to tide her over through the pregnancy. Also, she has to leave the United States and reside in another country."

Then he turned to me and began gently untying my ankles and my wrists. Carefully he removed the gag from my mouth. He seemed completely exhausted and drained. When he looked at me, I could see the deep sadness in his eyes.

"I'm so sorry, Catherine. I'm sorry you had to witness all of this. I only want the best for you and Nikki. Please don't hate me. I couldn't bear that. Try to understand that I had to do this. It was a debt I owed to my friends, the Cappellis. They would have done the same for me." Then he kissed me softly on the cheek and turned to leave. I reached out and clutched at his hand.

"Johnny, wait. I want to, uh . . . thank you for saving Mark and Nikki." Tears of relief began to run down my cheeks.

"Oh, my dear, sweet Catherine. There's no need to thank me. I wish I could have saved you from the heartache you've suffered since you came to this island. A soul as pure as yours should never have to come in contact with the Carlos of this world. Good-bye." He touched my cheek tenderly.

"Johnny, one more thing. Where's Luca? Is he okay?"

"He's fine, my dear. He's completely unharmed."

I managed a weak smile, he gave me a slight wave, and he left.

I looked once more at Carlo. Diminished. Defeated. Destroyed. A pathetic shell of a man.

It was time for us to go. Rocko walked directly behind the handcuffed Alberto and Milo, with the gun still pointed at them, and I followed behind. I noticed that Dom remained in the library. As we walked out the front door into the bright sunshine, I looked everywhere for Luca. As we approached the cars, my heart lifted as I spotted Luca, bound and gagged in the backseat of the Lincoln. Quickly I opened the door and climbed in to untie his hands and pull the gag from his mouth. He breathed a deep sigh of relief.

"Are you okay, Catherine?" he whispered.

"I'm okay. Are you?"

He nodded solemnly and took my hand in his. I felt safe for the first time in days.

Eduardo got into the backseat on the other side of Luca. Inez sat in the front. We sat silently awaiting a driver. Soon Dom arrived and started the car.

"What will happen now?" I asked of anyone who would answer.

Finally Dom answered me. "Kerosene. We poured it all over the office. There's a timing device attached to some explosives next to the door of the office. It's set to go off any minute now. When it blows, Carlo will have a chance to watch the flames spreading out to consume him. Then other explosions will go off in different parts of the house." We all turned to look out the car windows at the house. Suddenly a huge blast shook the car. The beautiful house, the Tara look-alike, burst into flames. A few minutes later another blast went off, and then another, and then another. The entire house was engulfed in flames. It was a chilling sight. Silently we watched the burning house for a few minutes, and then Dom drove the car out of the drive and onto the road. No one said a word, but Luca gave my hand a squeeze.

"Dom, where's Johnny?" I asked.

"He's already left in his private helicopter. Oh, I almost forgot. I'm supposed to give this to you or Mr. Romano." Luca and I exchanged puzzled looks, as Dom reached back to hand us a sealed envelope. Luca opened it, read it, and then showed it to me. It read:

> Luca, I know that you have spent two long and grueling years undercover posing as an employee of sorts of Carlo's. First of all, I congratulate you for your ability to coexist with such a loathsome creature in order to complete your mission. Secondly, I salute you for your persistence and dedication geared toward arresting the lowlife drug dealers that Carlo has been doing business with for a long

time. If I had not intruded with my own personal vendetta, I'm sure you would have been successful in apprehending the other parties as well as nailing Carlo, too. In light of this, I hope you will accept my deepest apologies and hope that the following information will be acceptable to you and the FBI in place of your long-hoped-for plan. As you have probably determined by now, I removed you from our little kangaroo court so that you would not be a direct witness to anything that happened today in that house.

Sincerely,
Johnny

P.S. Take good care of Catherine. You know how very special she is!

P.P.S. I have already taken the liberty of making one phone call to the FBI to let them know exactly where the plane carrying the heroin will be landing once the drug dealers have determined that they can't land on the island. Your FBI will be waiting to arrest them on arrival. Using the fictional name of Johnny B. Goode, I told them I was a contact of yours and that you had instructed me to call and report this vital information. You deserve the credit for catching these guys, Luca. After all, you did all the hard work. Hope you don't mind the liberties I took. Also, knowing that you are an honorable man, I trust that you will not reveal my true identity to the authorities. Although you may not agree with my methods, I hope you approve of the end results. If I can be of service to you in the future, please don't hesitate to call on me.

With warmest regards,
Johnny

Below the letter was a listing of the names of the drug dealers who would have arrived on the island very shortly to deliver drugs to Carlo. There were also phone numbers, addresses, and locations of illicit drug warehouses in Miami.

CHAPTER 30

As soon as we reached the ferry, Dom and Rocko instructed us to board. The ferry itself was quite impressive. Large and brightly painted in red, white, and blue, it resembled a shiny, new, supersize toy. It was obvious that Carlo had spared no expense. Carlo's motto had always been "Nothing but the best, no matter what the cost, no matter who you have to squeeze to get it."

Luca and I watched as Milo and Alberto were immediately taken into custody by two other large thugs and whisked off to the bowels of the ferry. Suffice it to say that neither Milo nor Alberto looked the least bit happy about their futures.

As confirmed earlier by Inez, the other workers from the house were already aboard when we arrived. The group, consisting of around thirty people, included gardeners, housekeeping staff, and kitchen helpers. They were all Puerto Rican. Most of them young. As I looked at their faces, I wondered if they would have difficulty finding new positions. But I knew that wherever they worked, it would be better than what they had had to endure while working for Carlo, the madman.

Since it was a warm, sunny day, many of them stood on the upper deck in the open air. The remainder sat in comfortable seats inside the spacious, windowed passenger cabin. All of them were in clusters, chatting quietly but amicably. All except Inez. She stood alone on the upper deck. As Luca and I slowly ascended the stairs to the deck, she marched purposefully toward me.

She looked worried and tired, her sharp features appearing more haggard than usual, obviously a result of the most recent unpleasant events in her and Elisa's lives.

"Mrs. Hanson, I . . . uh . . . I . . . I need to have a word with you."

"All right."

"I want to tell you that I'm sorry for the way I treated you. I . . . uh . . . I was acting on Carlo's orders. He had blackmailed me into doing awful things. Things that I'm really ashamed of. About two years ago, my husband was wrongfully convicted of killing another man in Miami. My husband was truly innocent. Shortly before the murder, my husband had gone to work for Carlo. God knows we had no idea of what we were getting into. Anyway, Carlo told me he would hire my husband a top attorney who would work hard to uncover new evidence and get my husband a new trial. He said he would do this and allow my daughter and me to earn an income if Elisa and I would agree to come and work for him. Two years passed, and we were no closer to proving my husband's innocence than we had been before. He just kept holding it over my head and threatened to stop providing my husband with legal help if I didn't follow his wishes. I was in a desperate situation. Now I find out that Carlo had hired a sleazy, no-good lawyer to do nothing on the case and see to it that my husband stayed in prison. Carlo had lied to me for years to keep us both under his thumb.

"I talked to Mr. Mancuso this morning, and he promised to hire new attorneys to help us out. We are hopeful of a new trial in which we can prove my husband's innocence, clear his name, and get him out of prison. I'm truly sorry for all the trouble I've caused you." She stopped for a moment. Her eyes filled with tears. "I want you to know also that I had nothing to do with Genesis's death. He was a good man. It was Milo who murdered Genesis under orders from Carlo. I found out about it afterward, but I was afraid of Carlo and what he might do to Elisa and my husband. That doesn't excuse my behavior, I know. I'm just very sorry, very sorry, Mrs. Hanson."

I had never heard her say that much at one time. It kind of shook me up.

"I'm sorry for the way Carlo treated you and your family, Inez. I hope everything works out all right for all of you."

She attempted a smile, nodded, and then added, "Oh, by the way, Mrs. Hanson. I packed all of your things, and they're in the baggage compartment of the ferry." Having said what she wanted to say, she abruptly turned away and went to stand at the railing. Luca and I exchanged will-wonders-never-cease looks.

As the ferry left the dock, Luca and I stood side by side, holding hands at the railing. We were both silent.

We watched the black billowing smoke pouring from the direction of the house. I felt very odd. I wasn't sure that all of this had actually happened. I had been living a nightmare, and it was hard to believe that the terrible ordeal was over.

Luca and I stood for a long time facing the shore until we could no longer see the island except for the telltale black smoke rising above it. Each of us was alone with his thoughts.

Finally Luca spoke. "Catherine, are you all right?"

"I think so. What happened today . . . everything that's happened since I arrived . . . it's so bizarre . . . so unreal, Luca. It's going to take a while before the reality of all that's occurred actually sinks into my brain. I'm totally exhausted. In a complete state of shock."

Luca nodded. "A lot has happened to you, Catherine. It'll take time to sort it all out."

He asked me to tell him everything that had happened in the house after Dom took him out of the library. I did my best to fill him in. As I told the story, I was incredulous to the events that I had actually witnessed. He listened attentively to my explanation.

Once again, we were silent as we each tried to assimilate everything that had happened.

"Luca, what are you thinking?" I asked.

"Well, the events of the last few hours came as a big surprise to me, too. I've been involved with Carlo's mess for two years, and all of a sudden, it's all over. Finished. Only it didn't play itself out the way I thought it would. Two years of pretending to be someone else is a long time. I'll have to adjust to being Luca O'Brien again. And now that I'm leaving the bureau, I'm in for a lot more changes. Good ones, I hope. I'm looking forward to that. I want a chance to see what it's like to live a normal life."

"Where do you go from here, Luca?" In that moment, I realized that I wasn't sure I wanted an answer to that.

"When we reach San Juan, I'll call the bureau immediately. Hopefully, they've got everything set up to arrest the perps and confiscate the drugs. I'll need to find out what they want me to do to wrap this whole thing up. We'll find out where Nikki is, arrange for you to see her, and make contact with Mark, too. According to what my superiors say, they'll tell me when I can proceed to DC, where I'll spend a few weeks being debriefed and tying up loose ends. After that, I'm off to a new life in northern California. There's a beautiful resort area on Lake Amethyst. An old friend of mine owns a great lodge. It's quiet and peaceful. I plan to vegetate for a while. I need time to think and figure out what I want to do with the rest of my life."

"Oh." That was all I could say. My heart was sinking.

"Catherine . . . there's only one problem."

"What's that?"

He turned his head to face me directly. "I . . . well . . . I . . . Damn it! I'm stuttering like some tongue-tied kid! Catherine, I'm in love with you." He paused for a few minutes before he spoke again. "Without you, nothing else really matters. I want you in my life . . . I've been . . ."

I interrupted him by placing my index finger against his lips.

"For an undercover FBI agent, you talk too much!"

He smiled and, drawing me close, kissed me.

As usual, I felt light-headed and breathless.

It felt so natural being in the shelter of his arms.

He kissed me again, and then we stayed together for a long time just holding each other close. Finally he spoke.

"Am I asking too much of you now to want to know where I stand with you, Catherine?"

"Luca, I'm confused about a lot of things. I've learned that my mother kept the truth about my father and my sister from me. My father was an adulterer who kidnapped my own sister. My mother lied to me about both of them. All of those years, all the lies . . . I don't undersand it yet. I may never understand it. I know it was wrong of my mother, and yet my mother loved me . . . but . . . there's one thing I do know, Luca. I'm not confused about one thing. And that is how I feel about you. We've only known each other for a short time, but I feel a closeness, a bond with you, that I know is rare. I'm in love with you, Luca. I don't care if it doesn't make any sense to the rest of the world. I know how I feel. You're the only thing in my life, besides my son, that does make sense."

"Good," he said, holding me close and sealing our declarations with another passionate kiss.

Holding hands, we watched as San Juan slowly came into view.

I sighed.

"What was that for?" he asked.

"That was a sigh of happiness. The first of many to come. I'm not used to that kind of happiness, Luca. It's been missing from my life for a very long time."

"Come here, you," he said, smiling and drawing me close.